Without Mercy

Alicia Dean

Published by Alicia Dean, 2015.

WITHOUT MERCY

First edition. February 8, 2015.

Copyright © 2015 Alicia Dean.

ISBN: 978-1508439516

Written by Alicia Dean.

Dedication:

For two of my four favorite attorneys, Stephanie Cox (who has never had a book dedicated to her), and Cana Wilson (miss you!).

Acknowledgements

Thank you to my sisters, Sheri Clements and Christi Perryman, for their assistance with my research questions and for their unending loyalty (they're my BIGGEST FANS). My beta readers, Faith Smith, Jessica Watts, Rebecca Ward, and Diane Burton. My always fabulous critique partners, Christy Gronlund and Kathy L Wheeler. And to Kim Hornsby for her fantastic proofreading assistance.

Chapter One

China Beckett darted a glance across the bank lobby toward the front door. What were the odds she could escape undetected?

Not good, she decided. Even if she managed to slip out without being seen, her absence would be noticed. And Sophie would have an aneurism.

Did she want to be a lousy employee or a lousy mother?

The choice was simple. She rose from her desk and headed past the teller line toward Sophie's office.

"Everything okay?" China's best friend and co-worker, Vanessa Hanson, said from behind her desk.

"Emma had an asthma attack. The school wants me to pick her up."

"Oh no!" Vanessa's green eyes widened. She looked toward Sophie's door and cringed. "Good luck with that."

"I know. Get ready for all hell to break loose."

"Yeah, well. Emma matters more than Sophie the Super Bitch." Vanessa gave a thumbs up. "Go get her, Tiger."

By the time China reached Sophie's door, a knot of worry had gripped the pit of her stomach. The thought of her little girl ill, wanting her mommy, made her heart race with anxiety.

The blinds on the large window leading from the lobby into Sophie's office were open. Through the slits, China saw Sophie at her desk. She couldn't just leave, claiming she hadn't been able to find her boss. She'd have to actually confront the she-devil.

Drawing in a deep breath, she rapped her knuckles on Sophie's door.

"Yes?"

China went inside, closing the door behind her. "Emma's ill. She's at school, and I need to pick her up."

Sophie's lip-sticked mouth compressed, deepening the smoker's wrinkles around it. "I'm sure the school can handle it."

China gritted her teeth. "If they could handle it, they wouldn't have called. I have to get her home. She needs a breathing treatment." The image of her tiny daughter lying in a hospital bed flashed through her mind. Her throat clogged with emotion. "She's been hospitalized three times, and she's only six years old. She needs me."

Sophie opened a drawer and retrieved a folder. She shot a glance at China before opening the folder and thumbing through the pages.

China recognized her own personnel file. *Great.* Did Sophie keep it handy for just such an occasion?

Okay. Message received. She missed a lot of work. But she was a single mother of a sick child and only took off when absolutely necessary.

"Let's see here." Sophie slid a pair of reading glasses on and studied the file.

Sophie was only forty-six, but her hair was mostly gray. She wore it shoulder-length, flipped up on the ends in a style that was too young for all that gray. She was tall and lithe and always made China aware of the fifteen pounds she'd put on in the last year.

As she waited for Sophie's reprimand, she shifted uncomfortably. The waistband of her skirt bit into her flesh, making her wish she'd worn something with a little more give. Enduring Sophie's lecture was bad enough without feeling self-conscious and restricted.

Sophie lifted her head and frowned, then looked back down at the paperwork. "You've missed four days this month. Last month you missed two. The month before that you missed eight, and the month before that..." She closed the file and shook her head, sighing heavily, as if sorely plagued by unfathomable tribulations. "That's not to mention the times you've been late."

"Emma's had a lot of problems. I—"

"We all have problems, China. For God's sake, if I took off every time one of my kids had the sniffles, I'd never be here." She folded her hands together and rested them atop her desk. "You just have to become a little more devoted to Greater Oklahoma Bank, concentrate more on your job. Let someone help you out."

China didn't remind Sophie that *she* had two healthy children, a husband, and a live-in nanny. It was easy for her to come to work on the rare occasions when her children were ill since there was always someone in the house to care for them.

"I know," China said. "My aunt normally helps out, but she's ill, and I didn't want to bother her." Aunt Lucy was almost fully recovered from the flu, but it was China's place as Emma's mother to take care of her when she could. Work was slow right now, and a few hours off wouldn't hurt anyone. "I'll work late tomorrow to make up for it."

"China, I know it's difficult trying to work and take care of a child alone. But look at it this way, how would you feed and clothe her, put a roof over her head, without a job? I promoted you to Teller Manager despite your attendance issues, because you're good at what you do. You're the best we've ever had, in fact. And that's why I've tried to be patient. However, if this keeps up, I can't promise you'll retain your position." She removed her glasses and pinched the bridge of her nose with her fingertips. "I'm sorry. But sometimes we have to make tough choices."

China glanced at the clock on the wall above Sophie's head. Almost ten minutes since the school called. Emma could have gotten worse. She couldn't continue debating with Sophie. Her daughter needed her.

"Look, I'm sorry, but I'm leaving to pick up Emma. If it means losing—"

A thunderous boom cut off her words. The office window behind her exploded, raining glass on her head, against her back. Breath seized in her lungs, and a cry ripped from her throat. She froze for a nano-second, then ducked behind the chair. What the hell...? A bomb?

Coming from somewhere far away, she thought she heard screaming, but couldn't be sure. An odd echo resounded in her ears. Everything was muffled, like she was underwater.

Sophie? She hadn't even screamed...

China gingerly rose and peeked over the desk. Sophie lay awkwardly slumped in her chair. A red stream leaked from a hole in her chest.

"Oh God." Her knees buckled, and she latched on to the edge of the desk. She dared a glance behind her, through the window, and the bottom dropped from her world.

Chapter Two

Three black-clad, hooded figures, each with a machinegun slung over their shoulder, roamed among the terrified employees crouched on the floor.

China dropped into a squat behind the chair, eyes tightly closed, back pressed to the desk. Broken glass crunched beneath her feet as she shifted, trying to make herself invisible. A scream strangled her throat. She clamped a hand over her mouth to stop it, and wet stickiness clung to her palm.

Was that...?

She pulled her hand away and held it in front of her face.

Blood. She gagged, trying to swallow back a rush of bile. She looked down at her clothing, and a strangled sob escaped.

Oh, God. She was wearing Sophie's blood.

She squeezed her eyes shut again, praying the shooter hadn't heard her scream. *I'm going to die...I'll never see Emma again...*

And, it was all her fault. She shouldn't be here. Shouldn't even be in the States. She should be overseas. A missionary, like her parents. God was punishing her, and she didn't blame him.

But why had he punished Sophie?

She tried not to look behind her, but her gaze was drawn against her will. Sophie's body lay half-in, half-out of the chair. Her eyes were open, staring, as if surprised. Blood had spread on her pale yellow blouse in a cookie-sized circle.

"Down!" a voice barked.

China jumped, even though the man couldn't have been speaking to her. His voice came from the bank lobby. He only sounded close because the window was no longer there.

"If you do what we tell you, no one will get hurt."

Right. They'd hurt Sophie without giving her a chance to do what they told her.

She needed to get help. If she used the bank phone, they might see the line light up. Her cell... No, her phone was in her purse, at her desk.

"Everyone on all fours, faces to the floor."

A different voice this time. Accented. Fainter than the first.

Sophie's cell phone might be in her purse. But where was her purse? One of the drawers, most likely.

Slowly, staying low to the floor, she duck-walked around Sophie's desk, then eased the lower right drawer open.

A Coach bag rested at the bottom. *Thank God.* She rifled through the contents until she found Sophie's phone. Her hands trembled so violently, it almost slipped through her fingers as she punched 9-1-1 into the keypad.

"You can come out now," a man's voice called. She startled and cried out. The cell slid from her hands and thumped on the floor before she could press the send button.

"China. Now!"

Dear God, he knew her name.

She looked over her shoulder. One of the bank robbers stood on the other side of the broken window pointing a handgun at her.

She tried to stand, but her legs trembled, and she couldn't make them obey. The man raised the pistol. "I said now."

Gathering strength, she pushed to her feet and walked slowly toward him. Beyond his shoulder, in the bank's lobby, her coworkers were scattered on the floor like Muslims at a mosque. Two of the thugs hovered over them. A fourth robber China hadn't noticed before stood near the entrance to the bank. This one was smaller, curvier beneath the black clothing. A woman.

China's escort motioned to Sophie's door. She stepped through, and he snatched her arm and led her to a chair next to Vanessa's desk.

"Sit," he commanded.

Her knees gave out, and she dropped into the chair. Her gaze swept over her co-workers. Vanessa lifted her head, her terrified gaze meeting China's.

"China!" she called, and started to rise.

The robber closest to her friend raised his gun, pointing it at her head. "Down!"

Chills raced through China's heart. "No," she screamed. "Please."

The gunman hesitated. Vanessa pressed her face to the floor, and China's captor made a gesture with his hand. The rifle lowered, and she sagged with relief.

"Is everyone out here?" The man's shout reverberated around the room. "Anyone still in the offices? The bathrooms?"

No one replied.

"You." He walked over and nudged Abel Brenneman with his foot.

Abel slowly lifted his head.

"Anyone else here?"

"Not—not that I know of."

"Who can get into the vault?"

"I—Angela has the key," Abel said.

Angela lay crouched a few people away. She lifted her head. "That's me." Her voice quivered.

"Up."

She stood and one of the gunmen—shorter than the one who held China—grabbed her arm and led her to the vault. Another gunman joined them.

The shaking girl made a few failed attempts, but finally opened the vault. The men followed her inside. In moments, they emerged, the two robbers holding bulging bags.

"Back on the floor," the short one ordered.

Angela obediently knelt and put her face to the ground.

The robbers backed toward the exit, waving their guns.

They stopped, the one in the rear glancing outside. Obviously having decided they were clear, he motioned with his hand and shoved the glass doors open.

China held her breath, praying they wouldn't hurt anyone else. When they disappeared through the door, she let out a sigh of relief.

"They're gone." Her voice was barely above a whisper. She cleared her throat. "They're gone."

Her co-workers, a few at a time, rose on unsteady feet. Others stayed on the floor until their companions reached out to help them. China snatched up Vanessa's desk phone and punched in 9-1-1.

Vanessa rushed to her. "Are you okay?"

"I'm fine—" Her words were cut off by the operator.

"9-1-1. What's your emergency?"

"We've been robbed." As the words tumbled from her lips, the true horror sank in. "Oh God. We've been robbed. We're at Greater Oklahoma Bank. The south branch."

"Name, please?"

"China Beckett."

"We have your location and are dispatching emergency units, China. Are the robbers still on the premises?"

"No—I mean, not in the bank. They're gone."

"Is anyone injured?"

Injured? She thought of Sophie's dead, staring eyes.

"My boss...the CSO...uh, Customer Service Office...Sophie, was shot."

Vanessa gasped and shoved a hand through her blonde hair. Her gaze went back to Sophie's office, then returned to China. "Sophie?"

China nodded.

The 9-1-1 operator said, "Is she alive?"

"No," China whispered.

"I'll stay on the phone with you until the responders arrive. Are you okay, China?"

"I'm okay."

Vanessa rested her hand on China's shoulder. "Are you sure you're okay? You're bleeding."

She shook her head, covering the mouthpiece. "It's not my blood. It's Sophie's."

Vanessa squeezed her eyes shut, then opened them and glanced toward Sophie's office again.

"Here." China handed Vanessa the phone. "Stay on the line with them. I need to call Lucy to pick up Emma."

Vanessa nodded and took the receiver.

China headed to her desk on legs that shook so badly they barely supported her.

Sirens sounded in the distance, getting closer and louder as she fumbled her cell phone out of her purse.

Aunt Lucy answered on the first ring. "Hello, China doll, how are you?"

China swallowed the knot in her throat. "The bank was... We were robbed."

"Oh my!" Her aunt's voice quivered. "Are you okay? You weren't hurt?"

China's body went cold...freezing cold, then shook, her teeth chattering so hard, she struggled to get the words out. "Yes— I mean, no, I wasn't hurt. I'm okay. Can you get Emma? She's had an asthma attack at school."

"Yes, of course."

The front door burst open, and two cops rushed in, guns drawn, followed by two EMTs pushing a stretcher.

"Love you, gotta go." China ended the call, weak with relief. Help had arrived.

She shot a glance to Sophie's office and shuddered. Help had arrived all right, but too late for Sophie.

Chapter Three

An hour later, China waited in the bank's conference room, wearing a T-shirt a female police officer had loaned her after they'd taken her clothing for evidence.

The EMT's had checked her over and cleaned the blood from her skin. The other employees were questioned and allowed to leave, but then, they hadn't been in the room when Sophie was murdered. All China wanted to do was get home to Emma. Her heart ached to hold her little girl.

A man with receding, sandy blond hair and a rumpled, baggy suit strode in the room and flipped open a badge. "Miss Beckett? Detective Boyle. I need to ask you some questions."

"More questions, Detective? I gave the officers everything but my bra size." Her fear had ebbed, leaving exhaustion and numbness in its wake.

The detective gave a small, grim smile. "I apologize. I know this is grueling, but it's necessary. I just need a few more minutes of your time." He took out a notepad and settled in the chair across from her.

"Of course."

"Name?"

Really? He'd called her Miss Beckett, so he must know her name. "China Beckett."

"You work here at the bank?"

"Yes. I'm Teller Manager."

He jotted something. "I understand you were in Mrs. Oswald's office when she was shot."

Sophie's dead, staring eyes flashed in her mind. She flinched and gave a quick nod.

"Right across from her, a mere, I don't know two, three feet away?"

She swallowed hard. "Yes."

"But the suspects shot past you and killed Mrs. Oswald?"

"Yes."

He pursed his lips and scowled. His mouth opened, but before he could speak, Vanessa's husband, Miles, appeared in the doorway.

"China, you okay, hon?" Miles was also a detective. China wished he'd interview her instead of this stranger.

"I'm okay."

"Hanson," Boyle said. "You know this woman?"

"She's my wife's friend. Our friend." Miles moved to her side and took her hand, giving it a squeeze, then looked at Boyle. "Can we do this later?"

"I just have a few more questions."

"I'll stay with you." Miles took the seat next to her. His easy, confident smile was comforting, and she nodded gratefully.

Boyle scowled, but didn't protest. "Take me through the robbery, step by step."

China drew in a deep breath. Slowly, she recounted the events, seeing it all once more in her mind as she relayed details. Everything, from the time she took the call from the school and went into Sophie's office, to the time the robbers left.

Boyle nodded slowly, looking perplexed, as if listening to someone describe a UFO sighting. He remained silent for a few moments. "Are you a gambler?"

"Gambler?" She looked at Miles, who frowned at the detective.

"Yeah. You know, casinos, slots, card games, that sort of thing." Before she could answer, he went on, "I've been to Vegas a few times, but with casinos popping up all over the place, not much sense in that. I can stay close to home and give my money away, know what I mean?"

China nodded, although she had no idea what the hell he was talking about.

He lifted his brows. "So, are you? A gambler, that is?"

She shifted irritably. Small talk about freakin' gambling when all she wanted to do was get the hell out of there? "No. Not really. I've been to a few casinos, but not much of a gambler. Why?"

"Just wondered. You know, if you were always this lucky or if it was just today."

"Lucky?" She snorted a disbelieving laugh. "I was almost killed. You call that *lucky*?"

He nodded, and his brows crawled farther up his forehead. "Yeah, *almost*, right? I mean, you're standing there, closer to the robbers than Mrs. Oswald. An easy target. There for the pickings. Yet." He shook his head and grunted out a chuckle. "They shoot past you and kill your boss. Either they targeted her on purpose and didn't want to hit you, or they're lousy shots. Either way, that would make you one lucky young woman."

"Boyle—" Miles started, but the detective held up a hand.

"Please. Let me question the witness."

Miles clamped his lips together and scowled.

A trickle of unease skimmed China's flesh. The detective seemed to be taunting her. Accusing her of something?

He studied his notebook. "Is there anything you noticed, anything you...recognized about the suspects?"

She shook her head. "They wore dark clothing and ski masks. I can't even describe them. Not at all. There were four of them. Three men and a woman."

"Any visible tattoos or scars? Think carefully. Anything at all identifiable about them?"

"No. I'm sorry."

"Take your time." His voice was suddenly solicitous. Trying to throw her off?

China focused, picturing the robbers in her mind. They all looked like replicas of one another, different shapes and sizes, but all dark, menacing, vicious clones. "Nothing."

"Anything distinguishable about their voices?"

"One had an accent."

"What kind of accent?"

She shrugged. "I'm not sure. Maybe French? He was smaller than the others. Smaller than the other men, that is."

"And one was a woman?" She nodded, and he wrote something down. "Anything else?"

"I can't think of anything. Except..."

"Yeah?"

She took a deep breath, hesitating.

"China?" Miles said gently. "If there's anything at all..."

She slowly released the breath. "He knew my name."

Detective Boyle did the brow-raising thing again. "Who knew your name?"

"The robber. The first one. The one who told me to come out of the office. He called me by name." The two men exchanged looks. "I thought maybe they knew *all* our names, but that's not likely, is it? How would they know which one I was, even if they had all the employees' names?"

"Good question." Detective Boyle scowled for a few seconds, tapping the pencil on the notepad.

China lifted a trembling hand and brushed her hair back. The EMT hadn't quite gotten all the blood. What remained had started to dry and a few flakes fell onto her lip.

"Oh, God," she cried, swiping at the blood—the dried remnants of Sophie's death. She shuddered and rubbed her mouth over and over. "Get it off of me, please, just get it off of me."

"Shh, it's okay. It's all gone." Miles put an arm around her. "Boyle, that's enough for now. If you need more later, I'll bring her down to the station."

The detective seemed to consider for a moment before nodding. "Okay. But I will need to speak with her again." He looked at China. "You're not going out of town any time soon, are you?"

Her chest tightened, and tears clogged her throat. "No."

He stood. "You're free to go. I'll be in touch."

Miles helped her to her feet and led her through the hall out the back door of the bank. Vanessa was waiting, and China's legs weakened with relief. She needed her friend, needed to be surrounded by people who loved her.

Vanessa hurried to her and pulled her in for a tight hug. "I'm so glad you're okay. That was the most..." Vanessa's body trembled. "...terrifying thing. I can't imagine what it must have been like to be there when Sophie..."

Boyle had followed them outside. He leaned against the building, watching.

China ignored him as she returned Vanessa's hug. She released her friend and sniffed back tears. "Yeah, it was awful." She rubbed her forehead with a shaking hand. "I just need to get home. Need to get to Emma."

"Of course. We'll drive you."

China shook her head. "Thank you, but it's okay. I can drive."

"You shouldn't—"

"Please. I'm fine. Really. I just need to go."

"Okay." Vanessa squeezed her hand, her green eyes darkened with concern. "You sure you'll be okay driving?"

China dried the tears and forced a smile. "I'll be fine."

Suddenly, she had to get away. From everything. Everyone. Even well meaning Vanessa and Miles. But mostly, from the not-so-well-meaning Detective Boyle.

Chapter Four

China slid into her Camry and turned the key in the ignition with fingers that still trembled. Would the shaking ever stop?

"China. Now."

She started, jerking her gaze to the back seat.

No one. Just his voice in her head—calling her by name. She shivered. He'd known her name. How?

Did that mean he knew where she lived? That he would be back to finish the job?

No. If he'd wanted to kill her, he'd have done so in the bank. Bank robbers didn't go after victims. They took the money and ran. They were probably near the Texas border by now. Heading to Mexico. They wouldn't be back. Wouldn't come after her. She had to get ahold of herself before she saw Emma.

She checked her reflection in the rear view mirror and gasped. Blood splatters clung to her dark hair, glinting like rubies when the sunlight hit them. Her blue eyes were dull, hollow, the dark smudges beneath them giving her the appearance of a corpse.

No wonder everyone treated her like a victim. She looked like a disaster survivor. She pulled an antibacterial wipe from the canister she kept in the car and did her best to clean off the blood. She couldn't let Emma see her like this. She would freak.

Once she'd gotten all the blood she could see, she backed out of the parking lot and pulled out onto the street. Her cell rang, and Aunt Lucy's number showed up on the caller ID. She punched the answer button.

"Hi, honey," Lucy said. "I was just checking on you. Thought I'd hear from you by now. Is everything okay?"

"Yeah. It took a while for the police and EMTs to finish up with me."

"EMTs? I thought you weren't hurt."

"I wasn't, it was—"

Sophie's blood. All over me. In my hair, on my clothes...in my mouth.

She shuddered. "I'll explain everything later. Listen, I need to go home and clean up before I pick up Emma."

"Take your time, sweetie. I'm anxious to see you and make sure you're okay, but this little one can stay here as long as you need her to."

The one-story log ranch house sat several yards back from the dirt road, hidden behind a forest of towering, leafy trees. Inside, Royce Dolan and his team gathered around the large oak dining table. They'd already discarded their masks inside the van. Wouldn't do to drive around looking like bandits.

He addressed the team, "Okay, gents—" His eyes went to Layla, "—excuse me, and ladies."

Layla inclined her head. She had long, thick black hair and startling emerald eyes. Her skin was the color of bone, and her blood-red lips were full, the kind a man couldn't help but imagine wrapped around his cock. A pentagram tattoo on her left cheek—a symbol of her devotion to the Prince of Darkness—was the only blemish in an otherwise perfect face.

Royce cleared his throat and continued, "Nice job. That was just the first phase, though. We still have a lot of work ahead of us." He tossed an envelope to each of them. "Your shares of the two mil. More to come when the big job's done."

Dan Bishop, a black man the size of a mountain and Royce's best friend, smiled as he thumbed through the cash. "Only bad thing about this is sharing it with a bunch of whiteys." He looked at Layla. "And with the devil."

Layla smiled and ran a hand along Bishop's cheek. "You ever done it with a daughter of Satan, preacher boy?"

Bishop jerked away from her touch. "Don't intend to. Burning forever in the fiery pits of hell wouldn't be worth it. No matter how good the sex."

"Tell me something." Marcel Dupree lounged in his chair, one arm slung over the back. He was a small Frenchman with a receding hairline, shifty eyes, and thick lips that were always moist from his licking them. He glared at Bishop as he drummed his fingers on the envelope lying on the table in front of him. "Why is it that Mr. Dolan here is your best friend, yet you despise white people? Did you even notice that he is white or are you too fucking stupid? Or, perhaps it is because he enjoys taking it up the ass and you enjoy giving it to him?"

Bishop lunged to his feet and headed around the table toward Marcel. Marcel flinched, seeming to shrink even smaller than his five-four frame.

"Bishop, simmer down," Royce said.

Bishop leveled a gaze at Marcel, then slowly retreated, dropping back down into his chair.

Royce grimaced. For a group of people who argued so much, they worked together like a well-oiled machine. As long as they limited the bickering to their down time, Royce could deal with it. He'd worked with them all before. He knew their strengths and their weaknesses. Marcel was a twisted, soulless pervert, Bishop a religious fanatic, Layla a devil worshipper who sometimes disappeared to reunite with her fellow-satanists. Aggravatingly, right in the middle of an assignment. But each had skills and attributes critical for a successful mission. He just hoped they could get through it without killing one another.

He looked at each one in turn, until he had their undivided attention "I told you this when you took the job, but it bears repeating. There are only three rules. Rule one, do what I say. Rule two, do *exactly* what I say. Rule three, there will be no, and I mean *no*, turning on each other. If you think you're going to make your cut bigger by taking out one of the team, think again. Any of you kills one of the other guys...or lady." He shot a grin at Layla. "You get nothing. Not a cent." He shrugged. "And, who knows? Maybe you get taken out, too. There's no room for traitors in a mission."

"You are not the one in charge." Marcel's eyes narrowed. "Why do we have to do what you say? Maybe we only want to take orders directly from the boss."

Royce leveled a glare on him. "Maybe you can go fuck yourself."

His smile revealed crooked, yellow teeth. "Maybe I would rather fuck the mark." He licked his lips and grabbed his dick. "That Beckett woman is a fine piece of ass."

"Four rules," Royce amended, his voice low and hard. "No one lays a finger on her. You so much as sniff her perfume, you're a dead man."

"Why is this? You have designs on her yourself?" Marcel smiled. "May I watch?"

"The boss says no one touches her. So, no one touches her."

Marcel crossed his arms and scowled. "How come Gunnar is allowed to stay with the woman?"

"Because you have no self-control," Layla spat. "You force yourself on women because you can't get any of them to fuck you willingly."

"I am more man than you have ever had, cunt. Perhaps, you want me to show you?"

Her scarlet lips stretched into a feral sneer. "How about if I cut your heart out and serve it for breakfast?"

Marcel smirked. "I thought you were a vegetarian."

Her shoulders lifted in a languorous shrug. "You're right. I'll feed it to my dog."

"Kiss my ass, whore."

Bishop scowled. "You people have to use such vulgar language?"

"What is the matter, preacher?" Marcel smiled. "We offend you?"

"The fact that you're alive offends me, little man."

"Damn," Royce snapped. "You guys in grade school or what? We have a job to do. We'll be spending a lot of time together in close quarters. I don't intend to play nursemaid to you assholes. Figure out a way to get along."

"I have an excellent idea," Marcel said. "The boss does not need to know how much the take was. We can split most of his share."

Royce turned his gaze to the Frenchman, more disgusted with each passing second. "You know, for a Poindexter looking motherfucker, you're not too bright. The news will report how much was stolen. Besides, that's not how this take goes down. If we can't trust you, you're expendable."

"You know something?" Marcel said. "I do not think there is another guy. I think *you* are the one who is calling the shots."

"Yeah?" Royce leaned down until he was a few inches from Marcel's vile breath. "Does it matter? You take orders from me. Period. Don't try to think too much, you might hurt yourself. All you gotta do is listen. Clear?"

Marcel's watery eyes glared back, and he stuck out his lower lip. "Fine. So, everything, including the big take, splits six ways, *oui*?"

"That's it. In theory."

"In theory?"

Royce nodded. "Each person's split will end up being more by the time this is over. Not all of us will survive the mission."

Marcel laughed. "Why would you say that?"

"Because, I know the guy we're up against."

"So?" Marcel looked around the table. "The *guy*. Do you people hear this?" He turned back to Royce. "There are six of us, *monsieur*. One of him."

Royce had worked with him before. Saw him annihilate a dozen guerillas in under two minutes with nothing more than a knife. He was taking a big chance he'd be one of the ones who didn't survive, but the money made it worth it. Hell, the adrenaline rush alone sucked him in. He chuckled and shook his head. "I know. *Only* six of us."

Chapter Five

China's house was too quiet. She put on an Elvis Presley CD—finding comfort in the music she and her aunt had listened to when she was growing up—and turned the volume up as loud as it would go. She was heading up the stairs when it occurred to her that the music would mask the noise of an intruder.

Debating for just a moment, she decided the silence was worse, and left the music on. "Danny Boy" blasted around her as she reached the top of the stairs.

Her house was a multi-level, thirty four hundred square-foot Tudor with five bedrooms, a pool, sauna, and hot tub. The front was secluded by an overhang of trees, and the back yard opened up into a wooded area. The home was much more elaborate than she could possibly afford on her salary. There were months she could barely make the utilities, and last summer she hadn't opened the pool because she couldn't afford the upkeep. But at least she didn't have to pay a mortgage.

She'd always counted herself lucky that Gary had left her the house as compensation for his abandonment. But now it felt like enemy territory, and the spacious rooms seemed to be nothing more than good hiding places for intruders.

In the bathroom, she turned the shower on as hot as it would go and stripped, stepping quickly inside. Steam surrounded her, the spray so strong, it stung her skin. But that was okay. It meant she was alive.

She wasn't sure how long she'd been standing under the water. It had turned cold, yet she remained. The strains of "Love Comin' Down" penetrated through the closed door. She considered getting out, but the cold water was starting to numb her, and that was what she needed. To forget, not to feel for a while.

"China?" A man's voice bellowed her name at the same time the bathroom door flung open, slamming against the wall. She screamed as the shower curtain was yanked back.

The scream died in her throat when she recognized Steve.

His face twisted in concern. "Good God, China. Are you okay?"

She couldn't answer. Tears streamed down her cheeks, and her body trembled. She didn't even care that she was naked.

Steve reached behind her and shut off the water. He grabbed a large bath towel and wrapped it around her body, then helped her from the shower.

"Sweetheart." He shook her shoulders gently. "Talk to me."

She stared at him in silence, drinking in the familiarity of his guileless, boyish features, his reddish-brown hair, and the nearly invisible freckles on his nose, at the goatee he'd grown when the guys at the fire station took to calling him Opie.

"How did you get in?" she finally said.

"I banged on the door, but you didn't answer. I have a key, remember?"

"Oh. Right." She'd given him a key, because he watched the house for her from time to time when she went out of town.

"I heard what happened. Are you—"

"Please," she cut him off. "Don't ask me if I'm okay. If I have to answer that question one more time, I'll explode."

He smiled. "Okay. I won't ask." He rubbed his hands briskly along her arms and for the first time since the robbery, she began to feel warm.

"Thank you," she whispered. She leaned her head against his shoulder and inhaled his familiar scent—Brut cologne and a hint of the hand-rolled cigars he occasionally smoked. Steve was a good friend and had been there for her through some tough times, but none as tough as this.

His arm tightened around her, and she became aware of her near nudity. Her face heated. He'd just seen her *naked*. She pulled away from him. "I need to get dressed. Go get Emma." She had a sudden, compelling, desperate desire to see her daughter. To hold her small, soft body in her arms.

"I'll drive you."

She shook her head. "No, please. I'll be fine."

"I'll just stay here while you're getting ready, then. So you're not alone in the house."

"Okay, sure. Thanks."

He followed her through the bathroom door that led to her bedroom. "I'll wait downstairs." He headed to the door.

"Steve?"

He paused and turned back. "Yeah?"

"Do you think God is punishing me?"

He frowned. "What?"

She shrugged. "My parents are across the world doing His work. Growing up, Destiny traveled with them and did the same. I was such a wuss that I stayed with Aunt Lucy most of my life."

He chuckled. "So, you're trying to say that your sister, Destiny, is a better person than you are?"

Well. Maybe *that* was a stretch. At eighteen, Destiny—older by two years—had left missionary work and in the fifteen years since, had been hell-bent on making up for lost time. Her life's goal seemed to be to party her ass off and seek every pleasure life had to offer, regardless of whom it hurt, including Destiny's fourteen-year-old daughter, Spencer, whose father—wherever and whoever he was—didn't even know she existed.

"I don't know. It's just that with everything that's happened, I just wonder. First Aiden died, then Gary deserted Emma and me. Now this."

Steve shook his head and folded his arms over his chest. "Aiden was a mercenary in some of the most dangerous places in the world. His entire life was a risk. As far as Gary is concerned, you married a man you didn't love, and he wouldn't know a good thing if it bit him on the ass." He crossed the room and looked down at her, brushing a lock of hair from her eyes. "And a bank robbery is just some random crime. You think God sent those bastards to your bank?"

China smiled. "Now you're making me sound silly."

"Well, if you think someone like you deserves to be punished by God, then you are silly."

She wished his words provided the comfort he'd intended. Still, she was grateful for his presence, his friendship. "Thanks." She squeezed his hand. "I'd better get dressed."

China said goodbye to Steve and slid into her car. She checked her purse to make sure she'd brought her cell and saw a missed call from Lucy. She tried to call her back, but there was no answer. A niggle of worry seeped in, but she pushed it aside. Lucy had probably just been calling to make sure she was okay. Her aunt didn't answer because, half the time, she didn't pay attention to her phone.

Sunlight warmed her face through the windshield as she drove. The sky was a clear, gorgeous blue. She tried to concentrate on the lovely May weather and not on what she'd seen that morning. Tried to keep telling herself that, just as Boyle said, she had been lucky. She was alive to see the beautiful day.

Sophie hadn't been so fortunate.

She was two miles from Lucy's house when her aunt called back.

"Hi, China doll, I'm sorry I couldn't reach you earlier."

"I guess I was in the shower when you called. I tried to call you back. I'm almost there."

"Almost where?"

"To your house. Where else?"

"Didn't you get my message?"

She stopped at a red light. "No. I didn't listen to my messages. Is something wrong?"

"Nothing's wrong. You know I love to see you anytime, but I didn't want you to waste a trip over here if you were just coming to get Emma."

"What are you talking about? Waste a trip?" She gritted her teeth and prayed for patience. Her aunt invariably took forever to get to the point.

"I mean, because Emma's not here."

Her heart slowed, then thumped loudly in her ears. "What do you mean, not there?"

"She's with that police officer. The detective."

"Detective Boyle?"

"Let's see. I don't recall his name, but that doesn't sound right."

The light turned green, and China pressed the accelerator. "Why is she with a detective, Aunt Lucy?"

"Well, because you sent him over to get her."

"What?" Her knees weakened, and she lost her breath. "Lucy, I did not send a detective over to get her. I didn't send anyone. You let her go with a stranger? Without calling me?"

"Oh, my. I tried to call you, remember? He was a policeman. He had a badge."

Chills raced over her skin. Why would the police pick up Emma?

"I need to call Miles and see what's going on."

"Is everything okay?"

"I—I don't know. I'll call you back."

China's fingers could barely function as she punched in Miles' number. Before she completed the digits, the phone shrilled in her hand. She jumped and almost dropped it.

The caller ID showed her home number. Dear God. Who was at her house?

She jammed the answer button with her thumb. "Hello?"

"Miss Beckett."

"Who is this?"

"You do not know me." The voice was deep, heavily accented. Austrian? German? Swedish? "Emma is here with me. You must please come home now."

Chapter Six

From somewhere deep in the Tanier jungle surrounding the prison, the chirp of a red-tailed monkey filtered through the hut window, followed by the low roar of a large cat.

Warden Kirabo Masawi's ebony skin gleamed with sweat, the lazily spinning ceiling fan the only source of air in the stifling room. Still, compared to the sweltering cage Stone had lived in the past seven years, the temperature felt like winter.

As Kirabo handed him his release papers, he said, "Mr. Stone, tell me. Are you happy to be free?"

Stone let out a sound that was meant to be a derisive laugh but came out more like a growl. "Tickled pink, Kirabo."

Kirabo's white-toothed smile took up the entire lower half of his dark-skinned face. "You were treated well, no?"

Treated well? Imprisoned seven years for a crime he hadn't committed. Food, sunlight, water, and various other luxuries withheld as punishment for all misdeeds, great and small. Beatings, solitary confinement, lice, disease. Oh yeah, treated well.

At least they'd rewarded him for good behavior. He lifted a hand and fingered the gold earring in his left lobe. A gift from Sabra, who was one of the few rewards he'd been given. A woman provided for his pleasure, only to be cruelly taken away when her entire village had been murdered six months ago.

He missed her, but tried not to think about it. She'd really been nothing more than a prostitute, but she'd cared about him and he her. What they'd shared hadn't been love, but it had been real. And now she was gone. He gave himself a mental shake, pushing back the grief. A man who lived as he did couldn't afford attachments. He'd known better. Or, at least he should have. China had taught him that lesson well enough.

"Treated like a king, dude," he said to Kirabo. "Thanks for the hospitality." Stone hefted his pack onto his shoulder and tipped the warden a two-finger salute. "See you around."

"But you will not be around, yes? You are returning to States?"

"No. I won't be around. It's just an expression. Yes. Returning to the States."

Where he could take a real shower for the first time in years. He'd lived with his own stink for so long he could no longer smell it, but he knew it was there. He wanted a good old American shower where he'd use too much hot water and soap up with Irish Spring until the bar was no bigger than a credit card. The hell with conserving resources. He hadn't used any of the US resources for seven years, so there should be a large chunk coming to him, and he intended to take his share.

"A good woman and a job await you, yes?"

"Yes," Stone said, simply to end the conversation. The job part was true. His buddy, Wesley, was not only holding money for him, he had a job set up for Stone in Texas. Now he just had to get there. *Straight* to Texas. No way in hell would he stop in Oklahoma. No matter how badly he craved seeing her. To give her a piece of his mind. To maybe make her suffer just a little of what he'd suffered.

But he wouldn't. China was married to someone else. Had a kid with the guy. But even before that, she'd betrayed him. While he lay near death in a hospital, she'd high-tailed it to the US. And he was thrown in a Tanier prison. He'd be damned if he'd ever look her in the face again, even if just to tell her what a lying, deceitful bitch she was.

Ice chilled China's blood. "Who is this? The police?"

"I am not police. They must not be called. No one must. You will come here right away. Alone."

"I don't understand. Who are you? You're at my house? I just left there."

"Emma and I arrived only moments ago."

Panic threatened to choke off her words, but she took in a deep breath and said again, "Who is this?"

"Everything will be explained."

"Is Emma okay? You haven't hurt her? Please don't hurt her."

"She is well. No more questions. You must come quickly, but do not exceed the speed limit. You must not encounter police. Goodbye."

"Wait—" But he was gone. China stared at the phone, her mind spinning with disbelief. What the hell was happening?

The blare of a horn made her snap her attention back to the road. A large tree loomed in front of the windshield, and she jerked the wheel back until the car was once more in its lane.

Good God, she'd forgotten she was driving.

She sucked in a deep breath and gripped the steering wheel, attempting to keep an eye on the speedometer. In spite of the desire to rush home to Emma, she knew it was urgent—critical— that she follow his instructions to the letter. The man hadn't been kidding around. He had her child. Her baby.

"Oh, God. Emma," she whispered. "Please be okay. Please, baby. Hold on. Mommy's coming."

Staying under the speed limit took every ounce of will power she could muster as she made the seemingly unending drive home. The world around her turned surreal, like she was an observer rather than a participant. Cars whizzed by, people meandered along the sidewalks. The stores, gas stations, businesses she passed. All were pieces of something she was no longer a part of. They were from the old world, the one that existed before an unseen danger had decimated her life.

She turned onto her street, her gaze immediately going to her tree-shrouded house at the end of the road. Funny. It looked normal. But a stranger—a deadly one—was inside with her baby, and this whole mess was far from normal.

Barely able to draw a full breath into her constricted lungs, she whipped into the driveway. Slamming the car into park, she flew out of the car and rushed to the front door.

"Emma!" she screamed, flinging the door open and running through the foyer into the living room.

Emma sat on the couch watching *Sponge Bob Square Pants.* Her startled gaze flew to China.

"Momma. What's wrong?"

A man stood at the opposite end of the couch, too close, *much* too close, to Emma.

"Emma," she whispered, relief sweeping through her. *Emma was alive.* Everything would be okay.

Emma scrambled from the couch and flew into her arms. "I missed you."

"Oh, baby." China clung to her and squeezed. "Are you okay?"

"Unh-huh. I'm okay."

China pulled back. Her eyes drank in the sight of her daughter. Strands of Emma's brown, curly hair clung to her chubby cheeks. Big, round dark eyes—so like her father's—seemed even larger behind the magnified lenses of her glasses.

"What took you so long to get here?" Emma's small face scrunched into a frown.

"I had...uhm...a little...trouble. At work. A problem came up." Sophie's bullet riddled body flashed through her mind, and she pushed the image aside. "How's your breathing?"

"It's good now. Miss Sally got me calm by singing." Emma glanced at the stranger, then back to China and lowered her voice. "I know I'm not supposed to go with strangers, but Aunt Lucy said he was a police and I should go. Am I in trouble?"

"No, sweetie." China hugged her again. "No. You didn't do anything wrong."

Emma pulled back and touched the tears on China's cheeks. "Why are you crying?"

China quickly brushed them away. "It's been a stressful day. Grown up things, honey. Momma's okay."

She looked up at the intruder. A blond man, wide-shouldered and as tall as an oak. One side of his face was movie star handsome with a chiseled jaw and eyes as blue as the sky. The other side was marred by an eggplant-colored scar that went from the corner of his eye to his jawbone, like beauty and the beast all in one face.

It was bizarre, having this strange, scary man in her home. Crazy to be comforting her daughter when she had no idea herself what was happening. Telling Emma she was okay, when she as far from okay as she could be.

China came to her feet and faced the man, pulling Emma against her body, both hands on her shoulders. "Who are you? What the hell is going on?"

"Please. Have a seat."

"Are you out of your mind? Don't offer me a seat in my own damned home!" The fear she'd felt for the past six hours turned into fury. "I want to know what's going on, and I want to know now!"

Emma turned a puzzled glance to her. "Momma? What's wrong?"

She squeezed her shoulders reassuringly. "Nothing, honey. Everything is fine."

"Yes, that is correct. All is well." The big man nodded. "There is no need to become agitated. Everything will be explained in due time. There will be more men here soon. My job is to stay with you to make sure all goes according to plan. In the event it does not, my job is to—take care—of you both."

Her heart dropped into her stomach. He said it so calmly, as if offering a stock tip.

She eyed the door. The man hadn't shown a weapon. She and Emma were closer to the front door than he was. If she was quick, she could—

"Do not try it."

Her gaze whipped back to the stranger. He'd turned his body slightly. Enough that she could see a gun tucked into his waistband. No way could she make it out the door without him gunning her down, and Emma, too.

"You cannot escape. There are many others. We would find you. You must simply follow orders."

"What orders? Why? I don't understand."

"As I said, more will be explained. Please be patient."

"You were the ones who robbed the bank."

"No more questions."

China clenched her jaw. "It wasn't a question."

Emma pulled away and looked up at China. "I'm thirsty."

"Come on. I'll get you a snack." She shot a look at the man, but he didn't seem inclined to stop them. He followed them to the kitchen. She sat with Emma while she had her juice and apples. Silent tension filled the room. Even Emma's normal chatter was missing. Her inquisitive gaze moved back and forth between the man and China.

After finishing only half her apples, Emma said, "I'm done. Can I watch *Sponge Bob*?"

"Sure. Yes. Come on, sweetie. I'll watch it with you."

They went into the living room, and Emma climbed onto the sofa next to China. "And Gunnar?"

"Gunnar?"

She twisted around to look at the man. "Him. Gunnar. Can he watch it too?"

China swallowed back a rush of tears. "Oh. Yeah. Gunnar, too."

She didn't see him move, but sensed when he came around the couch and settled into the easy chair.

China took Emma's small hand in hers and forced her attention to the TV, trying to focus on the wide happy smile of the sponge who lived in the sea.

Chapter Seven

The third straight episode of *Sponge Bob* was winding to a close when Gunnar stood and looked toward the kitchen. "They have arrived."

"Who?"

"The others."

China hadn't heard a phone ring or seen him take one out, so she wasn't sure how he knew.

"They will be in the kitchen. You must go to them."

Torn between not wanting to leave Emma alone with this man, and not wanting her to encounter whoever might be waiting, China hesitated.

"You will leave Emma with me." Gunnar seemed to read her mind.

She bit her lip and started to protest, but she didn't have a choice. If he wanted to harm Emma, he would do so whether China was around or not. She rose to her feet. "I'll be right back, sweetie."

Emma barely nodded, her attention still glued to the television.

In the kitchen, two men stood near the center island. One was tall, with a close-cropped beard and piercing gray eyes. The other was short with messy hair and large, gold-rimmed glasses, behind which, hazel eyes glittered with a light that wasn't quite sane. A laptop case hung over his shoulder.

She was sure the taller one had been the robber who'd led her out of the office. When he spoke, she knew she was right.

"I apologize, China. I'm sure this hasn't been an easy day for you."

"What the hell is going on?"

"Royce Dolan."

He stuck out a hand, and she looked at it, then back up to his face. "You've got to be kidding me."

He grinned and dropped his hand. Cocking his head toward the short man, he said, "This is Marcel."

Marcel licked his lips, and his watery gaze moved slowly over China's body. "Pleased to meet you." He smiled. "*Very* pleased to meet you."

Marcel was the one who'd pointed the gun at Vanessa, she was certain. His voice sounded familiar, and there was a hint of the accent she'd caught when he'd spoken during the robbery.

Had one of these two been the one who'd shot Sophie? She wasn't sure which of the robbers had pulled the trigger. That had happened before she'd even laid eyes on these men. Before she knew there *was* a robbery.

Royce went to the refrigerator and swung the door open. A sheet of paper fluttered before settling back down. One of Emma's coloring pages of the Disney princesses, held to the fridge by her magnetic school photo. China cringed. This animal touching those precious items, getting near them, seemed like a sacrilege.

He bent inside. "No beer? You need to go shopping." He turned back to look at her. "You'll have a number of guests to entertain over the next several days."

"Guests? *Entertain?*" She crossed her arms over her breasts and squeezed her fists, partly to block Marcel's gaze, and partly so she'd have something to clench. "I don't know what kind of demented game this is, but—but—"

"Calm down," Royce said. "No need to get worked up. Obey our orders, and we'll all make it through this." He shut the refrigerator door and pointed to the kitchen table. "Please, have a seat."

Hesitating just a moment, China sat. If she were going to disobey, it wouldn't be on something this minor. As her aunt liked to say, *learn how to pick your battles.*

"Momma?" China whirled to find Emma, with Gunnar just behind her, standing in the doorway, looking around the room at the men. "Who are they?"

"They—they're friends of Gunnar," China said. "Go back into the living room."

"Why can't I stay?"

"I'm dealing with some grown up stuff. Please just do what I say."

She frowned, sticking her lower lip out in a pout. "Okay. But I'm hungry."

"You just had a snack. We'll have dinner a little later."

Emma's long-suffering sigh followed her as she stomped out of the room. Gunnar disappeared along with her. *Lovely.* Her daughter had a looming, menacing, dangerous bodyguard. What a comfort.

When Emma was gone, Royce settled in the seat across from China, while Marcel remained standing behind her. She shifted nervously as something unpleasant slithered over her skin.

"Cute kid," Royce said.

The words shot fear through her heart. She jumped to her feet. "You leave my child alone. I swear to God, if you touch—"

He held up his hands. "Settle down, China. I can assure you, you're in no position to make threats. Sit down." He waited, and when she didn't move, he bit out, "I said, sit down."

She dropped into the chair and pressed her palms against the table, resisting the urge to lunge at him.

"That's better." He gave a curt nod. "I hope you understand what we expect from you."

She slid her hands from the table and wrapped them around her trembling body. Her breath stalled, and she shook her head. "Actually, I have no idea." Her shoulders trembled, and sobs caught in her aching chest. She shook her head over and over. "I have no idea what's going on, what you want from me."

"Right now, we want you to get ahold of yourself. Becoming hysterical will help no one."

Her gaze jerked up to him. She swiped tears off her cheeks and barked out a disbelieving laugh. "Are you kidding? My boss was murdered before my eyes, and criminals are in my house, with my child, and you want me to get ahold of myself?"

"For the sake of your daughter, I would highly advise you do just that."

Another threat to Emma. How could she protect her daughter against these vicious killers?

She sucked in a deep breath, let it out slowly, swallowed back tears. "Okay, I'll try. Please just tell me what you want me to do, then leave."

"I'm afraid this won't be over quite that quickly. All you need to know for now is that we expect your total cooperation."

"Cooperation in what? I don't understand any of this. What do you want? You robbed the bank because of me? Shot Sophie because of me?" Guilt stabbed her heart. She hadn't liked Sophie, not at all, but the poor woman was dead for God's sake. And it somehow had something to do with her. She pushed the thoughts aside. Nothing she could do about that. For now, she had to focus on keeping Emma safe.

"The robbery was only a small part. You will know more when the time is right. For now, you need to understand that we expect complete obedience."

"Obedience? You invaded my home. Threatened my life. My *daughter's* life." She ran a wobbly hand through her hair and shook her head. "You want me to do what you say and won't even tell me why you're doing this. This is too bizarre. Too much. I can't—" She sighed, shook her head again. "I can't do this. I don't understand why."

"Perhaps this will help." Royce motioned with his hand, and Marcel came around to place the laptop case on the table. He slid out a computer and booted it up. His stubby fingers clicked a few times on the keyboard before he turned the laptop around facing her and Royce.

The screen filled with what seemed to be a live feed of a coffee shop. At a small round table next to the window, a professionally dressed man and woman leisurely sipped from cups. Only a few other patrons were in camera range. One was a teenage boy who stood behind the couple, staring up at the menu, the other a young mother with two small children at a table nearby. China frowned. She didn't know any of them. "I don't know what you want. What am I supposed to be looking at?"

"Which one?" Royce asked.

"Which one what?"

Royce tapped a finger on the screen, first on the man, then his female companion. "Which one do you want to die?"

China's gaze flew to his face. "Die? Neither. Are you out of your mind?"

He flashed a smile that would have been attractive had it not been tinged with such evil. "Quite possibly. But that's beside the point. Which one? You must make a choice."

"No." Her head whipped from side to side in vigorous denial. "No. This is insane."

"If you don't choose, both will die."

"You can't," she whispered. "You won't."

He let out a sigh. He seemed to consider for a few seconds then once again motioned to Marcel. Marcel took out a phone and punched the keypad several times.

"Watch," Royce said.

She turned back to the screen, not wanting to see, but unable to look away.

There was no sound, but white flashes streaked across the screen. Glass shards burst like fireworks, and the two people jerked. Dark splotches painted their chests, and pandemonium broke out. People lunged from tables, most of them diving to the floor, but one man rushed to the couple and bent over the woman.

"Oh my God." China slapped a hand across her mouth. Shivers raced over her flesh. "You killed them."

The man on the video raised his head and shouted something, then the screen went black.

"No, I didn't kill them," Royce said. "You did."

Chapter Eight

Somehow China kept a scream from escaping. *Emma is in the next room. Can't frighten her.* She gasped for air, unable to escape the reality of what she'd witnessed, to tame the horror bubbling within her.

"You killed them." Her lips were numb, and the voice trembling out of her didn't sound like her own.

"Yes. You could have stopped it. Or, at least, saved one of them."

"What?" Her eyes were still glued to the blank screen. "You're blaming me?"

He shrugged. "We have a point to make."

"So you murdered two innocent people?"

"But you didn't know them."

She swung her gaze to him. "Am I supposed to thank you for that? That you killed *strangers* in cold blood? That I caused the death of these people?"

He laughed. "You keep changing your mind. Did I cause their deaths or did you?"

"You killed them." She couldn't seem to stop saying it. Her breathing panted out of her in short gasps. Spots danced in front of her eyes. *Don't pass out, Emma needs you...* She clenched her hands together and looked up at Royce.

His smile chilled her already frozen heart. "Better than killing someone you love. And we haven't done that. Yet."

Yet. She shuddered. "But you will."

Royce shrugged. "All you have to do is go about your normal life and follow instructions we'll be giving you. Gunnar will stay with you to make sure of that. We will be around. Watching. If you tell anyone what is going on, your daughter will die." He held his cell phone in front of her face and flipped through a slide show. Her gut clenched as she recognized the people in the photos…Aunt Lucy, her sister, her niece, Steve, Vanessa. "Remember, we're watching. Everyone. The police won't be able to get to them all quickly enough. Don't try to slip anything by us. You can't be sneaky enough or clever enough to best us, so the wise thing to do is accept your new circumstances. Obey us and wait for all this to be over. If everything goes well, you and your daughter will live."

She shook her head back and forth over and over. "I don't know what you want."

"I just told you. That's what we want for now, and that's all you need to be concerned about."

Her cell rang, and she glanced at the display. Steve.

"Answer," Royce said.

"I don't want to talk to him right now."

"Answer." His tone made it clear he wasn't asking.

With a trembling finger, she punched the answer button and lifted the phone to her ear.

"Hey, sweetheart," Steve said. "How are you?"

"Fine."

"You don't sound fine."

Royce leaned in to listen. His warm breath touched her neck. The smell of cologne—Attitude by Armani—a fragrance she normally liked, now made her stomach roil.

"It's been an awful day," she told Steve. "But I'm okay. Emma's okay. We're fine."

"I thought I'd come and stay with you. My shift's over, and I don't have to be back at the station until Thursday."

"*No*. Uh, no. That's not necessary."

"At least let me come by and make sure you two are okay. Safe."

Safe. We are so freaking safe. Before she could stop it, a giggle escaped.

"China?" Steve's voice held a hint of concern. "I'll be there soon."

"No, please. You don't need to."

"I want to," Steve said. "Let me come over. Be with you guys."

Royce nodded and mouthed 'say yes.'

She shook her head, but the warning look in Royce's eyes made her say, "Okay. Sure. That would be great."

"I'll bring dinner."

"Yeah. Thanks. See you soon." She ended the call and jerked her gaze to Royce. "Why? Why would you want him to come over while this...this..." She waved a hand around the room, even though Royce and Marcel were the only visible signs of the nightmare she'd suddenly been thrust into, "*this* is going on?"

"Everything must appear normal."

Another hysterical giggle escaped, and tears filled her eyes. How would she hold it together?

Because, if she didn't, Emma would be at the mercy of these maniacs.

She squeezed her eyes shut, then opened them and sucked in a deep breath. Standing, she faced Royce. "Okay. You want normal, no problem." Forcing bravado into her tone she didn't feel, she said, "But I promise you, if anything happens to Emma, you'll have to kill me, too, because no amount of threats or torture will make me do a damn thing you say."

Royce and Marcel left, but Gunnar stayed behind. He would apparently be a permanent fixture until this nightmare ended.

He piled ham, cheese, and pickles on a slice of bread, slathered another slice with mayonnaise, and closed up the sandwich. He headed toward the staircase, turning to face her before he went up. "You must not say a word to anyone. I will be listening."

"You have the house bugged," she guessed.

"Details need not concern you. All you must remember is that following instructions is a critical necessity."

China nodded, but she didn't need that reminder. The carnage she'd witnessed on the laptop was all the incentive she needed. She wouldn't tell a soul. The problem was keeping her talkative daughter quiet.

In the living room, Emma was still mesmerized by Sponge Bob. At times, China worried that Emma watched too much TV, but right now, she could only be thankful. The cartoon was keeping her occupied and hopefully would prevent her from noticing what was going on in her home.

Settling onto the couch, China pulled Emma onto her lap. "You know how important it is to keep a promise, right?"

"Yes." She nodded solemnly, making her glasses slide to the tip of her nose. China absently pushed them up.

"The fact that Gunnar is here and that those men came to visit is a very, very big secret. It's important that no one else finds out."

"Why?"

China sucked in a deep breath. How to explain life and death to a six-year-old? How to explain that they'd been cast into some horrific Twilight Zone that even she didn't understand?

"It's a grown up thing that I can't fully explain. I just want you to understand that you cannot, absolutely cannot, mention this to anyone. Not to Aunt Lucy, not to your teachers, your friends at school, and not to Steve."

"What about Spencer and Aunt Vanessa and Uncle Miles?"

"No. Not to them either. No one, Emma, do you understand?"

She nodded slowly, but she really didn't understand. How could she?

"Do you promise me? Promise and swear that it will be our secret?"

"Yes. I promise."

China hugged her tightly. "That's my big girl."

The doorbell rang, and Emma jumped from China's lap and ran to the door. China followed.

Emma swung the door open, and her face broke into a gap-toothed grin. "Steve!"

China's heart ached at her enthusiasm over Steve's visit. Just like Emma's immediate acceptance of Gunnar. She was hungry for a father. Gary had been that for a few years, but China hadn't been able to give him enough of herself. Hadn't been able to love him enough. He wanted the part of her she could never give. The part that would always belong to Aiden.

Now Emma was left without a father and she clung to every male figure that came into their lives. Another reason not to get involved with Steve. China didn't want to get Emma's hopes up only to have them dashed when she couldn't hold onto love.

Steve strolled in carrying a large pizza box with Emma practically tripping over his heels.

"Pepperoni!" she shouted gleefully. "I wonder if Gun—" She stopped, turning a horrified gaze to China. China's breath stalled in her chest.

"What's that, honey?" Steve asked, looking down at Emma.

"I wonder if...if I can have two slices."

"Sure, there's plenty." He gave China a puzzled look, and she shrugged, letting the breath slowly escape.

"Kids." She forced a smile. "I'll get the sodas. Let's eat in here in front of the TV."

Steve and Emma stared at her as if she'd suggested they tap dance on top of the pizza box. For her to allow food in the living room was unusual, but then, everything about this day had been unusual. She didn't want to sit at the kitchen table just yet. Not in the spot where she'd watched two people violently slaughtered for her benefit.

She grabbed two Diet Pepsis and a Sprite from the fridge. She took them, along with paper plates and napkins, into the living room. The three of them watched television, and China tried to force down some food, but every bite stuck in her throat like a lump of wet cardboard. Steve shot a concerned glance at her over Emma's head, but he didn't say anything about her lack of appetite.

Most likely attributing it to the robbery, he also didn't question her silence, her mood. She was sure she did a poor job of hiding her relief when he stood and said he was leaving. Not that she wasn't glad for his company. She was. The thought of her and Emma once more being left alone with the maniac upstairs was not appealing, but having Steve here, waiting for something to tip him off, something to go wrong, had her nerves strung tighter than the skin of an onion.

"Are you sure you'll be okay?" Steve asked when she walked him to the door. "I can stay here tonight if you need me."

The look in his eyes said he'd stay every night if she'd just say the word. She couldn't, though. Hadn't been able to yet and definitely wouldn't start now when doing so could get her and Emma both killed.

"I'm okay, really. Thanks, though."

"You'll call me if you need me?"

"I will."

He planted a quick kiss on her lips before leaving. She shut the door behind him and went back into the living room. Gunnar was already there.

"You both did well," he said.

She ignored him and took Emma's hand. "Time for your bath, sweetie, then bed. Let's go upstairs."

Emma turned to Gunnar. "Night, Gunnar. Sweet dreams."

His brows drew together briefly. He gave a quick nod. "I will see you in the morning."

As China made her way up the stairs, she could feel his gaze on her and Emma. Any moment, she expected to hear the sound of gunfire. Her back tingled with the expectation of the impact of a bullet. She didn't fully relax until she was upstairs and had closed the bathroom door behind them.

Chapter Nine

China sat on the edge of the bed while Emma took her breathing treatment, her eyes big and vulnerable above the mask.

Her heart ached every time she saw the apparatus strapped to Emma's tiny face. She'd taken the treatments since she was an infant and had always been good for them, sitting still and quiet even though, in the beginning, she had no idea what was happening. The fact that she had now grown accustomed to them was almost as heartbreaking as her needing them in the first place.

After removing the mask, China leaned forward and placed a kiss on Emma's forehead. She smelled like soap and shampoo, and China wanted to sit here with her forever, absorbing her youth, her sweetness.

A knock sounded at the door just as they were finishing Emma's favorite bedtime story, Cinderella.

"China?" Gunnar called from the other side of the closed door, the sound making her heart jump with trepidation. It was odd to hear her name coming from this frightening stranger.

"Yes?"

"You are almost done?"

"I'll be right back, sweetie," she said to Emma.

When she opened the door, the light from the hallway behind Gunnar lit his white-blond hair like a halo—angelic features on the devil.

"Done?" China said quietly. "I'm tucking my daughter in. Then I'm getting ready for bed myself and coming back in to sleep with her. Is there something you need?"

"You will not sleep with her."

"What?"

"You do not normally, correct?"

That was correct. China didn't normally sleep with her. She used a baby monitor to check her breathing. On days when Emma showed severe signs of asthma problems, China would sleep in her room, but those times were rare.

She thought about lying, but figured these guys knew more about her than she would have dreamed. She couldn't take the chance they'd catch her being untruthful. She wasn't sure what the consequences would be.

"No, I do not."

"All must be as normal. Emma will sleep alone."

A terrifying thought surfaced. Did Gunnar plan to sleep with *her*? No one was here to stop him from doing whatever he wanted. She was at his mercy. Nausea rose in her throat.

As though he read her thoughts, he said, "I will be sleeping in the guest room next to yours. I only require a few hours' sleep and will be on guard most of the night. Please do not worry."

He said it as if his presence was a comfort. *Right*.

She nodded. "I'll just say goodnight to Emma, then."

He returned her nod, and she closed the door and went back to Emma's bed. Eyes drooping with fatigue, Emma gave a small smile, and China bent to place a kiss on her forehead. "Sleep well, angel. Love you."

"Love you, Mommy," she whispered.

China's heart clenched. Emma only called her 'mommy' when she was ill or sleepy...or afraid.

The next day, China wanted to keep Emma out of school and stay home from work, but she couldn't. Not under the pretext of living normal lives. The bank wasn't open to customers, but all employees were expected to come in. The bosses wanted to talk to them, check on their well-being, inform them of developments. China knew much more than she wanted to about this whole disaster.

She dropped Emma off at school and drove to work. Her coworkers' movements were almost robotic. Their glassy eyes held the same terror she was sure was reflected in her own. Only she had even more cause than they did. Who knew that yesterday's robbery would be only the beginning of the nightmare? That it wouldn't be the worst thing that happened to her that day.

Vanessa came over to her desk and wrapped her in a tight hug. As if by unspoken agreement, they looked at Sophie's office, at the empty space where her window used to be.

"I can't believe it," Vanessa whispered. "She's dead. Murdered. I keep thinking of all the awful things I said about her."

"*We* said about her," China whispered back. They'd called Sophie everything from Super Bitch to Dragon Lady to Silver Succubus...and worse. And now she was dead. China tried not to think about it.

The bank president, Richard Lewiston, came out of his office into the lobby. "Everyone, can I please have all of you in the conference room?"

He'd been out of the bank at the time of the robbery. Lucky, lucky man.

Obediently, they all made their way into the conference room amidst the sounds of nervous throat clearing and rustling as people settled in chairs.

Richard looked sympathetically at his employees, then took a deep breath. "First of all, I want you to know how very sorry I am about what happened yesterday. About the robbery itself and the tragic loss of Sophie. As horrible as her death was, I thank God there weren't more casualties and that all of you are safe." His eyes landed on China, and he gave her a small smile. She felt all eyes turn to her, but kept her gaze straight ahead. "We'll resume business tomorrow. The police may have more questions for all of you. I've told them we'd be available at any time to assist with the investigation. These criminals are still out there, and the most important thing right now, other than the mental health of all of you, is for these men to be captured and brought to justice."

China squelched a hysterical laugh. These men were 'out there' all right. Just not as far as Richard, or the authorities, might think.

"We'll need your full cooperation with the police," Richard continued. "China, they specifically want to speak with you again." His handsome faced drew into a look of sympathy. "They asked if you could come by the station this afternoon."

A cold weight settled in her stomach. She would have dreaded talking to the cops no matter what, but now, knowing what she did and knowing she couldn't tell them, couldn't ask for help, would make the situation ten times worse.

Richard ended the speech by telling them they'd all be required to go through trauma counseling. A psychiatrist would be appointed, and a schedule would be set up so that each of them saw the doctor once a week. Their appointment times would be handed out the next day at work.

Subdued and morose, the employees slowly left the conference room. They were all free to leave, although China would be expected to stop by the police department.

"China?"

She turned when Richard called her name. "Yes?"

"Can you step into my office, please?"

She did, and he closed the door.

"Please, have a seat," he said. When she settled into the chair across from his desk, he sat in his own and steepled his fingers beneath his chin. "I know you were there when Sophie was shot. In her office."

"Yes."

"I'm sure that was especially traumatic for you. I can't imagine what it must have been like."

She nodded but didn't trust herself to speak.

"If you feel you need extra sessions with the psychiatrist, please let me know. We're family here at GOB, and we want to make sure you get through this."

Really? Then want to come to my house and run off the psychos who have invaded my life like ants at a picnic?

"Thank you. I appreciate it," she said.

"You will let me know?"

"Yes."

He nodded and stood. "That's all. Just take care of yourself."

She gulped back a sob. "I will. Thank you."

He walked her to the door and took her hands in his, giving them a squeeze.

Vanessa was waiting to accompany her to the parking lot. Thank God for her presence, her friendship. Even though she couldn't confide in her, couldn't really turn to her like she wanted to, just having her around was a comfort.

"You want me to go with you to the station?" Vanessa asked when they reached China's car. "Maybe I could make things easier, you know, because of Miles."

"No, thanks. I appreciate the offer, but it's not like I'm in trouble or anything." At least, not with the police. "I'll be fine. I'll answer their questions, pick up Emma, and go home and relax."

For just a moment, she was tempted to tell Vanessa what was going on, but she couldn't. Royce had been very specific in his instructions and very explicit in his example.

Chapter Ten

Detective Boyle met her in an austere, colorless lobby that held a loveseat and four chairs arranged around a scarred coffee table.

"Come on back, Miss Beckett."

China followed him into a small room with a bare desk and two chairs. When they were both seated, she waited for him to speak. Not knowing what to do with her hands, she used them to fiddle nervously with her purse strap.

Boyle opened a file and flipped through a few sheets of paper before addressing her. "Now, let me go over your statement and you tell me if there's anything you've thought of. Maybe something you...accidentally left out."

She noticed the slight hesitation before 'accidentally' and her discomfiture grew.

"Or perhaps there's something else you've remembered," he continued. "That okay with you?"

"Yes." The words came out as a croak. She cleared her throat and tried again. "Yes. That's fine."

"Okay, you say you were in Mrs. Oswald's office asking to leave early to pick up your daughter at school. You didn't know the bank was being robbed until Mrs. Oswald was shot."

"That's right."

"And you didn't know the robbers. Didn't recognize anything about them?"

She was able to answer truthfully by concentrating on the 'didn't.' At the time of the robbery, she didn't know them. "That's right. I didn't know them. Why would I?"

His shrug was too casual for her liking. "No reason. It's just that they shot right past you and killed your boss. A woman you've had differences with in the past."

"I wouldn't really say differences."

"What would you say?"

"I don't know." She shrugged and let her gaze wander around the room before coming back to Boyle. "She was a tough boss. A lot of people had conflicts with her."

He arranged his face into his trademark perplexed expression. "Yet *you're* the only one who was in the room with her when she was shot."

She gasped. "Are you insinuating I had something to do with Sophie's murder?"

He turned an innocent look her way. "I'm insinuating nothing of the kind. Why would you think that?"

"I just thought...you sounded like..." She blew out a breath. "Never mind. Please, let's just hurry and get this over with."

"As I was saying, you were spared. The robbers called you by name. They seemed to almost defer to you in a way."

"Defer to me?" Her laugh was short and devoid of humor. "I was nearly killed. They murdered my boss in front of my eyes. Pointed a gun at my best friend—"

"And didn't shoot her when you told them not to," he cut in.

"Dear God! You think they were following my orders?" She shot to her feet. "Do you think I'm *glad* they shot my boss? This is bullshit. Are you charging me with something? Do I need a lawyer?"

"Do you?" He didn't wait for an answer. "Take it easy, Miss Beckett. Please sit. I'm not accusing you of anything. I'm simply trying to solve a crime. Trying to catch some bad guys. You want to help me with that, right?"

More than you could possibly know. She now wished she'd let Vanessa come with her, although the detective probably wouldn't have let her sit in on the interview.

He stood and held a hand out toward the door. "Come with me. I'd like to show you something."

China followed him into a large room that held a long table with chairs on either side. At one end of the table was a small television. Detective Boyle walked over to the television and pointed at the chair nearest it. "Sit, please."

She did, and he turned the power on the TV, then pushed a button on a remote. A grainy, black and white image appeared on the screen. The quality wasn't state-of-the-art, but she recognized the scene. The bank. The robbery.

This time, she was able to see the shooting taking place, not just the end results. The guy who'd pointed the gun at Vanessa—and not the one who'd been China's escort—had pulled the trigger. Had killed Sophie. Marcel, she was certain. She watched the glass shatter. Jerked when Sophie's body jerked and blood blossomed on her blouse—dark gray now, not the vivid red she knew it to be.

There seemed to be no way the gunman could have missed her. She was standing there. Right there in front of Sophie's desk, nearly blocking Sophie from the robber's view, yet the bullets had gone straight past her and into Sophie's body.

Her insides trembled with remembered terror. She stuck the knuckle of her index finger between her teeth and bit down. Tears filled her eyes, spilling down her cheeks, over her fingers. "Oh, God, Oh God, Oh God," she whimpered over and over.

"You really should take it up," Detective Boyle said.

"Huh?" She dropped her hand from her mouth and turned to him, seeing his face through a fog of horror and disbelief. This couldn't be happening. The robbery, the men, the hell that her life had become. It couldn't be happening. "Take it up?"

"Gambling. You should take it up. I mean, with your luck and all, you'd make a killing." He studied her, his brows reaching for his hairline. "No pun intended."

Chapter Eleven

Emma wrestled her backpack into the car and climbed in after it. "Is Gunnar still here?" Her voice held a hopeful lilt that made nausea rise in China's chest.

"Yes. He's still here."

"Does he live with us now?"

"He's staying for a little while."

Emma nodded slowly. "Chelsea's getting a new daddy soon."

Oh, shit.

"Emma. You don't think Gunnar is going to be your daddy, do you?"

She shrugged but didn't answer.

Biting her lip, China searched for the words that would make Emma understand that 'getting a new daddy' wasn't all that simple.

"Honey, Gunnar can't be your daddy because we don't know him. He's a stranger, right?"

"Not anymore. If he's a stranger he wouldn't live at our house."

She had her there. "Okay, maybe not really a stranger, but he's someone we don't know that well and...well...mommies have to date a while before making someone a new daddy."

"Can you date Gunnar?"

"No." She shuddered at that nightmare.

"You've already dated Steve and didn't make him my new daddy." She stared out the window, her tone and posture giving out vibes of petulance.

"That's right. Because Steve and I are just friends." China slowed and pulled into the parking lot of a convenience store.

She wanted to have this conversation while she wasn't operating a moving vehicle, and put it to rest before they got home. "Emma, look at me." She did, but her lips were pursed into her pissy, 'I'm not listening' expression. "You have to understand that you may never have a new daddy. It's a big decision, and I don't want to do it unless I feel like it's going to work out. When things don't work out, life can be very difficult."

"Like with Gary?"

"Yes. Just like that."

"Why did he leave us?"

Good question. She'd arrived home from work one evening to find Gary gone. He'd taken his belongings and left a brief note telling her things weren't working out, he was moving his medical practice to San Francisco, she could keep the house, and he was sorry. She hadn't heard a word from him since. Her attorney had handled the divorce without her ever seeing or speaking to Gary. It was as if he'd never really been in her life.

"Sometimes people are just unhappy and want a different life."

Her brows drew together. "Did I make him unhappy?"

A lump rose in her throat, and she reached out to pull Emma close. "No, sweetie. Not at all. You made him very happy. You make *me* very happy."

"You make me happy, too." Her small arms tightened around China's neck and she whispered, "I wish my real daddy didn't go to Heaven."

Fighting back tears, China whispered back, "Me, too, sweetheart. Me, too."

When they arrived home, Gunnar was waiting in the living room. "I trust your day was good."

"As good as can be expected," China said tightly.

"Your visit with the police went well?"

A chill coursed through her. They were definitely watching her. But it wasn't like she hadn't already known that.

"I didn't tell them anything."

"Of course you didn't." He inclined his head, utterly confident in the hold he and his gang had over her.

Her eyes went to the large silver cross sitting on the table behind Gunnar. A gift from her parents. All their gifts had a religious theme, and other than the personalized bible they'd given her, the cross was her favorite. Somehow, its presence always gave her a sense of security, made her feel closer to her absentee parents. But with this frightening stranger in her home, that comfort was a mere wisp.

"Can you help me with my homework?" Emma asked him.

"Emma, no!" China said before he could reply. "Gunnar is busy. I'll help you with your homework."

He looked at China for a moment, then at Emma. "Your mother will help you. I will prepare dinner."

China held up a hand in protest. "No. Please. I'll fix dinner." She just wanted him out of her life, and if she couldn't have that, she'd rather pretend he didn't exist. She damn sure didn't want him fitting in to their cozy little family dynamic.

"You have worked all day," Gunnar said. "I will prepare dinner while you and Emma do homework."

Like everything else, this was obviously not a request.

Gunnar cooked spaghetti and meatballs with garlic bread. The meal was surprisingly good. A man of many talents—cook and killer extraordinaire. The thought took away China's appetite, and she only managed to choke down a few bites.

After dinner, she was loading the dishwasher while Emma watched Sponge Bob. The doorbell pealed and China jumped, nearly losing her hold on the dinner plate she was rinsing. The idea of company dropping in while she and Emma were being held hostage in their own home hadn't really occurred to her.

She dried her hands as she headed to the door. Through the peephole, she saw her niece, Spencer.

"Oh, no," she whispered.

"Who is it?" Gunnar said from behind her.

"It's my niece. She babysits for me every other Tuesday while I meet my friends for drinks."

He nodded. "Give me a moment to vacate the room then let her in."

She shook her head. "No. I'll tell her I'm ill or that I'm not up to it because of the robbery."

The doorbell rang again, and Spencer called out, "Aunt China?"

"Normal," Gunnar hissed. "You will go out. Let her in once I'm gone."

"Aren't you worried I'll go to the police? Slip someone a note to let them know about you and your buddies?"

The corners of his mouth lifted in an almost smile. "Are you really that foolish?"

No, she wasn't. Even if she managed to get help, there was no way the cops would catch all of them. Someone would be free to come back. To kill her and Emma.

Gunnar disappeared, and China opened the door, forcing a smile for Spencer. She was a pretty fourteen-year-old, tall and leggy, with shoulder-length chestnut hair. A sweet, kind-hearted girl with a mother who didn't appreciate her. Destiny had a history of jumping from man to man, bringing them in and out of Spencer's life without a qualm. The men always came first, and Spencer was left to fend for herself.

"What took so long?" Spencer moved past her in search of Emma.

"Sorry, honey. I was in the kitchen loading the dishwasher. Didn't hear the bell the first time."

China followed her into the living room where Emma launched herself into her cousin's arms. "Spencer! Spencer! Spencer!"

Spencer laughed. "Chill out." She looked at the TV. "Sponge Bob? Awesome! I haven't seen Sponge Bob in *forever*."

Emma giggled. "Yes you have. We watch it *every* time."

Spencer ruffled Emma's hair, then turned to China. "You'd better get ready. You're not going like that, right? Might be some hotties out there." Her voice became solemn, and her eyes misted with tears. "Are you okay?"

"I'm fine. What about you? Are you crying?"

She shrugged. "I was just thinking about how you almost died. I don't know what I'd do if something happened to you. I mean, then there'd just be Mom and me." She stopped, took a deep breath, looking uncertain and miserable. "I didn't mean that. I just meant..."

"I know what you meant. I'm fine." China hugged her. "I'd better go finish those dishes and change. Can't have the hotties seeing me like this, right?"

Spencer grinned. "I'll finish the dishes. You get ready."

"You sure?"

"Sure."

"Thanks." China headed upstairs, but she'd never felt less like going out. Gunnar appeared suddenly in the hallway, startling her, and she gasped.

"All is well?" he asked.

All was *not* well. The thought of leaving the two people she loved most in the world with this stranger, this *killer*, was more than she could bear.

"Please," she said. "Just this one thing. Let me cancel. I can't go out tonight. Besides, Vanessa probably won't want to, anyway. Not after the robbery."

"There are others to be going, yes?"

"Yes, but—"

"You will go."

This was too much. Too crazy. Desperation welled, and she blurted, "What do you want? Please tell me, what are you doing here? What do your people expect from me?"

"Please calm yourself. You will find out in due time. It is not my place to say."

"But it *is* your place to take over my life, terrify my child?"

"Emma is comfortable with me."

"She's six years old. She doesn't know you're a murderer. Doesn't realize we're in the middle of some crazy nightmare."

"I have asked you to calm yourself. I do not ask more than once."

The look in his eyes, more than the tone of his voice, convinced her he meant business. In spite of his serene facade, the man was a violent criminal. She would be wise to heed his warning.

Chapter Twelve

China was surprised to see Vanessa at the bar when she arrived. The others were there, too—Stacy and Karen from the bank and Tamara and Beverly, friends from China's book club. They ordered their usual pitcher of beer, but the normal upbeat chatter was notably missing from their gathering.

"How's Emma?" Vanessa asked.

At home with a killer. "She's okay. No more problems with her asthma."

"How are you? How did your talk with the detective go?"

China shrugged. "I couldn't give him any more information. Nothing helpful anyway."

Vanessa shuddered and took a sip from her glass. "I hope they find those assholes. I dread going to work. I know it's not likely, but I can't shake the feeling that they'll be back."

"Yeah, I know what you mean." China grimaced.

Vanessa squeezed her hand, and once more, China had the urge to confess everything to her best friend. But she didn't have the urge to sign Vanessa's death warrant. Or her own. Most definitely not Emma's or Spencer's.

Her gaze drifted to the television in the corner. A female Hispanic reporter, wearing a burgundy pants suit and a solemn expression, stood in front of a coffee shop. In the background, yellow crime scene tape fluttered in the breeze, and police officers milled about. A cold, hard knot balled in her stomach. Although the sound was muted, she knew what they were reporting. She didn't need the scoop. She'd seen it with her own eyes.

"Did you hear about that?" Stacy asked. "A couple gunned down in a Java Hut. Apparently a sniper. No one knows why. They still haven't caught the guy."

The others joined in on the discussion, but China remained silent. The waitress, a perky blonde wearing black shorts and a tight white shirt, brought over another pitcher of beer. "Guy over in the corner sent this to you."

China's gaze followed where the girl pointed, and the knot in her stomach froze. Royce. She hadn't noticed him before, because his table was nestled in a dark corner. He smiled and lifted his glass in a silent salute. Her jaw tightened, and she clenched her glass so hard she thought it would shatter.

"He's hot." Karen's eyes rounded in excitement. "Wonder which one of us he's into?"

Vanessa frowned. "He's nice-looking, but creepy. He's been watching us ever since we came in. You think we should call Miles?"

"Call Miles?" China echoed. "Why would we do that?"

"I have a bad feeling. I don't like the vibes he's giving off. I think maybe we should call the police."

China forced a laugh, hoping she didn't sound as nervous as she felt. "And tell them what? A guy bought us beer? Maybe they'll call in SWAT."

"Well..." Vanessa said slowly. "I guess I'm being overly suspicious. Hazards of being married to a cop."

"Yeah," Tamara agreed, lifting her glass toward Royce and mouthing a thank you. "Besides, no sense in chasing off an eligible guy. His species is endangered enough already."

Royce inclined his head toward them, letting his eyes rest on China a few moments longer than the others. Then he stood, threw some bills on the table, and walked out the door with the air of a man who'd accomplished his mission.

"Huh," Karen said, sounding disappointed. "Guess he wasn't into any of us."

"Like I said, a freakin' weirdo," Vanessa muttered.

China felt Royce's presence long after he was gone and, although she tried to force it, she couldn't pretend to be involved in the conversation, couldn't pretend to enjoy the evening.

"I think I should get back home to Emma." She rose from the chair.

"You're not driving yourself, are you?" Vanessa frowned. "Miles will pick us up."

"No need. I only had one glass of beer. I'm good to go."

"Are you sure? I'm ready to head home, anyway. We can bring you back to get your car tomorrow."

"No. That's okay. I can drive myself." It wasn't a good idea to let Miles and Vanessa come to her house. Even to the driveway. She said goodbye and hurried to her car.

When she got home, Emma was asleep, but Spencer was watching *Big Brother* on TV. Spencer loved all those reality shows, and China recorded her favorites for her, even though she herself couldn't stand them. Her idea of entertainment wasn't to watch a bunch of losers make fools of themselves, airing the details of their personal lives for all the world to see. Why would she be interested in other people's drama? Especially now when she had enough of her own.

"Is your mother coming to pick you up?" China asked.

Spencer shook her head. "Her latest boyfriend, Tracy, is coming to get me." She rolled her eyes and punched out a message on her phone. "I just sent him a text. He'll probably be here soon."

They chatted until a horn honked. Spencer grabbed her purse, kissed China on the cheek, and dashed out the door. China watched her leave, remembering the photos Royce had shown her. Fierce protectiveness surfaced. She loved Spencer as though she was her own, and she would do anything to keep her safe.

The shrill alarm pierced the morning, jerking China from a dream about Aiden. He'd shown up at her door, dark eyes smiling. In his thick Irish brogue, he'd said, *"No more worries, lass. I'm here now."* Relief and love filled her heart. She'd thrown her arms around his neck, clung to him tightly—she could almost feel his warm, strong body—and whispered, *"Come meet your daughter..."*

In her sleep, she'd been cocooned in sweet, safe warmth. Maybe if she stayed in bed and lay very still, the dream wouldn't leave.

It didn't work. The illusion fled, and there was nothing left but to face reality. Annoyed and exhausted from another restless night, she stumbled from bed and down the stairs.

Gunnar was sitting at the kitchen table.

"Today is your first instruction," he said.

"Oh, goody." Did Gunnar recognize good ole American sarcasm? She jerked a mug from the cupboard and sloshed strong, hot coffee in it.

"You must find out which day the Norman, Oklahoma branch will have the most money on hand."

Ice surrounded her heart. "You're going to rob another bank?"

"I did not rob a bank."

She let out a frustrated sigh. He was like some kind of robot, processing information in the most literal sense.

"Your *gang* is going to rob another bank?"

"It is not for you to ask questions. Only to follow instructions."

Dread welled in her chest as she took a gulp of the hot brew. She couldn't be a part of this. Couldn't aid in another robbery. Another murder. She shook her head. "I can't. I just...can't."

"You dare to refuse? Do you think we are playing?"

She remembered the web cam feed. The image of the couple she'd sentenced to death. "I know you're not playing."

"The deaths that have taken place so far have been those you are not particularly close to, true?"

She nodded.

"They will rob the bank no matter what. They wish to have information that will gain the most profit. If you do not get this for them, the next victim will be quite different from a boss you were not fond of. You are very close to your aunt, am I right?"

Fear moved through her, tingling along her scalp. "You won't... Please don't hurt Lucy."

"Perhaps she will not feel much pain. Perhaps she will. I cannot make any promises about that. But I *can* promise you that she will die."

Dizziness crowded her vision, and she clung to the counter until her knuckles turned white. *You have to do this, you have no choice...*

Emma came into the kitchen, and China took a steadying breath to compose herself. Emma's Dora the Explorer pajamas were stretched tight on her belly, and she carried her Reds build-a-bear she'd gotten last year when they went to Cincinnati to watch the Reds' series against the Brewers.

"Morning, sweetie." The words were raspy, stuck in her throat, but China forced a smile that felt frozen and stiff. She put her coffee down and took a bowl from the cabinet, pouring in Fruit Loops for Emma.

Emma climbed onto a chair next to Gunnar. China wanted to tell her to move to the other side of the table, away from him, but didn't. She put the cereal in front of Emma, then went back to the counter where she'd left her cup.

Emma slapped her bear on the table and it made a tinkling sound. China walked back to the table and stared down at the silver metal—singed black around the edges—hanging around the bear's neck. Aiden's dog tags.

She reached out a finger and touched the tags. "Emma, honey, why is Red wearing these?"

"She wanted to."

"Where did you get them?"

"From your room."

Gritting her teeth, she said, "You're not to get my things without permission. You know that."

"They're Daddy's."

"Yes, but they're not yours." She planned to give the dog tags to Emma one of these days, when she was old enough to take care of them. But not yet. She had told Emma most everything about her father, and Emma liked to pretend she'd actually known him. That he hadn't died before she was born. China had never been able to even show a photo to her. The period she'd spent with Aiden had been so brief, such a torrid, all-consuming affair, she hadn't taken the time to snap any photos, something she now regretted deeply.

"Give them to me. Now." Her tone was sharper than she intended.

"Let her keep them," Gunnar said.

"No!" Some small part of her questioned why she was being so adamant about something so insignificant when she was about to aid criminals in a bank robbery, but she couldn't seem to help herself. "She'll lose them."

He stared at her for a moment, then said to Emma, "Give them to your mother, please."

Emma's lower lip stuck out, but she yanked the chain from the bear's neck and thrust it at China.

China gripped the dog tags tightly in her fist, feeling an odd warmth coming from the cold metal, and turned her back so Emma wouldn't see her tears.

Chapter Thirteen

Stone straddled his Harley in a strip mall parking lot across the street from Greater Oklahoma Bank. He removed his helmet, squinting against the sunlight that bounced off the metal siding. Warm day for May. If it weren't for the cool breeze, he'd be sweating bullets in the leather jacket.

He now regretted parking so close to the Gray Goose, a bar roughly the size of a closet. Each time the door opened, loud music and voices floated out to him. It was starting to grate on his nerves.

A woman came out of a tanning salon and looked his way. He tried to smile, but he was sure it came across as a threatening sneer. She must have regretted the accidental eye contact, because she immediately ducked her head and hurried to her car.

He didn't blame her for being afraid. He looked like an escaped convict. His hair was too long and appeared to have been cut by a blind monkey wielding pinking shears. He hadn't shaved in days, which wouldn't have been so bad had it not been for the white scar that marred his lower lip and ran along his chin. Mangled flesh in the midst of his five-day beard was probably not all that appealing. The gold hoop earring completed the pirate persona he hadn't meant to cultivate.

He glanced back toward the bank and tried to control the way his heart rate shot up.

China.

She walked along the sidewalk, then stopped and turned in his direction. She seemed to be staring straight at him. They stayed frozen like that for a few seconds, then she continued walking, disappearing inside the bank.

He let out a breath, certain she hadn't seen him. His spot behind the SUV allowed him a more open view of her than she could have gotten of him.

She looked good. Great—he amended grudgingly—in creamy, white satin pants and a black blouse. Her body had matured, filling out in curves where there had once been angles. Her hair was shorter. He remembered it falling in long, soft, waves around her naked shoulders, her back arching as they'd made love...eyes closed, a small, dreamy smile playing on her full lips, the silky feel of the indentation in the small of her back...

Abruptly, he cut off the thoughts, shifting uncomfortably on the seat of the Harley, cursing his weakness. He wouldn't let himself remember the good times. Wouldn't think fondly of memories of China. He was on his way to do a job, nothing more. So why had he cruised by to ogle China? He'd promised himself he wouldn't think about her, let alone see her, yet here he was.

He sat there for another hour, spent half of it eavesdropping on an argument between a couple standing in front of the bar about her apparently acting like a whore, but he didn't catch another glimpse of China, which was just as well.

Shoving his helmet back on, he started his Harley and roared out of the parking lot, purging his mind and heart of the woman who'd loved him, then betrayed him and left him for dead.

China shivered when she stepped inside the bank, blaming it on the contrast between the warm day and the air conditioning in the lobby. But it was more than that. During her walk from the parking lot, she'd felt as though she were being watched. She'd looked around and hadn't seen anything, but the sensation lingered. This had been a different sort of being watched, not like the merry band of crooks she'd recently run up against, but something almost…supernatural. Like one of her aunt's favorite sayings, it was as if someone had walked over her grave.

In the break room, she poured a cup of coffee, her heart heavy with dread. How could she possibly go through with what Gunnar had told her to do? The real question was, how could she not? He hadn't exactly given her a choice.

She took her coffee to the lobby. The teller lines were nearly empty, partly because it was mid-morning on a Wednesday and partly because customers were skittish about coming to the scene of the crime.

The bank was eerily quiet, silence hanging over it like a shroud. Two of the tellers, Kyle and Nancy, were no-shows, leaving them short-handed, so China would have to work a teller window. They probably couldn't face coming back just yet. Maybe they never would.

When there was a lull with no customers in line, China put her closed sign in the teller window and went to her desk. Time to help some criminals wreak a little more havoc. Time to become an accomplice.

The branches had the most money on days when the casinos made their deposits. She just needed to learn what day that would happen in Norman. Picking up the phone, she dialed the first three digits of the Norman branch phone number. She stopped when an image of Sophie's jerking body flashed through her mind. The jerking, then the blood. Odd, but somehow, the jerking was worse than the blood. So violent, so invasive.

She had no doubt Gunnar would make good on his threat. She'd seen examples of how convincing they could be. Seen the results in 3-D clarity.

If she gave them the information, another bank would be robbed. Perhaps another person would die. Although, actually, it wasn't a given that someone would die. They'd killed Sophie as a gesture to her. Sophie had been cruel to her and the crooks wanted to show how much of her life they could control. A sick way of sealing her loyalty. And, of letting her know they could have just as easily taken *her* out. Instead, they'd taken out someone they saw as her enemy.

If she didn't give them the information, Lucy, and perhaps Spencer, or even Emma, would die. There was really nothing to think about.

Swallowing back the guilt, she dialed the Norman branch and punched in Melissa Campbell's extension.

"Hi, China. Haven't talked to you in a while." Her cheery voice increased China's guilt. God, how could she do this? "You okay? I know the robbery must have been awful. I can't even imagine."

No, but you will soon.

"I'm okay. Yes. It was awful. Especially Sophie."

"God. I know. I'm so sorry."

"Yeah. Thanks. Listen, I need to find out what day the casinos deposit. We're going to need to break some big bills, and you'll have a lot of change on casino days."

"Yeah. We will. Sure. They deposit on Thursdays."

Tomorrow. No time to brace herself, to mentally prepare. Although, how she'd possibly prepare for something like this, she had no idea.

"Okay." Her voice shook, and she wondered if Melissa noticed. "Thanks. I'll give you a call, and we'll work it out."

"Sounds good. Take care of yourself and let me know if there's anything else you need."

China squeezed her eyes shut against the flow of tears. "I will. Thanks."

She didn't have time to think about how much she hated herself, or whether or not she'd actually be able to give the crooks the information. The last part of the day was busier than the first, thankfully, and all she could focus on was taking care of the customers.

"Afternoon, China." She looked up to find Stan Epperson, one of their regulars, at her window. His gaze kept drifting to Sophie's boarded-up office. "I need to make a withdrawal."

"Sure." She looked at the account card he held and keyed his account number into the computer.

"Awful. What happened was just awful." He shook his head to emphasize.

She wanted to scream, *you think that's bad, let me tell you what's happened since, what will happen next. You ain't seen nothing yet.*

She forced her hands to pull out each bill and count. Tension caused her fingers to stumble and threatened to cloud her vision. She drew in a deep breath and recounted. It took three times before she got it right. She had to hold it together. The people she loved most depended on her.

With a murmured apology, she pushed Stan his cash. He left with another sympathetic tsk tsk.

She stared unseeing at the computer screen. No other customers in line, now would be a good time to catch up on some of the work that had fallen behind. But she couldn't move. Her muscles had locked. Her mind wouldn't allow her body to perform mundane tasks when her world was exploding around her.

"China?"

A voice from behind startled her, and she jumped, then let out an embarrassing yelp.

"You okay?"

It was Richard. She hadn't heard him walk up.

"Stupid question," he went on. "None of us are really okay. Sorry, didn't mean to scare you. Just wanted to remind you about your counseling session this afternoon."

She nodded. "I'll be there. Thanks."

"Remember, you can tell her anything. Anything at all, and it will be held in the strictest confidence. I want my employees to be able to talk about their feelings without thinking it's going to affect their jobs. Nothing you say will leave that office."

Nothing you say will leave that office...

A ray of hope entered her chest.

"Thanks, Richard." She smiled broadly.

Maybe there was something she could do after all.

Chapter Fourteen

The counselor's office was three blocks from the bank. On the day of their session, employees were allowed to leave two hours early and stay on the clock until their regular quitting time. China had to admit, the bank had been more than generous, more than kind since the robbery.

China sat in the waiting room, chewing the pad of her thumb, anticipation and fear battling inside her. This was it. Could she tell the psychologist what was going on? *They* wouldn't be listening here, no way.

This was her opportunity. She would ask the woman to call the police. She would tell her to have an officer meet China at a neutral location. It would look like a chance meeting, and she could tell him what was going on. Beg for help.

"China Beckett." The receptionist—a thirtyish woman with upswept brown hair, large-framed glasses, and a kind smile—gestured toward a hallway behind her desk. "Right this way."

China followed her pointing finger. A tall, slender blonde wearing a bronze blouse and black slacks stood in an open doorway. With a sympathetic smile, she approached, inviting China to open up. It was a sign. This was her savior.

"I'm Belinda Rogers."

China shook her outstretched hand.

"Come in." Belinda shut the office door behind them and when China was seated in the chair across from her, said, "Would you like something to drink?"

"Bottled water would be nice." She choked out the words, looked everywhere but directly at her.

Belinda rose and retrieved a bottle of water from a small fridge and handed it to her. China twisted the cap off and took a long swallow. Her mouth had gone dry, and a fine sweat broke out over her body.

"I know you experienced a severely traumatic event," Belinda said. She poised her pen over the legal pad in her lap. "Some of the things will be too painful for you to speak about, but if you can possibly bring yourself to do so, it would help you tremendously."

"There *are* some things I want to tell you." China swallowed some more of the water, gathering her courage. This was it. This was her chance to get out of this mess.

Belinda nodded, gave a gentle, empathetic, 'rest your burdens on me' smile. "I understand you were the one in the office with Mrs. Oswald when she was killed. That must have been devastating."

"It was." China swallowed back tears. "I-I can't get it out of my head," she whispered. When would be the right time to ask for help? Was it the right move?

"How are you sleeping? Do you have nightmares?"

My life is a nightmare... China closed her eyes and took a deep breath. "I can tell you anything, right?"

"Absolutely."

China sat forward in her chair and leaned toward the psychologist. Even though she was certain the office wasn't bugged, she kept her voice to a low whisper. "I need your help. This is going to sound bizarre, but I'm telling the truth. You have to help me. The men who robbed the bank are holding me and my daughter hostage. They've killed other people besides Sophie. They're threatening—"

As China spoke, the benign expression melted from Belinda's face, but it wasn't shock that replaced it. She now looked at China with what could only be fear...and something else. The tightening of her lips showed a hint of determination, resistance.

"I can't help you." Belinda also whispered, but hers was harsh, angry.

"What?"

"I need you to go. Now."

"But...I'm telling the truth. You have to believe—" But China could see by her expression that she did believe it. That she'd already known. "Wait. You... What's going on?"

Belinda lifted her chin and stared at her without speaking.

"Oh my God, they got to you, didn't they? You're working with them?"

"I'm not working with them, but they contacted me." Tears filled her eyes, and she shook her head. "I'm sorry." She looked away, to her desk to where a framed photo of three smiling children rested. "I have kids. I can't."

"They threatened your children?" China's desperate gaze shot around the room, and she lowered her voice. "Are they listening?"

Belinda shook her head. "I don't think so. I don't know. But they said if I did anything to—" She stood abruptly and stalked to the door, then swung it open. Hand on the knob, she said, "I just can't. Please leave. I'll tell your boss you're doing well. That further counseling isn't needed" She winced and paled. "You and I both know it's best not to see one another again."

China stood on shaky legs and moved to the door. Lightheadedness made her pause in the threshold. Without looking at Belinda, she headed down the hallway.

Her chest pounded, and chills raced up and down her arms. Nowhere to turn. It was all so...hopeless.

She hurried past the receptionist and back to the bank parking lot and slid into her car. Lucy had picked up Emma from day care in case the session ran long. China was suddenly anxious to see them both.

The house where China had spent most of her childhood was a single-story white bungalow with dark pink trim. Inside, the décor was crazily mismatched, much like Aunt Lucy herself.

China let herself in, smelling something chocolate when she walked through the door. Emma appeared from the kitchen, Lucy following behind. Lucy's disheveled, bright red hair—a less than stellar dye job—reflected the rays coming in from the skylight overhead. That same light made her heavy make-up unflatteringly stark. Her short, rotund body was forced into a multi-colored jump suit, the overall effect making her look like a chubby, lovable clown. In her hair was the ever-present hairband adorned with orchids—Lucy's favorite flower.

Dark smudges clung to the edges of Emma's mouth as she ran into China's arms for a hug.

"Brownies?" China asked, and Emma nodded happily.

"Come in. Sit." Lucy ushered her into the living room, and China sat on the forest green sofa. Emma climbed up and snuggled next to her while Lucy left the room, returning shortly with a plate of brownies.

When she was small, Lucy had baked often. None of the made from scratch stuff, though. She'd baked solely from mixes, but it didn't lessen China's enjoyment. Lucy could have fed her cardboard slathered in icing, as long as she did it with her loving smile and the stories. The stories were the best part of snack time.

Like the day China had been whining about her name. "It's a stupid name. *China*. Yuck. Why couldn't they have named me something cool like they did Destiny?"

"Your parents named you that because you were conceived in China. Count your blessings, young lady," Lucy had said with a twinkle in her eyes. "Shortly thereafter, they were in Yugoslavia."

China smiled now at the memory.

"I'll be right back with a glass of milk," Lucy said.

"You don't have to serve me. I can get it myself."

Truth was, she didn't think she could eat or drink anything. The more she thought about what she was about to do, the more tense she became. Lumps of fear crowded the base of her throat, nearly choking her.

"Don't be silly. I love taking care of my girls."

She disappeared and returned in moments, handing China a glass of milk. China sipped at it and nibbled on a brownie. She tried to join in Lucy and Emma's light-hearted chatter, but she couldn't concentrate. Several times, Emma would repeat a question, her small face scrunching in irritation at China's inattention.

After an hour, China stood to announce it was time leave. What she really wanted to do was stay here in the safe, loving bosom of her aunt. But there was a psycho waiting for her at home she didn't want to piss off.

Aunt Lucy walked them to the door. "What's wrong with you, sweetie?" she whispered when Emma ran into the other room to get her bear.

"Nothing. I'm fine."

Lucy shook her head. "You're far from fine. No wonder, though, after the awful robbery. Land's sake, that had to be terrifying."

"It was. I still can't believe Sophie's dead. Murdered." She shuddered, not adding that the terror wasn't over. That it hadn't ended with Sophie's death. "I can't stop thinking about it."

Aunt Lucy nodded knowingly. "You're that way. Letting stuff fester. Feeling things so deeply. Even as a little girl, you would let stuff eat at you. Work on you. Always feeling guilty when the least little thing happened—not that this is little, mind you. I heard on a talk show that people who've been through this kind of thing can suffer from some kind of post trauma syndrome. You know her death wasn't your fault, right?"

Ah, but she had no idea just how much it *was* her fault.

"I know."

Lucy pointed over China's shoulder, and she turned to look at a painting on the wall behind her. The picture had hung there ever since she could remember. It was of a canal, somewhere in Italy perhaps, judging from the architecture of the shops. Gondolas rested along either side of the water. On one side of the canal was a lone woman. On the other, a couple with their backs to the woman were walking away.

"When you were a young girl, even this picture made you sad." Lucy smiled and shook her head. "You thought the young woman was in love with the man, and her heart was breaking as she watched him leave with another."

China smiled back. "You don't think so?"

Lucy shrugged and patted her hand. "I always just assumed they were shopping."

"It is time for the information," Gunnar said as soon as China and Emma walked in the door.

China glared at him over Emma's head. "Emma, go get your snack, sweetie."

When Emma skipped away, China brushed past Gunnar into the living room and slung her purse on the couch. Gunnar followed, and she whirled on him.

"You can't really expect me to give you information that will lead to another robbery. Perhaps another murder?"

"Your option is to cause the death of your aunt. Maybe Emma. What is your preference?"

Her jaw tightened. She was trapped. Helplessly, hopelessly cornered. Going against their wishes—their *demands*—meant people she loved would die.

She lifted her chin and glared at him, tears of rage filling her eyes. "Fine." She clenched her fists at her sides. "Tomorrow. The branch will have the most money tomorrow!"

Without giving him a chance to respond, she rushed upstairs and closed herself in her bedroom. Falling onto the bed, she sobbed until she thought her throat would burst.

Dear God. What had she done? What would happen now? And beyond? What more would these people expect from her?

She wasn't sure how long she lay there, how long she'd been falling to pieces when she became aware of pounding on the door.

For a moment, she considered not answering. She didn't want to hear anything Gunnar had to say.

"China." His voice filtered through the door. "You must open the door immediately. It is Emma."

Her legs went weak. She rose from the bed and stumbled to the door, flinging it open.

Gunnar stood on the other side with Emma in his arms. She looked so tiny, so vulnerable. So ill. Her face was pinched, her lips inside the mask white and slightly tinged with blue. She stared at China over the apparatus.

"Emma!" China reached out and pulled her from Gunnar's grasp. "Emma, honey, are you okay?"

She pulled the mask a few inches from her mouth. "I—" a deep breath. "—had a attack—" She put the mask over her face and breathed in, removed it again. "—okay now—" wheeze "—Gunnar helped."

China's gaze flew to his. He scowled, the birthmark on his face more pronounced.

"She needs to go to the hospital." China's heart beat unsteadily as she clung to Emma.

He shook his head. "She is better now. She is coming around to her normal color."

China looked back down at Emma and saw he was right.

"You must keep a closer eye on your little girl." He lowered his voice. "She could have died."

Letting her guilt turn to anger, China struggled with her own breathing as she spoke just as quietly, "And wouldn't that just suck for you and your cohorts? It would be a downright pity if you had to limit the people in my life you have to threaten me with."

Gunnar stared at her silently for a moment, then turned and walked away.

Chapter Fifteen

In the kitchen of Bishop's ranch house, Royce leaned back in his chair and rested a foot on the table, surveying his team. "The next job is tomorrow. Same plan."

"Do I get to kill someone again?" Marcel's eyes glowed with an insane spark.

"Not in the plan this time, but we'll improvise if the need arises. Sorry, Marcel, hate to spoil your fun."

Marcel shrugged. "Not a big deal. I find other ways to amuse myself." He picked up a DVD lying on the table in front of him. "Such as, with these."

Royce frowned. "What's that, porn?"

Marcel licked his lips and smiled. "Of a sort. Probably not the kind of porn you are accustomed to."

"What you got there, sicko?" Bishop's dark face glowered.

Marcel turned to him. "You ever heard of a crush movie?" Bishop shook his head, and Marcel's smile widened. "It shows women. Nude women. Sometimes wearing heels. Others do it barefoot. They crush small animals under their feet."

Layla jumped up so fast her chair toppled to the floor. She advanced on Marcel, pure venom shooting from her cat-like eyes. "I will crush *you*, you twisted little fuck."

Royce had seen a lot of sick things in his life, had *done* a lot of sick things, but even his stomach roiled. "You're a demented motherfucker."

Marcel threw his head back and bellowed a laugh. "You people astound me. You have no idea what you are missing." He looked up at Layla, who hovered over him, breathing heavily.

"You are a fucking Satan worshipper, no? You dare to berate me with morality? Do your people not sacrifice animals?"

"No," Layla spat. "We sacrifice stupid little weasels like you. We gut them like the pigs they are."

"You know," Marcel ran his tongue over his lips and waved the DVD in her face. "This evil, Princess of Darkness thing is somewhat of a turn-on. Perhaps we shall fuck as we watch?"

Bishop rose and moved next to Layla, looming over Marcel. "You get that crap outa my house."

"Ah, come on. It is erotic. You cannot imagine the rush."

Bishop reached out and clamped a hand the size of a dinner plate around Marcel's neck. "I got a shitload of explosives in the basement. Nothing I'd like better than to set 'em off with your scrawny ass right in the middle of it."

"Hey, hey." Marcel tugged at Bishop's wrist. "Back off, Sambo."

Royce came to his feet and reached his hands out in a calming gesture. "Bishop, come on. Let him go."

Bishop glared at Marcel, tightening his grip so hard that Marcel's eyes bulged, then released him.

Marcel rubbed his neck, his wild eyes moving around the room. "I am going to watch the DVD while I have my way with the Beckett bitch. Just you wait and see."

Royce leaned in close enough to smell the garlic on Marcel's breath. "If I were a betting man, I'd bet you won't live to see another birthday."

"You believe this is true?" Marcel asked with a smug smile.

"I *know* it's true. I'm gonna make sure of it."

For a moment, the smile faltered, and the insane gleam disappeared. Marcel's eyes dulled into flat planes of fear. Then that odd, demented excitement was back. "It is against the rules. You cannot kill a team member."

"That's *during* the mission. After, all bets are off."

Marcel gulped, his Adam's apple bobbing. He spoke in a strangled whisper. "Not if I get you first."

Royce straightened, moving back from Marcel with a smile. "May not wait til after. Might be worth losing a few mil to waste your ass now."

"Why does the boss even have this creepy little shit-for-brains on the team?" Bishop said. "He's ignorant. No skills. Pretty much useless. A waste of space."

"Yeah." Royce shrugged. "But he's the kind who has no boundaries. Nothing he won't do."

"Yes," Marcel said. "And with a six-year-old involved, who knows? All of you, even Princess Lucifer here, might be too squeamish if the time comes." A smile spread across his face. "But as for me, if I end up taking the little one out, she will not be my youngest."

Steve came over that night. China had kept Emma near her all evening, hadn't let her out of her sight.

"Something wrong?" he asked when China let him in.

"Emma had an asthma attack today."

He followed her into the living room and squatted down to study Emma's face. "Are you okay?"

"I'm okay." She nodded. "Momma wasn't there, but Gun—" She stopped, looked up at China.

Again, the near slip up. This wasn't going to work. She and Emma would have to limit their socializing. It was too much to ask a six-year-old to be devious.

"But what?" Steve stood and turned to China. "You weren't there? Who was watching her?"

"I was here," China said. "She meant I wasn't in the room. I was upstairs. She...she did her breathing treatment on her own, and it was a little while before I realized anything was going on. By the time I did, she'd gotten it under control."

"You were very brave," he told Emma.

Emma smiled and lifted her chin. "I didn't even cry."

He chucked her gently on the chin. "Of course not. You're a big girl. Hey, I have an idea. Why don't I take you two out to dinner?"

China shook her head. "No. No, thanks. We've already had dinner."

"Ice cream?" His eyes were on Emma.

"Yeah! Ice cream!"

"No," China said again. Why did she always have to be the bad guy? "Emma's already had her snack and it's time for her bath. We'll just—"

"Did you hear that?" Steve interrupted. He leaned his head back to look toward the ceiling.

"What?" China's heart beat in double time. Had Gunnar made a noise? "I didn't hear anything."

Steve moved toward the staircase. "I thought I heard something." He looked to the second floor. "Maybe I should go up and—"

"No!"

He turned back, frowning. "What's up with you tonight? You're as skittish as a kitten."

China shoved a hand through her hair and shook her head. "I'm just a little on edge. I'm sure you understand. The robbery, the scare with Emma. My nerves are a bit jangled."

He came toward her and held out his arms. "Come here." When she didn't move, he beckoned with his hands and stepped closer. "It's going to be okay."

Wrapping his arms around her, he pulled her tight against his chest. He smelled of hand-rolled cigarettes and the sandalwood aroma of the cologne he always wore, felt familiar and safe. Strong. Warm.

She let herself be comforted for a moment, but the mood changed when his hand slipped downward, pressing her lower back until their groins touched. Tensing, she shoved him away.

"What's the matter?" He scowled down at her, his voice sounding hurt.

China bit her lip and looked at Emma. "Emma, honey, go upstairs and get ready for your bath. I'll be up shortly."

When she was gone, China turned to Steve. His naturally ruddy complexion had darkened to deep red.

"Steve, I don't want to mislead you. We've been friends for a long time, but that's all we are. Friends."

"Yeah, so?"

"That thing just now. The way you touched me felt like something beyond friendship. It made me uncomfortable."

He huffed out a breath. "I thought maybe you needed me. I want to make you feel better."

"What you made me feel is that you might be taking advantage of the situation, of my vulnerable state."

"I didn't mean to." He pinched the bridge of his nose and shook his head. "Hell, China. I'm crazy about you, and I would never want to offend you. To drive you away. Please tell me I haven't done that."

She reached up and touched his cheek. "You haven't. Maybe I overreacted. I'm not myself these days."

He took her hand, placing a light kiss on her palm. "No. I understand. I just don't want to lose your friendship."

"You haven't. You won't."

"Promise?"

She nodded. "Promise. I need to get Emma in the bath. Maybe you should go."

"We're still good?"

"Of course. Call me tomorrow."

She walked him to the door, forgoing her usual peck on the cheek. There had been enough touching for one evening.

After he left, she headed upstairs, worried about the way they'd left things. Then just as quickly, she dismissed her concern. Steve should count his blessings—hope that hurt feelings were the only injuries he suffered before this was all over.

Chapter Sixteen

Stone wasn't sure why he insisted on this form of torture. He'd kicked himself in the ass for going by to see China at work, and now here he was, parked down the street from her house. Did he *want* her to see him? Was that it? He wanted a confrontation? Maybe he wanted to hear her side.

Ah, hell, who was he kidding? He wanted her to tell him it hadn't happened. That she hadn't left him to rot in an African prison and married, had a child, with another man.

Problem was, he had too much time to kill before the next job. He shouldn't have stopped in Oklahoma. Should have gone on to Texas, waited there.

He stared at China's house through the tall trees towering in the gloom of evening. It seemed she'd done well for herself, but he didn't know how on a bank employee salary. Of course, the man she'd married had most likely taken good care of her. At least, until he abandoned her and their daughter.

What made a man do that sort of thing? A divorce was one thing, but from all he'd gathered, when the guy left two years ago, he'd left for good. Totally dropped out of his daughter's life.

Stone wasn't a kid person. Had no desire to be a father, but if by some cruel twist of fate, he became one, he damned sure wouldn't desert the child. He'd do what he could to take care of it.

The door opened, and a man stepped out. China was framed in the doorway for just a moment, then she closed the door. The man stepped off the porch and took a tobacco pouch and rolling papers from his pocket. Shaking out tobacco into the paper, he rolled a cigarette. Aiden hadn't seen anyone do that since...

Blood pounded in his ears, and his grip on the handlebars tightened. It seemed the lovely China didn't have a problem replacing men once they were gone. She had Steve to count on. Steve to fill her lonely evenings.

At least she hadn't hooked up with a stranger. He had to give her that. Nope. She'd gone in for the kill—chosen his best friend.

China longed to take the coward's way out and call in on Thursday. After all, it wasn't like Sophie was there to give her grief. But, of course, Gunnar wouldn't hear of it.

"Normal," he'd said until she thought she'd go nuts from hearing the word.

News about the Norman robbery hit just before quitting time. Richard called them into the conference room to announce the disaster.

Once they were seated, his gaze roamed over each of them. "I wanted you to hear it from me first. Our branch in Norman was robbed earlier this evening."

Murmurs and gasps went through the room. The skin tightened on China's scalp, and her heart raced so fast she thought it would explode.

Richard nodded, his expression grave. "Fortunately, no one was injured this time."

No one injured. Thank God.

"Was it the same people?" Angela asked, her voice quivering.

"We don't know yet. The police are investigating, and we should know more soon. I'm not sure how much information they'll reveal. They won't want to jeopardize the case." He dropped heavily into the chair at the head of the table, as if no longer able to stand with the weight of it all. "One bright spot. If it is the same group, perhaps this second robbery will lead the police to catch them."

No one was injured. China tried to focus on that detail, rather than the knowledge of her role in it.

Several employees shouted questions, but China barely heard as Richard answered what he could. He spent a few moments reassuring them, encouraging them not to let the fear control them. Not to let it make them leave their positions with the bank.

He ended with, "We're a family. We'll get through this and whatever you need, we'll do our best to provide it."

Afterward, they filed out of the room like dazed plane crash survivors. China couldn't bring herself to look any of them in the eye.

That evening, Lucy kept Emma while China went to the grocery store. Gunnar had suggested she leave Emma there with him. She hastily declined, but worried he'd insist. He hadn't, and she was immensely relieved. Cold-blooded killers were at the very bottom of her list of preferred babysitters. A bitter burst of laughter escaped at her bizarre humor. She was losing it.

Of course, leaving Emma with Lucy didn't exactly provide a lot of comfort. They were vulnerable there. Lucy had already been threatened. Would they follow through with their threat even though China had obeyed their orders? The robbery had been successful, highly profitable—they'd stolen nearly seven million dollars—thanks to the information she'd given them. *Way to go, China.*

The fear that had become her closest companion seized her when she was only half way through her list. An intense, pervading urge to hurry gripped her. To get back and check on Emma and Lucy. She'd never been clairvoyant, but something was wrong, or maybe it was just an abiding terror that another person would die. Only this time, it would be someone she loved.

She shifted from foot to foot. The desire to abandon her basket and hurry to Lucy's strangled her. But Gunnar expected groceries. She pulled her cell from her purse and punched in Lucy's number. Thankfully, her aunt had actually answered this time and assured her that everything was fine. Emma was helping her make pudding. So *normal.*

Partially reassured, China managed to wait out the line. A thin, bird-like woman in front of her turned and smiled. "Crowded today."

"Yes." China gave her attention to the rag magazines in the rack by the register, hoping to discourage conversation.

It didn't work.

The woman nudged her on the arm. "I couldn't decide whether to get the round steak or pork chops." She held a package of meat out for China's inspection. "The pork was 5.19 a pound, and this round steak is a two pound package for 11.79. I can't figure out which is a better deal. Do you know? I never was good with algebra."

China wanted to shout, *"It's not algebra, stupid! Just shut up and leave me the hell alone!"* Instead, she said, "The pork. That steak would be almost six dollars a pound."

"Oh, my. That's not such a good deal. I'd rather have the pork." She looked ahead of her. She was next. "I'll be back before they get to me. Save my place in line, dear."

The woman had already placed some of her items on the belt, but China wasn't waiting for her to return after contemplating the economic value of pork versus beef.

She pulled the woman's basket back and shoved the items from the belt into it, something she couldn't have imagined doing just a few short days ago. But after being an accessory in a bank robbery, this crime was small potatoes.

The cashier had rung up half of China's purchases by the time the woman returned.

"Oh." She peered at China's groceries in dismay. "You went in front of me."

"I'm sorry. I'm in a hurry."

China didn't respond to the woman's grumbling. She threw her money at the cashier, grabbed her groceries and ran.

As she loaded the last bag into the car, her trepidation skyrocketed. She straightened from the back seat, and an arm shot around her waist—roughly pulled her into a body. With a yelp she tried twisting her head around, but a hand clamped over her mouth, bracing her head forward. Her knees started to give way.

Foul breath wafted over her as a voice hissed in her ear. "No scene, *ma chérie*. I have a knife, and it will not end pretty. I have wanted to do this since I first laid eyes on you in the bank. Pretend that you know me. That you are..." he chuckled. "...*friendly* with me."

Oh, God. One of the robbers. Not Royce. Marcel.

He released her mouth, and his hand glided over her stomach, then up, grazing the undersides of her breasts. She cringed, swallowing back the urge to puke. She glanced around the nearly empty parking lot, not sure if she was searching for help, or hoping there were no witnesses to cause a scene. The few people about paid them no mind.

He pinched her nipple, and she cried out in pain. "Just a little something for you to think about. Before this is over, before we are out of your life, I will have you." His fingers dipped lower, cupped her crotch.

"Please don't," she gasped.

He laughed against her ear. His fetid breath moved over her in waves. "Oh, I'll have you all right. Preferably while you are still alive. But I am not too picky. Tell anyone about my little visit, and I will kill you and your child."

He gave her nipple another squeeze before releasing her.

His footsteps receded. Unable to look around, trembling, she leaned with her hands against the driver's door and breathed in long, gulping breaths of air until she felt calm enough to drive.

The next night, China took Spencer and Emma to the movies. It was odd to do regular things, *normal* things, when this insanity was going on. Between her encounter with Marcel, and continually waiting for Emma to slip up, it was all she could do to get through each moment.

Finding a movie suitable for Emma that Spencer would also enjoy was not an easy task. Spencer agreed to see the latest Disney movie, pretending to do so as a sacrifice for Emma, but China guessed that, like her, Spencer secretly enjoyed them.

A light spring evening breeze blew, and the sky was a velvety black with stars scattered like tiny jewels. A beautiful evening, and Spencer was more cheerful than she'd been a few nights ago. It was almost easy to forget what waited for them at home.

They went for ice cream after the movie, then dropped Spencer at her house.

When they arrived home, China's muscles tensed with dread—a strange car was in the driveway.

Her heart raced. Royce? Marcel? She hadn't told Gunnar about Marcel's visit at the grocery store. She had a feeling the news would not be well received. Maybe she should. But her silence wasn't to protect Marcel, she just couldn't be sure how—or against whom—Royce would retaliate if she told.

She caught a glimpse of a man on the porch. He turned.

Detective Boyle.

She didn't know whether to throw herself at his mercy or jump back in her car and peel off down the street.

He smiled as she and Emma approached. Bending down with his hands on his knees, he looked into Emma's face. "And this pretty young thing must be Emma."

Emma's lips parted in a beaming smile. *Great.* Now Emma would want *him* to move in with them. He ruffled her hair and straightened.

"What can I help you with, Detective?" China asked.

"You have coffee?"

Her stomach muscles tightened. Gunnar was inside. Most of the time Gunnar met them in the living room. Did he know Boyle was out here? *What the hell.* Weren't the bandits supposed to know everything? She'd take her chances.

"Sure. Come in."

Despite her bravado, she glanced around nervously as they entered. The living room was empty, as was the kitchen.

"Go get your pajamas on, Emma. I'll be up soon to tuck you in."

"Night, Mister." She smiled up at Boyle.

"Macklin Boyle." He extended his hand to Emma. It was the first time China had heard his first name. Almost made him seem human—harmless. But she knew better.

Emma shook his hand, then trudged upstairs. China headed into the kitchen leaving the detective where he stood. She pulled instant coffee from the cupboard, not wanting Boyle to stay long enough for a pot to brew.

"How do you take your coffee?" she called from the kitchen. "Is instant okay?"

"Beggars can't be choosers." His voice came from directly behind her.

She whirled, her hand flying to her heart. "You scared me."

"Black."

"Huh?"

"I take it black. I guess it would make a person jumpy. All you've been through."

"Yes." She gritted her teeth. The way he hopped from topic to topic rattled her, which was probably why he did it. She handed him a mug. He took it and sat at the breakfast table.

"Nice house."

"Thanks," she replied cautiously, but she didn't think it was meant to flatter. This man did nothing without purpose.

She crossed her arms and leaned against the counter, waiting. For a split second, she was tempted to try to get some kind of message to him, letting him know of the trouble she was in. But the idea left as soon as it took hold. She had no idea how many people were involved, but she was chillingly certain they could get to the people she loved before the police could get to all of them.

He took a sip of coffee and looked around, slowly nodding. "Bank must pay you well."

Ah. There it was. "No. This was my husband's house."

"Widow?"

She'd bet he knew all about her, but answered anyway. "No. Divorced. Gary left the house to me."

"Free and clear?"

"Yes." She rubbed her hands up and down her arms. "Detective Boyle, is there something I can help you with?"

"Just following up." Another drink of the coffee. "You think of anything new to tell us?"

"No, I didn't and no matter how many times you ask, I won't."

"Won't?"

"I can't. I've told you all I know."

"Crazy stuff. The Norman branch getting robbed, too."

Her eyes slid to the floor as she nodded. Damn. That was a tell. She looked back up at him. "It's awful. I hope you catch these guys."

"It's the same guys?"

"What? I suppose. Why are you asking me?"

He shrugged. "You just seem so sure. I thought you might...know something."

"I just assumed...I mean...so soon after, and the same way." China threw her hands up in the air. "I don't know. None of the robbers have been apprehended, so who knows, right?"

He finished his coffee and stood. "Yeah," he nodded as he looked around some more, then his eyes narrowed on her. "Who knows?"

Chapter Seventeen

The next morning, when China entered the kitchen, she found Emma with Gunnar at the dining table, head bent over her paper, tongue sticking from the corner of her mouth in concentration. She lifted her head and brushed her hair from her face with the hand that held the pencil, then passed the paper to Gunnar.

Frowning, he studied Emma's work. A big smile split his face, making even the damaged side almost handsome. "Is this a drawing of me? Very nice work, Emma."

Her face broke out into an expression of pure delight. "Thanks, Gunnar. Now it's your turn. Want to color?"

"All finished with your homework?"

"Yeah. All done."

"Okay, then. We will color."

China poured a cup of coffee and sat in the chair next to Emma, watching the exchange in disbelief. How could a man like this be so gentle with her child? He was helping her with homework, *playing* with her, yet China knew, if he considered it necessary, he would kill her.

"I'm going to a party next weekend," Emma announced, her eyes intent on the coloring book. "It's Brittany M's party. Brittany C wouldn't invite me to her birthday. She doesn't like me." The tongue crept back out, and Emma's glasses slid to the end of her nose.

Gunnar reached out and pushed them back up. "Why does Brittany C dislike you?"

"Because I'm a four-eyes."

Gunnar scowled. "Does she call you that?"

Emma nodded, not looking up from her paper.

"She is not a very nice little girl," Gunnar said.

China nearly choked on her coffee. What would he do? Offer to assassinate the six-year-old as a favor to Emma?

"Emma, it's time to brush your teeth and get ready for day care." Although it was Saturday, China was scheduled to work. One thing she disliked about working for a bank—other than the whole robbery thing—was working every third Saturday. Weekends were short and precious enough without having to go into work. She usually left Emma with Lucy when she worked Saturdays, but her aunt had a hair appointment this morning.

"It's not time yet," Emma pouted.

"Yes, it is time. Do as I said."

Emma shot Gunnar a look from the corner of her eye. Was she looking for him to come to her rescue? For God's sake, what the hell was happening?

When Gunnar didn't speak, Emma said, "Can I finish my picture first?"

"Sure, honey." China forced a smile. "Finish your picture, then go up and get ready. I laid your clothes on your bed."

Emma must have been painting the Sistine Chapel, because an interminable amount of time passed before she was finished.

After she finally presented her completed masterpiece—a rainbow colored dog jumping in the air to catch a ball—for Gunnar and China's approval, she tromped grudgingly from the room.

Gunnar stood. "You have done well raising her."

"Thank you," China said tightly.

"What happened to her father? He left when she was small?"

She rose from the table and went to the microwave to heat her coffee, watching the turntable through the glass door. "Gary wasn't her real father. We married when I was pregnant with her, and yes, he left when she was four."

"Her real father?"

"He died."

"How?"

The microwave dinged. She opened the door and removed the mug.

"An explosion." The words hurt to say.

"The military tags? They are singed."

Her throat closed with unexpected tears, and it took a moment to answer. "He was wearing them when he died. Steve was his friend. He gave them to me. Told me Aiden hadn't made it. He did—" She hesitated, not wanting to tell him Aiden had been a mercenary, but not sure why. "He did overseas work. He and Steve were friends. Members of the same team." They'd met when China had been teaching reading to orphans in Abidjan. She had taken over as an interim teacher, helping out until the next group of missionaries arrived.

Having been abandoned as a child at an orphanage in Ireland, Aiden had a soft spot for the kids. He would come around from time to time, check on their safety, stand guard if rebel forces were thought to be in the area.

China met him during one of those visits. One look at him, and it was as if she'd been struck by lightning. Her entire being came alive, and the air sizzled with some kind of crazy connection, as if the universe were melding their souls together.

Aiden had resisted at first. A loner with no family, only a few friends, he didn't want to bond with another human being—especially not on that level. In spite of his reluctance, they'd fallen madly in love and had been almost inseparable until he left for the mission that ultimately ended in his death.

"Were they working together when your husband was killed?"

Gunnar's voice yanked her back to the present. To a world without Aiden. She swallowed a lump in her throat. "He wasn't my husband. We weren't married. Aiden didn't know I was pregnant. I didn't know I was pregnant until after he died."

Angrily, she stirred cream into the near boiling coffee. "Look. I really don't want to talk about this if it's all the same to you."

"All the same what?"

She closed her eyes and blew out a loud breath. "I mean, if it's okay with you, can we please not talk about it?"

"Okay."

"Why are you so interested, anyway?" She put the spoon in the sink and took a sip of the coffee.

"I am simply making conversation. Wondering about Emma's father. A child should have a father."

"Yeah, well, I've gotten out of the market."

"Will Steve someday be her father?"

She slammed the mug down on the countertop, sloshing a small bit of the liquid on her skin. She snatched a tea towel from a drawer and used it to vigorously punish the back of her hand. "Listen, I may have to put up with your presence in my home. The threats. The fear. But making small talk with you and answering personal questions isn't part of the deal, got it?"

"As you wish."

To her surprise, he didn't seem angry. Did he ever get angry? Or did he wear the same bland expression, speak in the same monotone even while committing cold-blooded murder?

In the break room at the bank, China filled a cup with too-weak coffee from the carafe, nodding at Angela when she entered.

"Awful about Abel wasn't it?" Angela plucked a Styrofoam cup from the stack and held it out.

China poured automatically, her mind barely on Angela's words. "What about him?"

"You didn't hear?"

"Hear what?"

When Angela didn't answer, China's gaze rose to her face. The girl's eyes were damp, her mouth drawn in a tight line. Dread moved through China and even before Angela spoke, she knew what she was going to say.

"He's dead. He was found murdered." She shook her head and brushed back a handful of auburn hair from her face.

China's legs turned rubbery, and she dropped into the nearest chair. "How?"

"Shot in the head."

"When?"

"He was found last night." She sniffed and wiped at her eyes. "Can you believe everything that's happening lately?"

"No. I can't." Her insides clenched. "I can't believe any of this."

"Almost like there's some kind of curse." She lifted her cup, hand visibly trembling, then quickly set it down.

Even though China had skipped breakfast, a surge of nausea rose. She lurched toward the bathroom, ignoring Angela when she called out, "Hey, China. Are you okay?"

China leaned over the toilet and dry heaved. Her stomach clenched and her throat spasmed, but she couldn't vomit. She rose to her feet and walked unsteadily to the sink. Splashing cold water on her face, she stared at herself in the mirror. The hollow-eyed look she'd noticed the day of the robbery was worse. She looked like an extra from *The Walking Dead*.

The door of the bathroom opened. Looking over her shoulder at the reflection in the mirror, she saw Vanessa and Angela come in.

"You okay?" Vanessa asked.

"I'm fine, just, you know..." She turned toward them and managed a weak smile.

"Richard said everyone should go home. He said no one would feel much like working today, and we should pay respects to Abel." Vanessa made a sound that tried to be a chuckle but wasn't. "At this rate, might as well just shut down the bank for good. A tragedy every few days is certainly taking a toll on business."

"Yeah," Angela agreed glumly. "Not to mention on our staff."

China left Emma at day care and headed straight home, intending to confront Gunnar about Abel's murder. She knew. Oh yes, she knew. They had killed him. Gunnar probably hadn't, but one of the other sons of bitches had done it. And for no reason.

"Gunnar," she shouted as she slammed the front door. "I need to talk to you!"

She stormed into the living room to find Royce and Gunnar seated on her sofa. Marcel was in the easy chair, and a woman she didn't know stood by the fireplace.

They all turned at China's arrival.

"What happened?" China demanded. "Why did you kill Abel Brenneman?"

Her eyes roamed over all of them, waiting to see who would answer.

After several seconds of silence, Royce said, "Manners, China. You haven't met Layla."

The woman approached, her movements smooth and liquid like a panther. She had pale skin and a pentagram tattoo on her left cheek. Her flowing black hair was the same shade as the tight pants and low cut silk shirt she wore. She held out a hand to China. Long, black-painted fingernails scraped China's wrist when she reluctantly shook the woman's hand. The red lips tilted at the corners as Layla slowly let her gaze roam over China.

Nausea rose in her throat at the woman's touch. She tried to pull free, but Layla's grip tightened and held. She slid a long look at China, from her toes, back up to her face. "So, this is what all the fuss is about." Her voice was a throaty purr.

China pictured her staring into a mirror asking who was the fairest of them all.

"This is China," Royce said.

"Pleasure," Layla drawled, slowly sliding her hand out of China's, leaving an unsettling sensation, as if those lethal nails still scraped along her flesh.

"Abel?" China turned to Royce, looking down to where he still lounged on the sofa.

"You didn't tell us about Marcel accosting you in the parking lot."

China shot a look at Marcel, noticing for the first time he wore a cast on his right hand. He glared venomously at Royce.

"How did you...?" She couldn't complete the question. No need to. They somehow knew everything.

Royce stood and rubbed his hands down the thighs of his jeans. "Although you and brainy-act here can't seem to understand, we're always watching. It was wrong of you to keep it from us."

China frowned. "I didn't...I never thought to..." She shrugged and ended weakly, "...tattle." Maybe she should tell them he'd threatened her, but the less info she shared with these maniacs, the better.

"His actions were reprehensible. That was not part of the plan. We have a strict set of rules."

A disbelieving laugh escaped her. "Rules? Well, I'm so glad to know you have a code of conduct. That'll make me sleep better at night." She rubbed a hand over her face, catching a faint, disconcerting scent she couldn't identify that must have come from Layla. She shuddered. "You killed Abel because I didn't tell you what this pervert did? Are you kidding me?"

"I'm quite serious."

"The logical thing to do would be to kill him, right?" China jerked her head toward Marcel.

"We need him for the mission. We had to settle for a broken hand. Trust me, it wasn't an experience he enjoyed."

Marcel's eyes were more sodden than normal behind the frames of his glasses. He stared sullenly at Royce, then his gaze moved to China. Deep hatred resided in the moist orbs...along with lust. Revulsion moved over her skin.

"I can't believe it." She shook her head from side to side, feeling the need to cry but tired of doing so. "I can't believe you killed Abel. Over this."

"Hey, look at it this way." Royce smiled. "At least he wasn't one of your favorites."

Chapter Eighteen

High-pitched squeals punctuated the hum of a lawn mower coming from one of the yards that backed up to the park. China sat on a bench and watched Emma zip down a slide, followed by her new companion, a pig-tailed, freckled girl a few years older than her. She hadn't known the girl before today, but Emma was a little like Will Rogers, except she never met *anyone* she didn't like.

China had asked the girl, Chloe, where her mom was, and she had pointed in the general direction of the neighborhood where the man was mowing. China couldn't imagine letting a small child go to the park without supervision, but maybe her mother could see Chloe from a window. Or, maybe she was just extremely careless.

Not wanting to leave Chloe alone, China had stayed at the park longer than she intended. A lazy, listless, contentment moved through her body, which was odd considering her current predicament. Maybe so many tragedies piled on top of one another were rendering her immune to emotion.

Right now, rather than fixating and grieving over the death of Abel Brenneman, she was slouched on the bench, the sun's warm caress making her eyelids droop. The children's squeals, the chirping birds, even the roar of the lawnmower were soothing sounds. She could almost doze off, even with the hard wooden slats pressing into her butt and back.

"Miss Beckett?"

Her eyes flew open, and she sucked in a breath, shooting up from the bench.

"Sorry about that. I seem to have a habit of startling you." Detective Boyle smiled, looking anything but apologetic. "Got a minute?"

She glanced over to where Emma and Chloe were now tossing gravel up in the air, giggling as it fell on their heads. "Girls! Don't do that. Someone will end up getting hurt."

Boyce nodded. "Good advice. Wouldn't want anyone to get hurt, would we?" He dropped onto the bench. "You mind?" He took out a cigarette. He didn't wait for her approval as he struck a match, his cupped hand protecting the flame from the light breeze. Once he had the cigarette going, he looked up at her. "You're right you know. Someone always ends up getting hurt."

China remained standing. "What can I do for you, Detective?"

"Still trying to solve a murder and two bank robberies. Now I got another murder on my hands. You ever heard that old saying, no rest for the wicked? I must be one wicked son of a gun."

"You're talking about Abel Brenneman?"

"Why? You know about another one?"

She frowned. "No. Of course not."

"But you do know about Mr. Brenneman?" Boyle took a drag off the cigarette, studying her through the haze of smoke.

Her neck tensed, but she tried to keep it from showing in her tone. "I know he was murdered. Nothing more. You're not going to trip me up if that's what you're trying to do."

His brows rose. "You think that's what I'm doing? What are you saying? You're too cunning for that to happen?"

Cunning? This guy was something else.

"No. I just don't know anything. You certainly seem to think I do, though."

"All I'm doing is trying to put all the pieces together. Cops aren't the smartest people in the world. They're just good at assembling puzzles. You ever work a puzzle, Miss Beckett?"

"I find them boring."

He smiled. "I just bet you do." He stood and dropped the half-smoked cigarette onto the thick grass and stepped on it with the toe of a brown shoe in need of shining. "You're probably used to a lot more *excitement* than a puzzle can give you."

She gritted her teeth so hard her jaw ached. "I'm not *cunning*, Detective Boyle, but I'm certainly not stupid. You seem suspicious of me, and I'd like to know why." A little voice in her head said, *maybe because you're guilty...* But she wasn't guilty in the sense he thought. She hadn't been involved from the beginning.

A shrug wrinkled the shoulders of his suit, the same one he'd worn the first day they met.

"They called you by name, Miss Beckett. *China.* You and I are getting to be good buddies and *I* still don't call you by your first name. But the robbers did. They knew your name. You were me, wouldn't you find that a little suspicious?"

"I'm the one who *told* you they called me by name. You were me, wouldn't that sound like I'm innocent?"

He looked down at her but didn't answer.

She crossed her arms and stared out over the park for a few seconds, then looked back at him. "Listen, I don't know what you think I've done, but if you suspect me, if you're going to charge me, just do it. Knock off these innuendos. These games."

Boyle squatted and picked up his cigarette butt, straightened, and flicked it into a nearby trash can.

"Nothing I hate worse than a litter bug." He shot her a grin. "Well, almost nothing. I'll be in touch, Miss Beckett. You have yourself a good evening."

The evening news showed a special feature on the recent bank robberies and killings.

Carmen Bainbridge, KDTV anchorwoman, stared at the camera with proper solemnity as she delivered her spiel. Her teeth were too big and her nose too pointy, but her dark eyes were engaging and held a vitality that penetrated the TV screen, making her seem prettier than she was.

"According to authorities, there are no suspects in either robbery and whether or not they are related is still under investigation. Police are also trying to figure out if the murder of a bank employee, Abel Brenneman, was in any way related to the recent robberies.

"Mr. Brenneman was found shot to death in his home in Norman late Friday night. Police have no suspects in that case, either. They are asking anyone with information about the robberies, or Mr. Brenneman's killing, to please come forward."

She went on, but all China heard was death, death, death. Her lassitude from earlier at the park was gone, spoiled by Boyle's visit, and by the reality of her plight.

Each day that passed, she grew to believe more strongly that the chances of her surviving were slim. What would happen to Emma? Gunnar seemed to have grown fond of her. Would he raise her himself? She'd meant it facetiously, but the disturbing thought wouldn't go away once she entertained it.

What a catastrophe.

She remembered how upset she'd been with Emma over the dog tags, and shame gripped her. Aiden was Emma's father. She should have his dog tags. Now. Not once she was grown. China may not be around to watch her grow up, and where would the dog tags end up then?

It was late, Gunnar had disappeared upstairs, and Emma was asleep. China went into her bedroom and slid open the drawer of the small, wooden jewelry box atop her dresser and retrieved the dog tags, then headed to Emma's room.

She stood for a moment, watching her daughter sleep, the moonlight from the window shining a strip of light on her round cheek.

"Emma," she whispered as she gently sat next to her on the bed. Emma didn't stir. "Emma, sweetie. Wake up."

Emma yawned and batted her eyes open. "Is it morning time?"

"No, honey." A shaft of guilt shot through her. She should have waited until tomorrow. Not knowing for sure if she'd see tomorrow had prompted her, but now she felt foolish. "I just wanted to give you something."

"What?" Without her glasses, Emma's eyes appeared even more vulnerable than usual.

"This." China held the chain out to her.

She sat up and reached out to take them. "Daddy's dog tags? For keeps?"

"Yes. For keeps."

Lying back down, Emma tucked the fist holding the tags under her chin. Her eyes drifted shut. "You're not afraid I'll lose them?"

"No. I know you won't."

"I won't. I promise."

China leaned over, brushed the hair back from her forehead, and kissed her goodnight. "Sleep tight, sweetie." But Emma was already out.

Rainclouds hid the sun, making the glass wall of the coffee shop a grayish color, rendering it nearly opaque.

The rain had held off throughout Sophie's funeral, although China had expected the heavens to let loose during the graveside service. She couldn't recall a funeral she'd attended where it hadn't rained. Thankfully, the list of funerals she'd attended was short.

"It was lovely." Angela's hands were wrapped tightly around the cup in front of her as if letting go would precipitate another tragedy.

"Yeah," Vanessa agreed. "A lot of people there. She had a big family. Tons of friends."

China didn't weigh in on the awesomeness of the funeral. Nor did she point out that much of the crowd had been media and curious strangers. She wasn't sure how a funeral could be 'lovely.' People seemed to say that about all funerals.

"I'm just glad it's over with." China lifted the mug to her lips and test-sipped the coffee. Strong and hot. Just what she needed to counteract the chill inside her.

"We'll have Abel's funeral next week," Stacy added glumly.

The bank had closed early for Sophie's funeral. China wondered if customers would start to complain about all the hours they'd been closed. So far, the people she'd dealt with had been sympathetic, patient, but how much longer would that last in the hustle bustle convenience-conscious world?

"Have the arrangements been made for Abel's service yet?" Vanessa asked.

Angela shook her head. "They're waiting for the coroner to release the body."

They lapsed into silence. China doubted that any of the coffee shop patrons had to wonder where they'd been. Four women wearing black clothing and morose expressions, talking about death.

She turned her attention to the scene outside the window. The dreary view was preferable to seeing her own pain reflected in the eyes of her friends. Lightning flashed across the gray sky, and the clouds opened up, dropping buckets of rain onto pedestrians who now hurried along the sidewalk.

"Can you believe what's happened with all the robberies and deaths?" Vanessa asked. "Miles said he's never seen anything like it, and he's been a cop for nearly twenty years."

China started to turn back to respond, but caught sight of a motorcycle in the corner of the strip mall parking lot and kept her gaze focused there. A man sat astride the bike, seemingly oblivious to the rain drenching his clothing. It was too far to make out his features, but there was something familiar about his posture, his demeanor, the set of his shoulders...

"Oh, God," she whispered. "Aiden."

Chapter Nineteen

Insane. You're going insane.

"What did you say?"

Angela asked the question, but China didn't look her way, didn't respond. Her gaze was glued to the man on the bike. He seemed to be staring toward the coffee shop and for one delusional moment, she really would have sworn it was Aiden.

Then, the man and motorcycle headed out of the parking lot, disappearing into the sheets of rain.

Not him.

She let out a breath. "Nothing." She shook her head. "Never mind."

No way had that been Aiden. He was dead. He'd died in an explosion seven years ago, halfway around the world. She was truly starting to worry about her sanity. To worry for Emma. What would happen to her if her mother snapped?

No. She wouldn't snap. She would hold it together for her daughter.

A disturbing realization came over her.

Had it not been for Emma, she wouldn't need to hold it together. She would just give up, let go, and happily sink into the welcoming arms of madness.

Son of a bitch. She'd almost seen him. He'd thought the rain masked his presence, but for a brief moment, he'd felt as though she were looking at him. *Seeing* him. He felt something travel between them like currents along a telephone line.

What was he thinking? This was dangerous. Foolish. Hopeless.

An encounter with China was the last thing he needed. There was still a week to go before the job started, but he didn't give a damn. Time to get his ass to Texas.

He sped back to the Best Western and tossed his few belongings in his bag. He had to get out of town. Now. Just get the hell out.

At the checkout desk, he pitched his key to the clerk, a young, acne-faced boy.

"Room 313," the boy said. "You have something here."

"For me?" Who the hell even knew he was here?

"Yeah." The clerk passed an envelope over the cheap countertop.

Aiden took it and stepped outside. He dropped his duffle on the ground before ripping the envelope open. He studied the contents—a note and a newspaper clipping of a story about a bank robbery that happened a few days ago. He'd heard about it on the news, then found out it was the bank where China worked. He hadn't learned that tidbit until after he'd seen her, knew she was okay. He hated to acknowledge the relief that made him feel.

The article mentioned that a female bank employee had been shot and killed. Another female employee witnessed the murder, had been in the office at the time. An unwanted twinge of fear clawed his chest. He hoped it hadn't been China, then wondered why he gave a damn. Another bank, a branch of Greater Oklahoma, had been hit a few days later. Odd. Coincidence?

It didn't matter. Not his problem. He had a job in Texas. End of story.

He unfolded the slip of paper and frowned as he read the typed note.

The witness from the article is your China. This is only the beginning. Next time we won't miss. Do as we say and no worries.

Make one wrong move and LOTS of worries. Don't leave town. We'll be in touch.

His chest tightened as he folded the paper and slid it back into the envelope with the article. What the hell was going on and what did it have to do with him?

He looked over at his Harley. Then back at the door of the Best Western. Stay or go?

He tapped the envelope against his palm. Could he really leave without finding out what this was about?

Folding the envelope, he stuck it in the back pocket of his jeans. With a sigh, he heaved the duffle over his shoulder and shoved the door open.

The clerk looked up with raised eyebrows. "Yes?"

"That note you gave me. Who delivered it?"

The man frowned. "Some guy."

"When? What did he look like? Did he say anything?"

"Uh...it was this morning. Early. He was just a messenger kid, I think." He blew out a breath between pursed lips. "He said some dude gave it to him and paid him to bring it in. That's all I know."

"You ever see the kid before? Know who he was?"

"No, man. I told you all I know. Anything else I can do for you?"

Aiden's jaw tightened as he reluctantly came to a decision. "I need to check in again."

"Sure. How many nights?"

"Not sure." He frowned as he scribbled his name on the form the clerk slid toward him. "Wish to hell I did."

Gunnar didn't meet them when they walked in the house. China frowned, unsettled. Not that she wanted him to be there, but she'd become accustomed to his presence. To the routine. Sort of like having an infected tooth extracted. You wouldn't be sorry it was gone, but you'd definitely notice its absence.

Emma switched on the television, and China went into the kitchen, then the dining room, but no sign of Gunnar.

Returning to the living room, she heard footsteps and turned to find Layla coming in from the hallway. China was no longer just unsettled. She was thoroughly creeped out.

"What are you doing here?" The words came out confrontational although she hadn't meant them to. At best, a conflict with the woman would be unpleasant. At worst, it would be deadly.

A brow shaped like a bat's wing rose. "I am here to watch over you."

"Where's Gunnar?"

"Royce needed him. He'll return soon." Layla strolled around the living room, black-tipped fingers grazing photos and knick-knacks on the tables.

Emma glanced at her with a puzzled frown. Then, with a scowl, turned her attention back to the TV. Even her chatty daughter didn't want to converse with this creature.

The woman stopped next to a table that held the cross China's parents had given her.

Fingernails clicked against the silver, and Layla's mouth turned down at the corners. "Such a useless symbol."

Her fingers moved to the bible lying beside it, and China cringed. She didn't want this evil woman touching the sacred items. Her hand hovered above the leather cover, but stopped short of touching it.

Green, soulless eyes rose to China. "You think this will protect you?" She laughed. "Nothing can, you know."

China shuddered, trying not to let the woman get to her, but she could almost feel the evil pouring from her. "When will Gunnar be back?"

Layla shrugged. "Not soon enough. I don't like this any more than you. Babysitting is not my choice."

China pulled her eyes away from the woman and said, "Come on, Emma. It's dinner time."

Emma slid from the couch and followed China into the kitchen. She was unusually silent, not open and friendly with Layla as she was with every other stranger she came in contact with. Not surprising. Animals and children could sense demons.

China made hamburgers and just as she and Emma sat down to dinner, Layla came into the kitchen. She looked at their plates, then at China, her nose wrinkled in disgust. "Devouring cow flesh? You realize an animal had to die for that, don't you?"

Emma's features crumpled. "We're hurting an animal?"

China shot Layla a scowl. "Honey, some people choose not to eat animals. They're called vegetarians, and that's okay. But, the people who eat animals are okay too. There's nothing wrong with it. Just like birds eat worms and bugs to survive and cats and snakes eat birds. People eat animals, too. It's the way God intended. Circle of life. You remember *Lion King*, right? That's what Mufasa meant."

Emma nodded, but she finished her macaroni and cheese without eating any more of the burger.

China also couldn't eat, not with Layla watching them, her venomous gaze as powerful as a punch to the gut. She pushed her plate away. If nothing else, this ordeal might serve as a weight loss program. Not one she'd recommend to her friends, however.

After a tense few hours with Layla alternating between cold silence and thinly disguised threats, China ushered Emma upstairs to get ready for bed.

"Who is that lady, Mom?" Emma asked as China tucked her in. "Why is she in our house?"

"She's a friend of Gunnar's. She came to visit us while Gunnar had to go somewhere."

"Is he coming back instead of her?"

"Yes," China answered, hoping it was true. A week ago, she'd never have dreamed she'd be wishing for his return.

After Emma's bedtime story, China kissed her goodnight and went back downstairs.

Layla was still prowling, back in the living room now.

"How are all of you able to come and go so easily?" China asked. "Aren't you afraid you'll be seen?"

The trees surrounding the house would provide some cover, and the rear faced a wooded area. Still, it seemed a bit risky.

"We are very careful. Perhaps we have something powerful watching out for us." Her lips curled with derision. "Like your God."

"You don't believe in God."

"I never said I didn't believe. I do think maybe he exists. If so, he is weak and foolish. Despicable."

China flinched, half expecting a bolt of lightning to incinerate the woman. "Wow. You must like living dangerously."

"What? You think your God will strike me down?" She threw out her arms as if in supplication and looked up at the ceiling. "Take me!" she shouted. "If you're so mighty, so powerful. Take me now." She waited a minute, then lowered her gaze to China, grinning. "Guess he either doesn't exist, or he's not as powerful as you give him credit for."

China allowed herself a smug smile. "Or maybe he prefers to take care of things on his own time table. Doesn't mean he won't take care of them."

Layla's eyes narrowed and, for the first time, her confidence seemed to falter. Then, the contemptuous smile was back in place. "We'll see, won't we?" She studied China. "Are you and Gunnar lovers?"

"What?"

"A woman gets lonely. Has needs. I thought perhaps you had taken Gunnar as a lover."

As repugnant as the thought was, China didn't bother to deny it. She didn't give a damn what this woman thought.

Layla said, "Royce and I will soon become lovers."

"Look, I appreciate the effort, but I'm not interested in engaging in girl talk with you. And, before you ask, I don't want us to braid each other's hair." The words came out before she could stop herself. She didn't know what had made her so bold. It wasn't much wiser to taunt Layla as it had been for Layla to taunt God. But, she was growing weary of the constant threats and living in fear.

Layla's brows rose. "Ah, so the little lamb isn't quite so meek. I like that. You're showing some backbone. It's much more fun to kill things that put up a fight."

China remained silent. She wasn't quite as bold as she'd thought.

Layla sighed. "Royce is married and ridiculously faithful. He marries elderly women for their money, but actually stays true to them. Until they die, that is."

China's interest was piqued in spite of herself. "He's done this often? Married wealthy women who've died?"

"Five times. Widowed four." She threw out a hand, the black nails fluttering like flies. "All elderly, all wealthy, all quickly expire. He's oddly faithful while they're breathing." She stared into space and said softly, "He will give in, though. I will have him." Her gaze shifted to China. "And you never will."

"For God's sake, of course I won't. Why would I?"

"Royce is very sexy. Very handsome."

"If you're into psychotic killers."

Another of the slow, malicious smiles. "Yes. As I happen to be." She fixed China with a hawk like stare. The depths of her eyes were filled with ancient secrets and rage. Her hand shot out and caressed a lock of China's hair. "He desires you."

China flinched and took a step back. Alarm fluttered in her lower abdomen. "That's crazy." Her voice came out low and shaking.

"Crazy, but true. He would have already had you if he hadn't been ordered—" She stopped abruptly—as if aware she'd said too much.

Ordered? All this time China believed that Royce was the one in charge. There was someone else behind this? Who? And why?

"Nevertheless." Layla's silky tones broke into her thoughts. "Consider this a warning. Stay away from him."

China let out a disbelieving laugh. "I'd love nothing better than to stay away from *all* of you."

Layla leaned close, until they were nearly nose-to-nose. "Just remember, Royce belongs to me. Understand?"

This time, she didn't flinch, tried not to show her fear. Layla's cloying perfume washed over her and still, she managed to hold her ground.

Layla finally moved away, and China let out a long breath. "I'm tired," she said. "I'm going to bed."

"I believe I'll go upstairs also." Layla bent and slid something from her boot. A small, black-handled dagger appeared in her hand. She smiled, running a finger slowly along the side of the blade.

Panic bubbled to China's throat. "What are you doing?"

"Emma didn't seem to Emma didn't seem to get the message earlier about eating slaughtered animals. I thought I might pay her a visit. Kids like show and tell, right? I can show her what I mean."

China's heartbeat stalled, and the blood in her veins froze. "You can't...you won't..."

"Oh, don't worry. It won't be anything fatal. I'll just give her a little sample of what the animals feel. Royce said we couldn't kill either of you unless he orders us to. Didn't say we couldn't play." She shot China a vicious glare and strolled toward the stairs.

"Stop!" China screamed. "Don't touch her."

A chuckle issued from Layla's blood red lips, but she didn't pause.

Looking around frantically for a weapon, China closed her hand around the cross. With a strangled cry, she lunged toward Layla's retreating back.

Chapter Twenty

The heavy cross landed against Layla's skull with a sickening thud. The force of the impact vibrated through China's hands and up her shoulders, and Layla crumpled to the floor at the bottom of the steps.

The cross fell from China's hands and landed on the floor with a thud. Her body quivered with aftershocks. Dear God, she couldn't believe what she'd just done...

She dropped to her knees beside Layla's still body. Pooling blood from beneath the mass of black hair was still spreading. Layla's face was more pale than usual. China reached out a trembling hand and touched the ghost white neck. A pulse beat...faint, but there.

Her heart tried to hammer out of her chest. She sat back on her heels. What now? She couldn't let Gunnar see Layla. Couldn't tell Royce what she'd done. If they killed Abel because China hadn't squealed on Marcel, what might they do for this?

When would Gunnar be back? He could walk in at any second. Panic set in. Rapid breaths came in short, shallow gasps.

What if Emma came down? Boyle showed up? Layla died?

If Layla died, China would be a killer. But then, in a way, she was already a killer. She was at least partially responsible for more than a few deaths. Innocent victims. Something Layla definitely wasn't.

She stared down at the still figure. *Hide her body, I have to hide it, at least until I figure out what to do...*

Snatching a green plaid throw from the back of the couch, she wrapped it round Layla's head to stem the bleeding, then grabbed her shoulders and heaved.

The journey was slow, but she managed to drag her to the patio door without losing the wrapping that kept her head from dripping a trail of blood along the floor. Every few moments, she stopped to rest, sucking in deep breaths of air until her strength came back.

Looking down at the still-unconscious body, she had an eerie feeling that Layla would wake, her demonic eyes would slap open, and a soul-chilling cry would emit from those thick, red lips...

China shuddered as she slid the door leading to the back yard open, then bent to her task once more. Layla's head banged against the bumps of the doorway, and again on the patio stones. She cringed. If Layla weren't unconscious, and if it weren't for the throw protecting her skull, the blows would seriously sting. When she woke up—*if* she woke up—she'd have a mother of a headache.

Sweat beaded on her forehead, and her muscles screamed from exertion as she painstakingly drug Layla over the edge of the patio, to the door of the shed at the back of the house.

The thugs came and went through the back yard. China glanced around. If one of them showed up now...

No. They mustn't. She had to hurry.

Digging the key from the top of the light fixture next to the door, China unlocked the shed and jammed the key in her pocket. She pulled Layla's body inside and kicked the door closed.

She let Layla fall to the ground and surveyed the shed. One small window set high in the wall of the shed provided meager visibility from the streetlights outside. The shed had electricity, but she didn't want to turn on a light and draw attention.

A musty smell hung in the air, faint remnants of odors China couldn't identify. Gary had turned the shed into a home gym. China had hardly come out here at all since Gary took off. Everything was just as he'd left it.

A weight bench secured to the floor over by the west wall was her best bet. After several more attempts of tugging and rolling, she managed to get Layla on her back atop the bench. A thump sounded, and something hit China's foot. She jumped back, her hand flying to her heart as she searched the ground for the object. She let out a shaky laugh. Layla's cell lay in the dust beneath the bench. She put the phone on vibrate, then slid it into her own pocket.

She couldn't leave her unattended without securing her. She quickly looked about for something to use as bindings and snatched a roll of duct tape off a shelf, securing Layla's hands and feet tightly to the bars of the weight bench. The tape was so tight it crimped the flesh on Layla's wrists, but her comfort was the least of China's concerns. Her immobility was much more important. She ripped off a large strip of tape and pressed it over Layla's mouth.

Sweat poured down her neck. Standing upright, she surveyed her handiwork.

This would have to do for now. So far, Gunnar had never ventured out here. Even if Layla regained consciousness, any attempt at crying out wouldn't carry into the house.

Satisfied, China hurried back inside. She halted at the entry to the living room. *The blood.*

Flinging cabinet doors wide, she rummaged for a cleaning solution. What had she heard took blood out of carpet? Club soda? Laundry detergent? No. That wasn't it. She couldn't recall, and she didn't have time to google it. She jerked out a bottle of carpet stain remover, grabbed a sponge, and went to work.

Five minutes later, after she'd scrubbed until she thought her arms would fall off, the stain appeared lighter. It was still there, but was more a pinkish spot that might be mistaken for Kool-Aid or juice. She wiped the blood spots from the heavy metal cross and set it in its usual spot on the table.

Had Layla left anything lying around? China peered around the room. Nothing. She couldn't recall seeing a purse or any other personal item. Her gaze fell on the knife, and she snatched it up.

She moved methodically through the house, room by room, searching for anything else that belonged to Layla.

Halting, she shook her head. What had she done? God. She was so calm. So matter-of-fact. Calculating. Perhaps her new companions were rubbing off on her. All she felt was numb. Not fear, not remorse, not worry.

Fuck them.

She'd played victim long enough. They could do whatever they wanted to her, but one way or another, she would keep Emma safe.

Realization struck. *She was free.* No one was in the house. She and Emma could leave, right now.

Her heart beat faster. Was it really true? She finally had an opportunity to escape? Even while at work, while taking Emma to school, she'd been watched, escape had been impossible. But now, they only *thought* she was being monitored. Now was the time to make her move.

Where should they go? The assholes had eyes all over town. Nowhere was safe, but anywhere was safer than under their demented control. If she and Emma did get away, what would it cost? Who else might suffer because of it? Lucy? Spencer?

She needed to grab Emma, then get Lucy and Spencer. She would take them with her. She wasn't sure what she could say to convince them to flee, but she'd think of something. Hell, she would tell them the truth. Whatever it took to get them somewhere safe.

She ran up the stairs to her room, flung clothes and Layla's knife into a small suitcase. She darted into Emma's room and grabbed clothes for her, shoving them inside the now bulging case.

Hurry, hurry, hurry...the words beat into her brain with the rhythm of her pounding heart.

She swept through the downstairs, grabbing Emma's asthma medication and inhalers from the bathroom cabinet.

She reached the bottom of the staircase, and heard it. A sound in the kitchen. She stilled, and the breath hitched in her throat. Layla? Had Layla managed to free herself from the shed? Was she coming through the kitchen now...enraged, seeking to wreak vengeance...

Forcing her breathing to slow, China paused to listen.

Heavy footsteps moved across the kitchen floor. The door swung open, and China let out a scream.

Gunnar stopped, staring at her, his face scrunched. "China?" His eyes dropped to the medication she held against her chest. "What is this?"

Despair made her weak, and she gripped the banister with her free hand. So close to freedom. She fought back tears of frustration.

"Sorry. You startled me. This is...Emma's medication. I—I'm taking it to the upstairs bathroom so it will be handy if she..."

His glance took in the living room, wandered toward the second floor. "Where is Layla?"

"I don't know. She was here when I went upstairs to get ready for bed." Too late she realized she was still fully dressed. "Then— uh—I decided to come down and get Emma's medicine before going to bed."

He nodded slowly. "I am sure she is around. I will find her."

"Okay," China said. "Goodnight."

She headed upstairs, her footsteps sluggish with disappointment. If she'd been just a little faster, if she hadn't bothered to pack clothes, she and Emma would be away now. Her chance was gone.

What would Gunnar do when he didn't find Layla? Not waiting to find out, she fled to her room. Layla's phone was still in her pocket. Opening it, she thumbed through the text messages as an idea came to her. Maybe she could at least stall the search that would inevitably ensue when Layla didn't show up.

She found Royce's number stored in the phone. After reading a few texts to get the feel for the tone and speech of Layla's messages, she composed a text to him.

Something urgent came up. I must attend to it. I won't have phone service for a while, but will be in touch when I do. Will return soon.

Nervously, she waited to see if Royce would respond as she changed into her pajamas. A few moments later, the phone vibrated. An unfamiliar number—Royce's most likely—appeared on the display, but she ignored the call. Not long after, the vibration started again. China picked up the phone to find a text message from Royce.

We need you. You have a job to do. If I don't hear from you soon, you will be replaced and lose your share of the take.

Good. Maybe that would buy her some time.

She was brushing her teeth when a knock sounded at the door. When she opened it, she found Gunnar scowling down at her. "I cannot find Layla."

China managed a casual shrug. "I'm sorry. Maybe she figured you'd be back soon and cut out early."

His thin lips pursed in concentration. "Perhaps. Layla is a bit—unstable. I'm sure she will return."

Thank God for Layla's unpredictability. "I'm sure she will."

"I will let Royce know. Perhaps she has returned to him." Gunnar stepped back and China closed the door, leaning against it as she took in deep gulps of air.

Would her text forestall Royce long enough for her to figure out a solution to this mess? Nothing to do but keep up the charade and hope they didn't search the property. If they went into the shed...

She sent up a silent prayer, although the way things were going lately, she was starting to wonder if God was listening.

Chapter Twenty-One

China barely closed her eyes all night, expecting her bedroom door to fly open and an enraged Royce to appear, demanding she confess to what she'd done to Layla. She only managed a few fitful hours of sleep before giving up and going downstairs.

She was drinking her second cup of coffee when Emma came in, rubbing her eyes as she climbed into a chair.

"Morning, sweetie." China stood, bending to hug her and kiss her cheek. "Hungry?"

She nodded sleepily, and China released her, then poured a bowl of cereal and a glass of juice. Emma sipped the OJ and seemed to perk up as she dug into her Fruit Loops.

Gunnar entered the kitchen. "Royce heard from Layla."

Emma spoke around a mouthful of cereal. "That mean black-haired lady?"

The corners of Gunnar's mouth lifted in what might have been a smile. "Mean? Did she harm you?"

China's heart lurched. Emma had no idea how close she'd come to being harmed.

"No." Emma shook her head. "She just talks mean."

"Yes. That is true." He turned to China. "Apparently, she had something to attend to. Odd. She didn't speak to you before she left?"

China hoped her frown matched his puzzlement. "As I said, she was here when I went upstairs."

"Did anything happen that I should know about?"

China busied herself with pouring a third cup of coffee. "No. Nothing. Is Royce concerned about her?"

"He is angry mostly."

But is he suspicious I had something to do with it? Maybe not. To Royce and the others, she was a mealy-mouthed puppet, too terrified to consider opposing them. Layla had underestimated her in much the same way.

She sat next to Emma, watching Gunnar from lowered lids.

He rested his hands on his hips, slowly taking in the kitchen, and she held her breath, praying no signs of her dragging the body remained.

Just play it cool. He would have no reason to suspect anything. She just had to play it cool.

"I have my book club tonight," she said to divert Gunnar from thoughts of Layla.

"Book club?"

"Yes. A group of us meet once a week to discuss a book."

He nodded. "You have completed the required reading? I know your life has been somewhat busy of late."

His concern with the mundane never ceased to amaze her.

"No, I haven't." This week's book was a coming of age story about a girl who lived in the Appalachian Mountains. Not only had China not read the book, right now, she couldn't even recall the title. "But we can still meet. They'll understand...you know...with the robberies and all. I can just listen to their discussion."

"Of course. You should not cancel."

Oh, don't worry, I won't. Even though she hadn't read the book, this meeting would turn out to be the most important one of all. In the wee hours, while she tossed and turned, her stomach churning at the fear her deed would be discovered, she had come up with a plan.

Emma played upstairs while China readied the snacks for her meeting. She ran damp palms down the thighs of her jeans. Her heart beat so loudly, she almost didn't hear the knock. Tamara was the first to arrive and the others, Beverly, Keisha, and Doris, came shortly after.

China deposited a platter of vegetables and dip on the coffee table. "I'm sorry. I didn't get a chance to read the book."

Tamara shook her head as she chose a celery stalk and plunged it in the dip. "Hell, it's no wonder." She took a bite and spoke as she chewed. "All you've been through, I'm surprised you're even having the meeting. We could have canceled, you know."

"No. It's okay. I need to stay busy. The distraction helps."

China offered drinks and once her hostess duties were out of the way, she settled in the easy chair. "So...since I didn't get to read it, fill me in. How was it?"

"Fantastic!" Beverly leaned forward, her face animated. "I couldn't put it down."

"I thought Kara Sue was a little cliché," Tamara interjected.

Keisha shook her head. "No way. She was a great character."

"No, I can see where she's coming from. I mean, come on, barefoot, pigtails, ma and pa?"

"That wasn't the point of the..."

And they were off.

China forced her expression into attentiveness and nodded or grunted from time to time when appropriate as she surreptitiously glanced around the room.

Of all the purses, Tamara's would be the easiest to get to. Tamara was focused on the discussion...and the food. She hadn't touched her purse, or even looked at it in the hour since she'd arrived. Plus, the bag was small. And she'd placed it on the sofa table behind her. With a little stealth and a lot of luck, she had a pretty good shot. Of course, it all hinged on whether Tamara's cell phone was in her purse.

"Excuse me," China said. "Restroom break. You guys keep talking."

"Actually, I need to go to the restroom, too." Tamara stood. "Should I use the one upstairs?"

"No! I mean, you're welcome to use the one down here. It won't take as long and you can get back to the discussion."

Gunnar was on the second floor somewhere. It was unlikely he'd be wandering the hallway, but she didn't want to risk it. Plus, *she* needed to be the one who went upstairs.

Tamara headed into the hallway, and China ambled toward the staircase, her eyes darting to the other three women as she passed the sofa table. None of them was looking. China unfastened the purse and brushed it off the table onto the floor.

"Oh, damn. Look what I did." A few amused glances were quickly tossed her way before her friends went back to the snacks. Squatting, China gathered the fallen items, sighing in relief when one of them turned out to be a cell phone. She stood when everything was back in place—other than the cell. That, she slid in the pocket of her jeans, hoping it wouldn't choose that moment to ring.

Hurrying upstairs, she slipped into the bathroom after making sure Gunnar was nowhere in sight. The assholes may have her phone bugged, but not likely they'd bugged all her friends' phones.

Taking a deep breath, she squeezed her eyes shut briefly, then dialed.

A male voice came over the line. "Hello?"

"Miles, it's me, China."

"Oh, hey, China. Didn't recognize the number."

"Miles," she whispered. "I need your help."

Chapter Twenty-Two

Once her guests were gone, Emma was asleep, and Gunnar had retired to his room, China made a plate of dinner, grabbed a bottled water, and headed to the shed. She didn't intend to starve her hostage to death, at least not yet.

She hadn't been out to check on Layla since she put her in the shed. Was the woman still unconscious? Had she died from her injury? The thought barely brought a pang of regret.

Part of her hoped Layla had regained consciousness, so that China would know she hadn't killed her, but another part of her—the part that was terrified of the woman, even though she was tightly bound—hoped she never would.

When she approached, she saw that Layla had indeed come to, but was still taped securely to the inclined bench. Above the duct tape, her eyes spat venom. Her hair was more wild than usual, and blood had crusted in a dark red streak from her hairline along her cheekbone. The musty air in the shed was now saturated with the odors of sweat and body waste.

"If you scream, I'll put the tape right back." China pinched the edge of the duct tape and ripped it from Layla's mouth. Gunnar wasn't likely to hear her if she screamed. But she had no intention of leaving the gag off for long.

Layla's mouth spread in a slow, cruel smile. "You know you're a dead woman, right? You and your little bitch daughter?"

Without thinking, China shot out a hand and slapped Layla across the face. Her head flew sideways, and a large red welt formed on the pale canvas of her cheek.

China clenched her teeth. "Don't ever say that again."

Her eyes glinted with amusement. "You have more backbone than I would have guessed. Didn't think a weak little nothing like you had it in you."

Taking a deep breath to get her anger under control, she removed the foil from the paper plate. "I brought you dinner."

Layla curled her nose at the pork chops, stuffing, and green beans. "I'm a vegetarian. I will not devour animal flesh."

"Then eat the stuffing and green beans."

"No doubt the stuffing is made from pork stock. The green beans shared a plate with the pork. I will not touch it."

China shrugged. "Then you'll starve."

"I *am* starving. How long have I been here?"

China ignored her as she replaced the foil over the plate.

"I could die from my injury you know."

China looked down at her and grunted a humorless chuckle. "Then you'd owe me one. You'd finally be with your master."

"You know nothing, you stupid cow." Layla jerked against the bindings, and her mouth pulled back, showing teeth like the snarl of an animal. "Royce will kill you and let Marcel rape your dead body."

China allowed a satisfied grin to touch her mouth. Leaning slightly forward, she made sure Layla was looking directly into her eyes as she whispered, "Or maybe, Royce will kill *you* when he learns I got the best of you."

With Emma buckled in the passenger seat, China searched the cars in the circle drive at the school until she spotted Miles' Buick. She pulled next to him and parked close enough that her passenger door was nearly touching his driver's door.

He rolled down his window. "Good God, China." His concerned gaze dropped briefly to Emma, and he lowered his voice. "Is all this for real?"

"Yes." She hadn't told him every detail in their brief phone conversation. Only that the robbers had been to see her and threatened her, and she wanted Emma away safely until it was over. She'd made him promise not to tell Vanessa. "What did you say to Vanessa?"

"Only that you needed a favor, and I'd be gone a few days. She demanded I tell her what was going on, but I didn't." He narrowed his eyes. "Maybe this isn't the best idea. Maybe we should let the authorities handle it."

"I can't." She couldn't count on the police believing her, on them taking action before something happened to her child. Plus, she wasn't sure who she could trust. There was no way to sort the good guys from the bad.

Her gaze swept the schoolyard and nearby streets. No sign of anyone, but that didn't mean they weren't there. She was hoping, if they were watching, they would be far enough away that they wouldn't notice Emma's quick shift from her car to Miles'.

"You don't understand. They have eyes everywhere. They'll kill Emma, Lucy, me, whoever they have to in order to make a point. Trust me on that."

From the back seat, she retrieved Emma's backpack, which was stuffed with a few changes of clothing, her inhaler, a toothbrush, and her favorite toy, Red, who once more wore Aiden's dog tags around his neck. China couldn't take the chance of packing actual luggage, but she wanted Emma to have at least a few things. Knowing Emma would have her daddy's dog tags with her brought a small measure of comfort.

"I know I'm asking you to take a risk by getting involved. I didn't know where else to turn." A sob burned her chest, and she swallowed it back. "I'll understand if you change your mind."

"No. I want to help you, and if you say we can't go to the authorities, we won't. But this isn't a permanent solution. Something needs to be done."

"I know."

"Once I have Emma safely settled with my sister, I'll come back. We'll figure this out."

China nodded. Miles' sister, Miranda, was a former cop who lived in Illinois, near Chicago. Emma knew her, so it wasn't as if she'd be with strangers. Of course, each person China involved was at risk, but she didn't know what else to do. It helped that Miles and Miranda were cops. At least they knew how to protect themselves, how to protect others.

China reached across the seat to Emma. In spite of her intentions to not cry, her throat closed. "Oh, baby." She choked back a sob and pulled Emma into a tight hug. "Mommy's going to miss you so much."

"I'll miss you too." Emma's voice quavered with tears, and China made a concentrated effort to control her own. Emma pulled away and lifted her small hand to wipe at China's cheeks. "Am I going away forever, Mommy?"

"Oh, no, baby. You're just going away for a quick, fun trip. You'll be back soon."

"Why am I going to visit Miranda?"

China had explained the lie once, but she did it again. "She needs your help with some projects. I told her what a big girl you are, and she said you're exactly what she needs."

An uncertain smile crossed Emma's face. "Okay. I *am* a good helper."

"Yes, you are, sweetie."

Before she lost what little nerve she had, China released her. She passed the backpack to Miles through the window.

"Come on, baby," she said to Emma. "This is going to be fun. You're going to crawl out the window, and Miles is going to pull you into his car without you ever touching the ground."

"Awesome!"

China planted one last kiss on Emma's cheek and lifted her toward the window. Miles reached out and pulled her through.

"Back seat, sugar. Buckle in," Miles said.

"Bye, Emma." China sniffled back a cry and tried not to let Emma see her tears. She leaned toward Miles. "Be careful, Miles. These are very bad people."

Miles nodded slowly. "Trust me. I know all about bad people."

She straightened and once more let her gaze sweep the area. Shrubs along the drive partially obscured the view from the street, but she couldn't shake the feeling the bad guys were out there. Watching.

"Not like these," she said softly. Wrapping her arms around her body, she shuddered. "You haven't met any like these."

All day at work, China fought tears. A gaping hole split her stomach, opened in her chest—a sense of loss so strong, it was a physical ache. Her baby girl was gone, and she had no idea for how long. Would she ever see her again? She'd never felt such pain, such unbearable loneliness. Not even when Aiden died. Then, she'd spiraled into a deep, numbing grief, licking her wounds and becoming as depressed as she pleased. Now she had to suppress her pain and carry on as though everything was normal. Her psychotic lapse when she lost Aiden had somehow made her grief easier to bear. Giving in to a mental breakdown most definitely had its advantages.

Counting the time Emma should have spent at day care after school, Miles would have more than nine hours to get her away. At the end of the longest, most excruciating day of her life, China drove home.

Gunnar met her in the living room. "Where is Emma?"

Ignoring him, she went into the kitchen. She stopped in front of the fridge, intending to down one of Royce's beers in one gulp, but halted with a pained gasp. Emma's rainbow dog hung on the door with her name scrawled in uneven, lower case letters.

China's knees buckled, and she grabbed the refrigerator door handle to keep from falling. Tears welled, pouring out of her in a weeping torrent.

"China! What is it? Has something happened to Emma?"

She hadn't heard Gunnar enter the kitchen.

Without turning, she said, "She's gone."

Gunnar stalked over and grabbed her arms, hauling her around to face him. "What do you mean, gone?"

Lifting her chin, she stared into his eyes. "I sent her away. Somewhere safe. I don't care what you do to me, as long as she's okay. I want Emma away from here until this is over."

His face darkened, and his hands tightened, digging into the tender flesh on the underside of her arms. She didn't care. Pain was a welcome distraction from the hole in her heart.

"What are you saying?" he growled.

"You heard me. You can let Royce know, we can carry on with the plan, and I will do as he says, but only if he agrees not to harm anyone else. If they hurt Aunt Lucy or Spencer, I won't do another damn thing for them. Not one. Got it?"

Gunnar shook his head. "You have no idea what you have done. Royce will not be pleased."

"I don't give a *damn* what pleases Royce. You tell him—" She jerked from his grasp. "Tell him what I said. Tell him now that Emma is gone, I will do as he wants only as long as Lucy and Spencer stay safe."

The anger on Gunnar's face faded, replaced by concern, which scared China more than the anger had.

"You don't understand how this works. No one tells Royce what to do." His shoulders dropped and he released her, then slowly shook his head. "Whatever happens next, it will not be pleasant."

China rose earlier than usual the next morning. She took a wrap filled with spinach, tomatoes, and cucumbers to Layla. She'd considered continuing to bring Layla meat dishes, and she could eat them or starve. But then, what would be the point in feeding her at all, knowing she wouldn't touch it?

Her hostage's mood hadn't improved, but China ignored her jibes. She fed the wrap to her to keep from having to untie her hands. When Layla finished eating, China slapped another strip of tape over her mouth and left without speaking.

Gunnar came into the kitchen nearly an hour later. He poured a cup of coffee, holding it in his large fist. "I must tell them today."

"I know." She poured a cup of her own, then looked at the breakfast table where Emma would normally be sitting, chatting incessantly between bites of cereal. Miles hadn't called yet, but she had told him not to. They had to be careful about making contact. He was to meet her at work today during lunch and report that he'd delivered Emma to Miranda and that she was safe. That everything was fine. Until China actually heard him say the words, she wouldn't feel certain.

"I cannot protect you," Gunnar said.

She snorted a laugh. "I didn't know it was your job to protect me."

"It is not my job. That is the problem."

Without responding, she left the kitchen and headed upstairs to shower.

Just as she finished dressing for work, the doorbell rang. Seven-thirty a.m. Who would stop by at this time of morning?

Curiously, she made her way downstairs and opened the door. No one was there, but a cardboard box sat on the doorstep.

Frowning, she glanced down both sides of the street but saw nothing.

Taking the box into the house, she set it on a table in the foyer and tugged the flaps open. When she looked inside, something tight and hot clenched in her stomach, and she nearly crumpled, staying upright only because of the white-knuckled grip she had on the edge of the table.

A low sound emitted from her throat, a gasping hiccup that would neither stop nor turn into a full sob.

When Gunnar took hold of her shoulders an interminable time later, she was still making that sound, and she couldn't stop. She also couldn't pull her gaze away from the contents of the package where Red, still wearing Aiden's dog tags, lay nestled in the bottom of the box.

Chapter Twenty-Three

"Did they kill her?" China's voice was strained, the words coming out as if pushed through a sieve.

"I do not know." Gunnar sat on the sofa next to her. The box lay on the coffee table in front of them.

"How could you not know?" She whirled on him. "How could you not fucking know if your people murdered my daughter? Where is she? Where is she? Where is she?" With each word, she slammed her fists into Gunnar's chest. He didn't move. Didn't flinch. Didn't try to stop her.

When she finished, spent and drained, he said, "We will have to wait for word."

Her cell phone rang, and she snapped it up and punched the answer button without looking at the display. "Hello?"

"China." Vanessa's voice sounded as cold as an arctic wind.

"Yes?" Her heart pounded like a bass drum in her ears.

"They found Miles."

"Was Emma with him?"

"No."

"Did he say anything about her? If she's okay?"

"No." That same, cold monotone. "He didn't. He couldn't, China." A gasping sob came over the line. "He's dead."

Blood rushed to China's head, and her hand trembled so badly she thought she'd drop the phone. "What do you mean?"

"Dead, China. Murdered. Surely after the past week, you're familiar with that word. Dead!" The last was a scream that turned into more screams. China waited, listening to Vanessa as she screamed and cried. She wasn't even worried about anyone hearing her end of the conversation. After what happened with Red and Miles, obviously they knew what she'd done.

When the torrent stopped, China said, "How? Where?"

"One of his cop buddies came by the house this morning. Miles was found in St. Louis. In his car. Shot to death."

"Emma?"

"Nothing was said about Emma."

China's gut clenched, her heart shifting between grief over Miles and terror for her daughter. "I'm so sorry. I don't know what to say."

Another sob. "Neither do I." The line went dead.

China called into work. The bank would be short-handed for sure, with her and Vanessa out, but there was no way she could go in. Not when her little girl might be dead.

By noon when she hadn't heard from Royce, when Gunnar hadn't been able to find out anything, she knew Emma was dead. She also knew it was her fault. She'd killed her daughter. Her precious, beautiful child. The tiny being God had placed in her care.

Her life was over. There was no way she could live with the pain. No way she wanted to. She briefly considered going out and releasing Layla. That would guarantee a certain death. But she discarded the idea. If for no other reason, she didn't want to give the bitch the satisfaction.

Half the morning she sat staring into the cold fireplace, the other half she listlessly wandered through the house. During one of her forays into the kitchen, she encountered Royce. His unexpected appearances no longer surprised her. She no longer gave a damn.

She stared into the piercing gray eyes. "She's dead, isn't she?"

He lifted a Budweiser from the fridge and twisted off the cap. Tilting the bottle toward her as if in a toast, he said, "It's five o'clock somewhere," then downed half the contents in one gulp.

"Tell me about Emma."

He rested his hip against the counter and crossed his arms, holding the bottle loosely between his thumb and finger, swinging it like a pendulum. "You follow baseball?"

A quick, jerky nod was all she could manage.

"When a batter has a 3 and 0 count, he should never, ever swing at that next pitch. Not unless he knows for a fact he can do something with it. Lot of times, if they swing, they end up swinging at ball four or knocking a little blooper into the infield and getting thrown out at first. This is like that. You were 3 and 0, but you took a swing."

She waited.

"Not a smart move, China. Tsk, tsk."

She tried to swallow back the knot in her throat, but it remained. "Is—my—daughter—dead?"

He sighed and straightened from the counter. Opening the back door, he motioned with his hand.

A bear-sized black man stepped inside. He was bald and wore a shiny, snug fitting athletic shirt the color of butterscotch candy. Sunlight glinted off a pair of small gold hoop earrings. Her eyes dropped to his side, and her knees buckled.

"Oh, God." She ran to Emma and scooped her up in her arms, squeezing, hugging, crying, and kissing her all at the same time. "Emma. Oh, baby. Are you okay, sweetie?"

"You're hurting me." Emma's muffled voice made China ease her hold.

Pulling away, she moved her gaze over Emma in ecstatic disbelief. "I'm sorry," she whispered. "I'm just so happy to see you."

Emma shot a glance up to the black man. "I was so scared, Mommy. He's a stranger, but he made me come with him." Tears welled, and she snuffled a sob. "They took me away from Uncle Miles. Then he got hurt. I think he went to Heaven."

Her heart seized. Had Emma witnessed his killing?

She turned to Royce. "Did she see?"

"No. We told her Uncle Miles was gone, but she didn't see him leave." He grinned and raised his beer-free hand, palm up. "You're welcome."

She glared but didn't speak.

"We're going to talk about this, China. For now, you may spend time enjoying your daughter, but trust me, this isn't over. Not sure what will happen. Maybe nothing. If you've truly grasped the severity, the *importance* of following orders, it's possible there may be no further consequences. I'm not sure if your friend's..." He looked at Emma. "...trip to Heaven convinced you."

Tingles of fear and relief spread through her chest. "It did," she whispered. "I promise, it did."

He slowly nodded. "Maybe. Since Layla's disappearance, we're a bit short-handed, but we plan to finish the job and nothing will stand in our way. It's important that we make that clear to you; that you understand."

"You have. I understand."

Royce moved to the door and paused. "For your sake, and for Emma's, you'd better hope you do."

After dinner, a knock came on the door. China ignored it, but whoever it was persisted. Each bang grew louder by the second. On leaded feet, China went to the door and looked through the peephole. She sucked in a deep breath. Detective Boyle.

Reluctantly, she swung the door open. His suit looked more rumpled than usual, and some kind of brownish stain spotted his light gray tie.

"Can I help you, Detective?" Her voice was flat, just like her heart. Relief at Emma's safe return was tempered with despair, with guilt, over Miles. She did her best to put him out of her mind. One tragedy at a time was all she could assimilate.

"May I come in?"

She nodded and stepped back so he could enter. Without offering him a seat, she crossed her arms and waited.

"My, my, Miss Beckett. You are having a bad run lately." His eyebrows rose. "You must have walked under at least a hundred ladders and had maybe a thousand black cats cross your path, am I right?"

She tightened her jaw and lifted her chin. "I'm not sure what you mean."

"You've heard about Detective Hanson's death, I'm sure. Come on, the robberies, the killings." He shook his head. "That is some bad shit, you know?"

Although his questions, his suspicions, were wearing on her last nerve, she really couldn't fault him. He was right to be suspicious. She did know what was going on. And, rather than helping to stop the horrors, she was aiding and abetting. With what choice, though? She was part of this dangerous charade until the bitter end.

"Yes, very bad."

He stuck his hands in his pants pocket and looked down at the ground, then back up at her. His brown eyes skewered her with mistrust. "I guess you're going to tell me you know nothing about it. About Abel Brenneman's death, Detective Hanson's death, the robberies."

The back of her throat ached with unshed tears. "I wish I could tell you." She met his gaze, willing him to read her sincerity, *her mind*. "I really, really wish I could."

He frowned and narrowed his eyes. "If you know something, you *can* tell me."

She let out a trembling sigh. "No. No, I don't know anything. I'm sorry."

More sorry than he would ever know.

China spent the evening with Emma, watching TV, helping her bathe, reading her a story at bedtime.

Once Emma had fallen asleep, and Gunnar had retired to his room, China snuck dinner to Layla. She had no idea what she was ever going to do about the woman, but she didn't dwell on it. One day at a time, one step at a time. That was her new mantra.

Layla finished eating and looked up at China. "What is your plan?"

She didn't answer.

"You know your conscience won't let you kill me. I bet you already feel guilty, so much that it's eating you up. Little Miss God-fearing China," she taunted. "But you weren't quite God-fearing enough to stay with your parents and do the Lord's work, were you?" She laughed, but it had grown weaker over the past few days. "Maybe you'd be more comfortable on our side, hmmm? Since you couldn't hack it as a missionary?"

"Shut up." China tore a strip from the duct tape.

"Tell me how it made you feel when your mother and father left you with your aunt. When you were a child and became ill. You almost died, but they wouldn't come back and be with you. Their work was more important than their own child. How did that make you feel, China?" she hissed.

Her hands dropped, and she stared at Layla. "How do you know about that?"

"We did our homework. Before we ever started the job. We made sure we knew everything about everyone." She laughed again. "But the intel we gathered isn't why I know you felt rejected. Abandoned. That, I guessed on my own. I mean, what child wouldn't?"

China was eight when she'd been struck with meningitis. The doctors were less than optimistic about her chance of survival, although she didn't know it at the time. Her parents hadn't come back to the States to be with her. Each time she woke and found Lucy there, but not her parents, she felt the agonizing pain of abandonment, the realization that if she didn't matter to her own parents, she must not matter at all.

"They were doing important work," China said unconvincingly.

"More important than their child? Serving a weak God? A God who doesn't deserve their devotion? If God is love, why didn't your parents love you?"

"They did love me."

"Right. That's why they spent so much time with you while you were young. Come on, isn't it time to let it out? Time to admit how angry that made you? Afraid God will punish you for resenting his most devout children?"

The old insecurities, feelings of abandonment left her numb, except for the ache lodged deep in her heart. "Who the hell do you think you are? You don't know them. You don't know anything." She almost didn't recognize her own voice. She sounded like a small child, begging a bully to leave her alone.

"Don't I?" Layla grimaced in the parody of a smile, making the tattoo on her cheek stand out in stark relief against her pale skin. The symbol mocked China's pitiful denials. "But then, that's what they all do, right, China? *Everyone* leaves you."

She compressed her lips and slapped the tape over Layla's mouth, silencing her, but the words followed as she hurried from the shed.

Chapter Twenty-Four

Work had been hell in the days since Miles' death. Vanessa was gone on bereavement and the other employees walked around as though aliens had stolen their souls and their bodies were now just empty husks.

Vanessa had begged China to tell her about the favor Miles had been doing, but China refused. Vanessa not only held her responsible for Miles' death, but she was angry that she wouldn't tell her the truth. China remained silent. She'd rather Vanessa be mad than dead.

Vanessa called on Saturday morning, a few hours before Miles was to be buried.

"Tell me the truth, China. Tell me what Miles was doing." Her voice rose. "What favor was he doing for you that got him killed?"

China swallowed back tears. "I'm sorry, Van. I can't." Doing so would put her in too much danger. She might lose her best friend, but at least her best friend wouldn't lose her life.

"Well, then there's nothing left to say." The hysteria subsided, and her voice became icy, robotic. "I've transferred branches. When I'm ready to come back to work, I won't be working with you."

"Vanessa. I know you're hurting right now but—"

"I don't want you at the funeral. I assume you'll respect my wishes."

"Vanessa, please—"

"Don't show up."

She started to argue further, but Vanessa had hung up.

As much as China loved Miles and as much as she wanted to tell him goodbye, she would stay away. Funerals were for the living, and Vanessa was right. China would respect her wishes. Although it wasn't the same, since China and Aiden hadn't been married for twenty years, she understood. She wouldn't have wanted to see the person responsible for Aiden's death at his funeral.

That night, she sat in Emma's room and watched her sleep, trying not to think of Miles and Vanessa, about everything that had happened these past few weeks, about how hopeless the situation had become.

She was growing increasingly worried that Emma would slip and say something. Gunnar living with them round the clock. Her adventure with Miles. Strange people in and out of the house. How could a six-year-old continue to stay quiet about so many changes? Of course, it was possible she'd said something at school, maybe even to her teacher or principal, and the adults had brushed it off the way adults have of only half-listening to children. Lucy would listen, though. But had Emma said anything, Lucy would have asked about it, so it was unlikely Emma had mentioned any of the recent happenings to her. They hadn't seen her since Miles' death, which was probably a blessing.

An hour passed before Gunnar knocked on the door and suggested China return to her own room.

Recognizing the early warning signs of a sleepless night coming on, she took two over the counter sleeping pills. Within moments after she went to bed, the medicine took effect and a heavy-limbed lassitude stole over her. Sighing, she gave into the luxury of not thinking and let herself drift.

Sometime later, a pressure on her shoulders snatched her out of deep sleep. Before she could scream, a hand clamped over her mouth.

Her eyes flew open, but she couldn't make out the figure looming over her in the darkness. Gunnar? He'd never entered her room before, other than to briefly check in during his nightly rounds. Besides, this man wasn't as large as Gunnar. Who was he? Had he done something to Emma?

Terror shot through her limbs. She bit at the hand and jerked her body violently, struggling and bucking as she tried to free herself. She gasped and drew back when her breasts brushed against the hard wall of her assailant's chest.

"If you're worried about being raped, love, I can promise you, moving like that is not the way to prevent it." The words were said in a hush, but the low, male timbre was familiar.

Her movements stilled. The voice didn't belong to Gunnar.

She blinked, trying to put the man's features into focus. When her eyes finally adjusted to the dimly lit room, her mind confirmed what her heart had known. With fingers that shook, she pulled the hand from her mouth. He didn't resist. He knew she wouldn't scream.

She stared disbelievingly into eyes that, though she couldn't see them clearly now, she knew to be as black as the night surrounding her.

"Aiden," she choked out. "You're alive."

Chapter Twenty-Five

China scrambled to her knees, her heart squeezing with joy.

"Oh, my God. Aiden. How...?"

Tentatively, in case it was another of those dreams that fled with the cruel light of dawn, she lifted a quivering hand and placed it on his cheek. Rough stubble grazed her palm.

Yes. Not a dream. It was real. *He* was real. Warm. Male. *Alive.*

She threw her arms around his neck, kissing his cheek, his forehead, his lips. "Oh, God. It's a miracle. You're alive."

He took hold of her arms and pulled them from his neck, then leaned back to look at her. "Yes, I'm alive. Disappointed?"

She frowned, still unsure this was real, that Aiden was here. Had she done just as she'd feared? Gone completely insane?

No. He was real. She'd touched him. She could smell him. His warm, woodsy male scent. She could hear him. That husky tone with the faint Irish brogue. She could see him, although the features were a little older, a little rougher, as if time and tragedy had carved a harshness in them that hadn't been there before. A jagged scar cut through the dark stubble on his face. She shuddered, not wanting to imagine how he might have gotten that scar.

Then his words penetrated, and she frowned. "Disappointed? What are you talking about?"

"You seem surprised I'm alive. I assume you thought I'd die in prison. The question is, are you happy or upset that I didn't?"

His body was close to hers, and she desperately wanted to lean into him, to maintain contact. She couldn't let him slip away again. But his demeanor didn't welcome the overture, so she resisted.

"Prison?"

He wasn't making any sense. Her mind couldn't process what was happening. She was still feeling the effects of the sleep aid, not to mention the shock of finding Aiden in her bedroom. Alive. The word kept beating into her head. Aiden was alive.

His dark eyes searched her face, a frown marring his forehead. He stood. "Maybe you should put on a robe so we can talk."

Automatically, she obeyed him, slipping from beneath the blankets. She grabbed her robe from the back of a chair and tugged it on.

"Aiden. I—"

He moved close and touched his fingers to her lips. "Is the house bugged?"

She shook her head. "I don't think so." She thought of what had happened with Layla. The hounds of hell hadn't descended upon her, so they must not be listening. "No. I know it's not."

He nodded and stepped back.

"What's going on? You were in prison?" She couldn't take her eyes off him. He wore faded jeans and a black button-up shirt. A small gold hoop glinted in his left ear, nearly covered by his longish dark hair. He looked different, but it was Aiden. Definitely Aiden. "All this time, I thought you were dead."

He threw back his head and laughed. "Right you did. That's rich. Didn't think it would catch up to you, eh? You ran off and left me in a hospital to die, and just assumed I would perish. No, love. That's not how the story ends. I survived."

His words were like heavy rocks pounding into her chest. She swung her head slowly from side to side. "No, Aiden. How could you think that? I didn't know you were..." Pain shafted through her, cutting off her words. All this time, he was alive, and he thought she'd abandoned him? "But the explosion. Steve said—"

He lifted his brows. "Steve? He told you I was dead?"

She nodded, her mind working this new information. Steve hadn't lied on purpose, had he? No. He wouldn't have done that.

He was grief-stricken at Aiden's death. No way would he have lied to her.

"So now, the two of you find comfort in one another's arms. How did you come to marry another gent in between?"

"I didn't... Steve and I are just friends. And, Gary—"

"Never mind. That's all in the past." He crossed his arms and studied her. "What I need to know is what the devil you're up to now, lass."

"What I'm up to? What are you talking about?"

"All this cloak and dagger stuff. The note at my hotel. I've been keeping an eye out the past few days. Seems you've made some interesting friends."

"Friends?"

"Royce, Bishop. I don't recognize the others, but I know those two well. We were a team once. What have you cooked up with the two of them?"

When his meaning registered, white-hot anger replaced her shock and happiness. She lifted her head and glared into his smirking face. "What are you accusing me of? I've been through hell the past few weeks, and since you know these men, it appears to have something to do with you. And you dare accuse me of being involved?" She jammed a finger into his chest. "You know them. They've threatened me and my daughter, killed people I love, and it's all because of you." Her body shook with rage, and tears made her voice quaver, but she didn't let them spill. "What did you do to them to make them want revenge? To make them come after your daughter to get it?"

Aiden's face paled, and he flinched. "Daughter?"

"Yes, daughter. What the hell do you think? If you've been watching us, then I'm sure you've seen my little girl. *Our* little girl. Emma."

"Keep your voice down."

"Fuck you! Did you hear me?" She grabbed him by the shirtfront. "Did you hear me? You almost got your daughter killed!"

He whipped an arm around her waist, pulled her against his body, and covered her mouth with his other hand. "Shhh," he whispered. "Calm down. You don't want to rouse any attention. You need to calm yourself so we can talk."

She jerked against his hold, but his arm was like a vice she couldn't escape.

"I'll release you when you are ready to discuss this calmly. When those stormy eyes are no longer shooting fire at me." His voice softened, and a brief smile touched his mouth. His grip loosened. A light caress on her waist shocked her, and the anger fled. She relaxed, letting her face fall against his chest. The tears came, her body shaking with the torrent.

He removed his hand from her mouth and slipped his arms around her. "Shhh, love. Don't cry now. It's okay."

"All this time," she sobbed into his chest. "I thought you were dead, and I've been trying to go on. Then these men appear and make our life hell. They murder people, threaten me, threaten Emma. They took her. Dear God. They took my little girl and killed Miles. Now, you're here and I thought you'd help, thought everything would be okay," she paused to take a breath that turned into a snuffle, "but instead, you're accusing me. You're angry and you hate me and you think I'm involved." She stiffened and leaned back from him, staring angrily into his face. "After all I've been through. You honestly believe I'm a part of this?"

He squeezed his eyes shut briefly, then opened them and shook his head. "I don't know what to think. None of that's important right now. What we need to do is figure out what we're going to do."

He set her away from him. She rubbed her hands up and down her arms, trying to warm the chill his absence left.

A few moments of silence passed between them, until she broke it by saying, "So, nothing?"

"Nothing?"

"No reaction about your daughter. I assume you didn't know you had a child and now that you do, you have no reaction?"

He gave a broad smile that made the scar on his chin look even whiter in the gloom. "I'm afraid I'll have to get back with you on that. For one, I think you're aware, I never wanted children. For another, I have doubts she belongs to me."

"Are you serious?" She grunted in disbelief, tamping back a burst of anger. "Of course Emma is yours."

"That's neither here nor there. Right now, I need you to tell me everything you know about this whole devilish mess."

She studied him silently for a moment, then all her anger dissipated. Regardless of his attitude, of his suspicions, Aiden was here. He hadn't died in that explosion.

She knew the kind of man he was. Even if he didn't believe Emma was his child, no way would he abandon them. They finally had someone they could trust. Someone who wasn't afraid of Royce and his evil comrades. Someone who would give his life to save another.

She told him everything that happened from the day of the robbery to now.

He listened, stopping her to ask questions from time to time, but mostly just listening. His brows rose when she got to the part about Layla. She thought she detected a hint of admiration in his expression.

"Do you think that was wise, going into the shed where you could be seen?"

She shrugged. "The property is surrounded by trees. I only went out a few times. I didn't want her to starve to death."

"Why not?"

She didn't have an answer to that one. "I don't know. I even made sure to accommodate her vegetarian life style so she wouldn't starve. Besides, I just felt a need to go out and check on her. I think part of me wanted to make sure she was still where I left her. I had visions of her breaking free from the shed and coming inside the house." She shuddered. "In the vision, she visited Emma's room first."

A look of sympathy crossed his face, then was gone as suddenly as it appeared. "No more, though. I'll handle this. I don't want you going back out there."

That was a task she'd gladly relinquish. She nodded. "Okay. So, what do we do now?"

"I'm not sure. I don't know what they want from me just yet. Until I do, until I know who all is involved, we have to be cautious."

"They could kill Emma. We have to do something."

Aiden shook his head. "They won't kill your child. They know your cooperation would end immediately if they did."

"You seem confident in that. Or is it just that you don't care if they do?"

He scowled. "Even if she's not mine, I don't wish to see her harmed. Although, it's becoming clear why you're trying so hard to convince me I'm her father."

"Oh?"

"You think that would guarantee my assistance."

"Will it?"

He shook his head. "If I decide to help, it will be because it's the thing to do, and because all this started on account of me. I would save a stranger's child as quickly as I would my own."

"In other words, her being your daughter means nothing to you."

He lifted his hands in a 'what can I say' gesture. "I'm afraid not."

His words sent a cold wind rushing through her soul, but she wouldn't argue. If he agreed to help them, she didn't give a damn if he believed Emma was his. Apparently, he had changed. Or, she never really knew him in the first place. She would never have fallen in love with this cold stranger.

"So, what now?"

"I don't know yet. I need to stay under the radar until we know more. I'll go check in on your guest. Make sure she's where she can't get away." He headed for the balcony and she noticed for the first time, the door was slightly open. That must have been how he'd gotten in. "I'll be in touch."

"You're leaving?"

"Yes. Why?"

"Why? My God. I thought you were dead. I haven't seen you in seven years."

"I told you, we'll talk more later."

"But...I..." she lifted a hand, then let it drop. "I want you to stay with me." She took a breath. "I don't want to lose you again." He laughed, and her anger rose once more. "What's so funny?"

"You want me to stay? In your bed?"

"I didn't...I just..." Her cheeks heated.

He stalked back to her and cupped a hand along the side of her face. His touch sent desire skittering along her nerve endings, while his words made her hate herself for it.

"If you need sexual gratification, you'll have to look elsewhere. I can't be falling for your charms again. It took me years to get you out of my system. Loving you makes me weak and foolish. For both our sakes, and for the child's, I need to stay sharp." His gaze raked her body. "I can't say you don't tempt me, love. But I'm not sure you're completely innocent in all this. Too much of a risk, you see. I'd as soon take my chances mating with a black widow." He grinned and placed a quick, hard kiss on her lips before releasing her.

She didn't respond. She was suddenly drained, exhausted. He headed toward the balcony's glass door. Sliding it back, he disappeared into the blackness outside.

Her heart slowed, then thudded to life again. In spite of the differences in him, in spite of the anger and coldness, Aiden was back. It was a miracle, one she'd never thought possible. Deep in her soul, she knew everything would be okay. Regardless of what happened now, tonight was much better than last night had been.

Tonight, Aiden was alive.

Chapter Twenty-Six

Stone slid over the side of the balcony and dropped to the ground. His heart and body wanted to climb back up and sate the hunger that had gnawed at his soul all these years. Seeing China only fed that hunger, like a shark sensing the presence of a sea lion. Escape was the only way he could resist her.

Damn the woman.

Above the tree line, a sliver of white moon edged from behind a cloud, then quickly retreated, as if allowing Stone privacy for his clandestine task. The back yard was shadowed in darkness, but eyes peering from the gloom could easily spot movement. He crouched low to the ground and started toward the shed.

China's voice came back to him...*I thought you were dead.*

Right. He'd believed her lies before and suffered the consequences. No way he'd go down that path again. Although laden with sweet warmth and skin as soft as an Irish meadow, the path was treacherous. Her sky-blue eyes and full, kissable lips had nearly done him in.

He had to forget the woman he once knew. Forget the passion. Forget the dreams of an eternity in her arms.

Things were different now.

Was the child his? A fissure of warmth bloomed in his chest, but he pushed it back. He didn't want a child. If it turned out she was his, he'd do the right thing by her, but to hell with getting swept up in the emotions of it all. He'd made that mistake with the mother. *Fool me once...*

And what about Steve? Why would he tell China he'd died? He and Steve had been heading into the city in Tanier. They'd rushed into a burning house to help the people trapped inside, and the next thing he knew, he was waking in the hospital. Things were chaotic at the time. Yet another civil war—something the people in the area had grown accustomed to—had erupted. The hospital was packed with the injured and dying.

Barely able to stand upright, Aiden had left, headed out to get the money and meet up with Bishop and Royce. In all the confusion, perhaps the doctor thought he'd died, or forgotten him completely. What was one more body, after all? Or, it was entirely possible Steve had lied to China. But for what purpose? He was interested in her, of that Aiden was certain, but her thinking Aiden was dead hadn't helped his cause in the least. She had, after all, married another man. They'd both been rejected by the lovely China.

He shook his head. Too much to decipher at the moment. Steve's motivations bore watching. But for now, he would reserve judgment.

He reached the shed and found the key to let himself in. A sour, foul smelling odor assaulted him. In the gloom, he could make out the figure of a woman lying on a reclined workout bench. What looked to be a hundred rolls of duct tape bound her feet and upper body to the bench. He moved closer. Long, dark tangled hair partially obscured a pale face. She lay perfectly still.

He thought she was dead until her eyes flickered, then opened. They were a hazy green, the whites marred with red streaks. She frowned, and the eyes took on a spiteful glare. Involuntarily, Stone shivered. He'd encountered some bad people in his time, but the malevolence in this one was like that of a creature from the depths of Hades.

"My name is Aiden Stone," he said.

Surprise appeared briefly in her expression, then the malice was back.

He nodded, satisfied. "So, you know who I am. In that case, you know I don't mess around. I want answers from you, and I'll do whatever it takes to get them."

Without trying to be gentle, he ripped the tape from her mouth.

She flinched, and her thick lips pulled into a snarl. "I'll die before I tell you anything." Her voice was weak, belying the aggressive words.

"Maybe I can coax you into changing your mind." He gave her the smile that had frightened the woman at the strip mall. The effect was lost on this one.

"There's nothing you can do," she spat. "I'd rather die than tell you anything."

"Some things are worse than dying, you know."

She made a sound that might have been intended as a laugh, but came out as a strangled growl. "Give it your best shot, cowboy. I am not afraid."

Stone leaned closer to examine her head. Blood matted in the dark hair and congealed in the wound. It was a wonder she hadn't died, or at least suffered brain damage.

He let out a low whistle. "Ouch. That must have smarted a bit."

She glared. "Your woman's a dead bitch, I hope you know."

"She's not my woman."

"Your whore, then."

He shrugged. "We've got more important issues to discuss." He pulled a chair over and sat, tipping back and balancing with his feet. He linked his hands behind his head as he studied her. "Way I see it, we have three options. Option A, I utilize my special talents and torture you until you talk. Problem with that is, you might let me kill you before you tell me what I need to know. Or, you might lie. Either way, I won't get the answers I seek."

He waited for a response, but there was none. Maybe she sensed it was an idle threat. He wasn't into torturing women. But this was no ordinary woman. She'd terrorized China and the child. If China hadn't stopped her, no telling what she'd have done to the little girl. He could see the evil residing inside Layla. It shone from her eyes. He smelled it coming from her pores, nearly overpowering the stench of her body.

"I'll admit, I'm not fond of that option. I don't really have the stomach for torture anymore. Getting old I guess." He flashed her a grin. Still no response. "Option B, you tell me what I want to know. You tell me all the players, how many assholes I'll have to deal with, where their headquarters are located, everything you know. I untie you, let you take a nice, hot shower, and change into fresh clothes. We'll clean and treat your wound. Once this is all over, I let you go. Option C, you don't tell me a thing. I'm forced to find out on my own." He met her eyes. "And I will find out. Tracking's one of my specialties. So I'll locate Royce and the others, no doubt. It'll just take a little longer without your help. Then, after I find them, I make it to where Royce thinks *you* gave up the info."

She laughed. "How do you think you're going to pull that off?"

"That's the easiest part of all. China has your cell phone. A properly worded text message would seal your fate."

Her smile faltered.

"You've known Royce for a while, right?" He didn't wait for a reply. "You know his reputation? I'm sure you've heard of his special brand of punishment. Not certain if it's just rumor, but the way I hear it, he peels the skin from his victims and leaves them outdoors for days, or however long it takes them to die. Exposed to the elements. Animals feeding on them." He forced a shudder. "Got to be the worst way in the world to go. Lucky ones don't last more than a few days. Royce did it to a guy just for stealing his woman. Wonder what he'd do to the person who betrayed him, ratted him out, and brought his whole operation to its knees?"

Her expression went rigid, the shadows beneath her eyes darkening. "Fuck you."

He frowned as if deep in thought. "You know, if I were you, I would choose Option B. A and C will only cause you a great deal of pain."

"You'll never find him." She lifted her chin and attempted a smug look, but the skin on her face visibly tightened, and her lips trembled.

"We'll see about that. You'd be surprised how ingenious I can be when I need to. I'll be back soon. If you're not ready to talk then, you can deal with Royce."

He let the chair back on all four legs and stood. Retrieving a roll of duct tape from the floor, he secured her mouth once more.

On his way to the door, he stopped and turned back. "Hmmm. A person who refuses to eat the flesh of an animal will have her flesh eaten *by* them." He lifted his brows. "Gotta love the irony, right?"

Emma danced anxiously from one foot to the other, making the hem of her blue ruffled dress brush against her legs. "Come on, Momma, we'll be late."

"I'm almost ready." China laughed. Her spirits were lighter than they had been in a while. She and Emma were going to church for the first time in months. Since she'd experienced a miracle, paying a visit to God's house was the least she could do.

Grabbing her purse, she joined Emma at the door. "Maybe after, we'll go for a drive."

Emma's face lit with excitement. "Can we go to McDonald's?"

"Sure we can." The mood China was in, she'd have agreed to almost anything.

They would barely have time for the extra stop. Gunnar had given his permission for this outing, but had insisted they be back by two. Most likely, while he was keeping sentinel on the house, someone would be dispatched to monitor their every move.

As they drove to the church, it was all she could do not to share her news... *Emma, your daddy is alive...*

The words fought to escape, but she held them back. She wasn't sure how Aiden wanted to play this, how long they had to keep it secret. Plus, there was the fact that he wanted no part of being a father. Emma had been through enough lately, she wasn't going to pile rejection from her father on top of it.

Fountain of Love Fellowship Church was nearly filled by the time they arrived, but she and Emma managed to squeeze into a spot near the back. The smells of numerous colognes mingled in the air. At the large piano on stage, Miss Crandall sat as she had for thirty years, although now the music dragged a little, and a metal cane was propped beside her against the bench.

China settled into the padded pew, marveling at the difference in the comfort level from when she was a child. The pews back then had been hard wood. Whether her parents were in the States or out of the country, they attended church regularly. China hadn't enjoyed it like Emma did. She was too afraid she'd do something to gain her parents' disapproval. Her childhood church visits consisted of interminable hours sitting stiffly on the uncomfortable benches, tensely praying she'd get through the service without screwing up.

This time was different. The music sent peace settling over her. The pastor spoke about faith. How fitting that she'd chosen this service to attend. God was telling her he would be there for them. No matter what, she could count on Him.

When it came time to pray, China was able to sincerely join in, asking God to stay by their side, to protect her little girl. And she fervently thanked him for bringing Aiden back.

After the service, they joined the line of parishioners waiting to speak with Pastor Timothy. The preacher was in his late twenties. His thick, curly reddish brown hair and easy smile fit his congenial personality.

Pastor Timothy had taken over the church a few years ago when the pastor China had grown up with—Pastor Denton—had retired. Pastor Denton had been kind, but his bushy gray eyebrows seemed perpetually drawn into a frown and all China could remember were his threats of eternal damnation. As a child, she had no idea what brimstone was, but she knew she wanted no part of it.

When their turn came, China stuck her hand out, and Pastor Timothy gripped it warmly in both of his. "China. So wonderful to see you. I hope we'll see you around more."

"Yes. I plan to come more often," she promised, briefly suffering a familiar twinge of guilt at her lack of attendance.

He bent to look into Emma's face. "Emma, you get prettier every time I see you."

She blushed and smiled shyly.

When the pastor straightened, he said to China, "How are your parents doing?"

"Good," she said, though truth was, she didn't know for sure how they were, or even where they were.

"I saw a friend of theirs a few days ago. He said to give you his regards."

Ice chilled in China's chest and she knew what he was going to say before he said it.

"His name was Royce Dolan. You know him?" Before she could respond, he said, "He asked me to tell you he was sorry he missed you. He's heading out of the country soon and promised to look your parents up. So, if you talk to them, be sure to let them know."

China replied, but in her terror-numbed state, wasn't sure what she said. Her peace had been replaced by abject dread. Royce's power was far reaching. She'd already been concerned about her loved ones who lived nearby, but he was letting her know that no one was safe. Even though they were worlds away, he could get to her parents, too.

The warm spring sun shone down on them as she and Emma headed to the car, but it might as well have been a black cloud for all the pleasure it gave China.

Emma kept up an endless stream of chatter as they drove, while China held a cramp-inducing grip on the wheel. The promise of sanctuary had been shattered, leaving her feeling abandoned and afraid.

Chapter Twenty-Seven

Stone propped the motel door open with a straight-backed chair. Since his release from prison, he didn't like to be in tight spaces. Needed a reminder he was free to leave anytime he wanted. Funny how the human mind worked. A tropical vacation to some remote island seems like the ultimate getaway, but you get stranded on that same island, unable to leave, and suddenly that little piece of paradise becomes unending torture. The difference was free will. Freedom. People who'd never lost it had no idea how precious it was.

He used the remote to turn on the television. Surfing through the channels, he was about to conclude that the airwaves had suffered a hostile takeover by reality shows before he finally found a ballgame. Reds and Braves. Muting the sound, he dropped to the edge of the bed and toed off his scuffed boots. He leaned against the headboard and propped his feet atop the bedspread, then dialed Wesley's office, where he was thrust into a world of infinite automated options.

With nothing to occupy his mind while he waited, his thoughts turned to China. He'd actually seen her, talked to her, touched her after all these years. Bittersweet, to say the least. Like glimpsing heaven while hell's flames licked at his feet.

What did she see when she looked at him? She'd been happy to see him at first. Actually seemed to still want him, but he'd put the kibosh on that pretty quickly. Didn't matter. Even if she did want him, once the shock of his return wore off and she got a good look at what prison had done to him, she wouldn't anymore. He rubbed a hand on his whiskers. Maybe he should shave now that he was back among the civilized. Maybe he should do it before he saw her again...

"Hey, *compadre*, what's happening?" Wesley's voice dragged his thoughts away from China.

"More than you'd believe."

"Try me."

He pictured Wesley on the other end of the phone. He'd be leaning back in his chair, his rattleskin cowboy boots propped on his desk—hair slicked back, business suit, goatee trimmed to perfection. Wesley out in the trenches was the exact opposite of his business persona. On a mission, the hair would be wild and long, the goatee a full-on beard, the eyes steely, determined, deadly. Stone had been glad, on more than one occasion, that Wesley was on his side.

"Can you run some names for me?" On the television, Joey Votto hit a three-run homer. Maybe this would be the Reds' year.

"What you got?" The sound of paper rustling came across the phone line.

"Royce Dolan, Dan Bishop, some guy named Marcel, a female, Layla, and a big, Swedish guy, Gunnar."

"Damn, partner. You ain't talking about choir boys. You got some rough hombres on that list. Bishop and Dolan would scare Satan himself. No last names for the others?"

"No. Sorry." He gave Wesley their descriptions and all the details he had. "Another thing. You know this city better than I do. Where do the low-lifes hang out?"

"What kind of low-lifes? The stupid criminals who spend as much time inside the joint as out, or the low-lying low-lifes who know what's going down? Not to say that a lot of them ain't dumber than hell, too."

Stone grinned. "The low-lying ones. The underbelly of the city. I need to find out if they've heard of any newcomers, any odd happenings, any rumors about who's behind the bank robberies."

"You want Farrell's. It's a bar just northeast of downtown. You can get anything you want there. Sometimes things you don't want. I'll get on the names right away. When you heading down south?"

"That's another issue altogether. I'm not sure. Might have to beg off the job."

"You're going to turn down an easy mil? All you have to do is accompany Rodriguez's family back to Mexico."

Stone grinned. Wes made it sound like delivering pizza, but they both knew it was a little more than that. The man was a powerful player in the drug cartel with many enemies who would love to get their hands on his wife and kids. "Still n' all, I'm not certain how long I'll be needed here. You remember China?"

Wes let out a derisive chuckle. "How could I forget? The one woman to break your heart, the one who made you start thinking of picket fences. Never thought I'd see the day you'd let a female tame you."

"Right. That's the one." Stone let the picket fence comment slide. Going all soft over China wasn't one of his prouder moments. "She's in a mess of some sort. She has a little girl now. They need my help."

"This mess have to do with those names you gave me?"

"'Fraid so."

"Damn. That's more than a mess. It's a full on Armageddon."

"See why I may not be available any time soon?"

"No big rush. I can find someone else, and there will always be another job waiting for you. I'd do it myself, but the government frowns on its employees moonlighting."

"Yeah. Especially if the employee is a big shot who runs the most successful covert anti-terrorist operation in the U.S."

"Stop. You're making me blush." Wesley chuckled. "Let me know what you decide, and I'll get back to you when I have something. You be careful, you hear?"

"Plan to."

"Don't get so caught up in watching *her* ass you forget to watch your own."

An image of China and her soft, smooth bottom briefly flashed in Aiden's mind before he pushed it away. "Not to worry. That's ancient history."

"Yeah. So is the sinking of the Titanic, but no one's forgotten that either."

China let Emma play on the McDonald's playground for a little while, but their deadline was approaching, so they couldn't stay as long as Emma wanted. Of course, no amount of time would be long enough. Emma would stay in the playground until she graduated if it were up to her.

Against Emma's protests, China hustled her into the car, and they headed home.

When they arrived, Steve's car was parked in the driveway. China nearly choked, and her heart took a dive in her chest.

Was Steve *in* the house? Had he encountered Gunnar?

With trepidation tightening her neck muscles, she parked and helped Emma out of the car. The sun was bright in the sky, nearly blinding her so that she didn't see Steve on the porch until she was almost to the steps.

She shot him a big smile, fueled by relief. His answering smile made her feel guilty. Then she remembered that Steve was the one who'd told her Aiden was dead. And Aiden was very much alive. She resolved to get answers without revealing why she wanted them.

"Hey, you two." Steve gave an easy grin, his hair glinting like copper in the sunlight. "Where ya been?"

"Church and McDonald's," Emma cried happily as they climbed the steps. She hugged Steve, and he reached out to peck

China on the cheek, but she avoided his lips by busying herself with unlocking the door.

He followed them inside and China said to Emma, "Go upstairs and change out of your dress."

Her lips curled into a pout. "Can't I keep it on?"

"No. It's for church. Get your play clothes on."

China didn't care that much what she wore, but she wanted a few moments alone with Steve.

After Emma had stomped upstairs, and they'd moved to the living room, she turned to him. "I need to ask you something."

"Sure." He frowned. "This sounds serious. Is everything okay?"

"Would you like to sit?"

"No, thanks." He remained standing, as did China. She was too filled with nervous energy to sit, too afraid of what she might hear.

She clasped her hands together and tipped her head back to look him in the face. "What happened the day Aiden died?"

"What?" He shook his head. "You know what happened. Why are you asking me this now?"

She couldn't continue to look at him as she spun the lie. Turning, she paced away. "I had a dream last night. It was so real... I just... I saw him dying, and I couldn't do anything about it. I think I'll forever be haunted by not having a body to bury."

"I understand. I feel the same way."

She stopped and faced him. "So, tell me again. What happened?"

"You don't want to hear this, China. Any more than I want to say it. It's just too hard." His jaw tightened. "I don't get why you're asking me this after all these years."

She slipped off her heels and kicked them under the coffee table, avoiding his gaze. "I was in shock that whole time. I barely remember how the events unfolded. I'm not even sure you ever told me the whole story. I'd like to hear it again."

"Are you sure it won't be too painful?"

"No, not sure at all." Her voice was a whisper. "But still, I need to hear it. Please."

Steve sighed and dropped onto the edge of the couch. He linked his hands between his thighs and stared at them as he spoke. "Aiden and I had both just completed separate missions in Tanier. We ended up in the same village and were setting out to travel back to headquarters together. We saw flames in a house and heard cries. We both ran in and saved the family, but the mother said her father was still inside—the man was in a rear bedroom, disabled. Aiden rushed back in, and I was following when, out of nowhere, the hut exploded." He paused and drew in a ragged breath. "I remember screaming for Aiden, not realizing I was severely injured myself. Next thing I knew, I woke up in a hospital. The doctor told me Aiden didn't make it." He looked up. Moisture glinted in his hazel eyes. "Telling you was the hardest thing I'd ever done. I waited a few days, until I was well enough to travel to Abidjan where you were waiting for Aiden."

His emotion was real. She remembered him arriving in Abidjan. Telling her that Aiden had died a hero. No way would she believe he had anything to do with Aiden's supposed death. But how could they have thought Aiden perished when he hadn't?

The depth of Steve and Aiden's friendship came back to her. Sometimes it was easy to forget he was grieving too. It was also easy to forget he had also been a mercenary. Should she tell him the whole story? Tell him about the mercenaries and the threats? That Aiden was alive? She wasn't certain Aiden would help them, but she had no doubt Steve would. Maybe he could hold his own with these guys.

The words formed on her tongue, but she bit them back. She couldn't risk Steve's life. He had been a soldier years ago, but the last six or seven, he'd been living a civilized normal life. A firefighter, yes, but battling fires was different than taking on a gang of demented, evil murderers.

"So you never saw his body?" she said instead.

He stood and stalked to the fireplace. His shoulders drooped.

"Steve," she whispered. "What is it?" He didn't respond. "Well?" she prompted.

"Leave it alone, okay?"

"I need to know. I need to hear this."

"I asked to see his body. I said I wanted to take him back to the States. That you would want to take him back." He sighed heavily. "The doctor put the dog tags in my hand and said, 'That's all that was left of him.'"

Chapter Twenty-Eight

"So, where do you think Layla got off to?" Bishop flipped a black queen up and scowled at the half-finished game of solitaire spread out before him.

"There's no telling. Probably some satanic convention or something."

"Yeah, probably. That's one fine looking woman, but she's evil as Hell, no pun intended."

Royce chuckled. "Amen, brother."

Bishop smiled as he flipped up an Ace and was able to clear an entire row. "What the hell, though, right? Means a bigger take for the rest of us if she doesn't show."

"Yeah, but it lessens our odds. I like four to one a hell of a lot less than five to one."

"Should be six to one, but I guess boss man gonna bark orders and not get his own hands dirty?"

"That's what he pays us for. It's about over, anyway, so not to worry."

"About over, but the hard part begins now. Robbin' banks and shootin' folks is tiddly winks compared to tangling with that Stone dude."

Royce leaned back in his chair. "Yep. I know what he's capable of. Thing is, we got him right where we want him. No way he's going to let any harm come to the woman or the kid."

"Why's that?"

"He was head over heels for China. You remember how he mooned over her when we did that last mission together. Then, she got herself knocked up, and he got himself thrown in prison."

Bishop's hand halted over the cards. "Kid's his?"

"Looks that way."

"Why didn't boss man just grab him when he walked out of prison instead of creating this big ole scheme? Not that I'm complaining, mind you. This way's a lot more profitable for me. Just curious."

"When Stone walked out of prison, he didn't have two coins to rub together. He may or may not have anything left from the last job. If he does, it's buried somewhere, and you couldn't torture the location out of him. This way, we have something to threaten him with. Boss thinks his family is his Achilles heel." Royce reached over and picked up a line of cards, placing them on top of a red ten. Bishop scowled harder. He hated it when he missed a move. "Besides, he's got this whole big plan, and it didn't include just taking Stone down right away. Wants to make him suffer some until he takes him out. Apparently, it's not just about the money."

"I hear it's about a woman."

Royce grinned. "Ain't it always?"

"What woman, though? That whore Stone was with in prison or maybe the Beckett woman herself?"

"Not sure. Not my place to ask. I just take orders."

Bishop tapped a finger against the table. "Hmmmm, but orders are to not harm the Beckett woman or her kid. So, maybe he just has a soft spot for women and children?"

"Or, maybe he's saving their demise until he can make it count against Stone."

The tapping stopped, and the big hand clenched into a fist. "I don't like that. Don't want no part of hurtin' a woman or a little girl."

"We won't have to. That's why the boss has Marcel around. If that's his plan, and I still don't know if it is, Marcel will do the dirty work. Boss'll just make Stone watch."

Bishop's head shook slowly from side to side. "Damn. Ugly business we got ourselves into."

"Ugly, but profitable."

"So, come on man, who's the dude pullin' the strings? You can trust me."

"Fraid not, my friend. We've shared a lot of things in our time, jobs, booze, women—"

"Yeah, but to be fair, I asked the Lord's forgiveness, and I didn't know you'd already had her."

"Would it have made a difference?"

"Woulda made a difference if *I'd* had her first. Then, you never would've had her."

"Why's that? The old once you go black you'll never go back thing?"

"Nah. Ain't nothing to do with being with a black dude. It's about being with *this* black dude."

Royce laughed. "Right."

"Serious, man. Before I settled down and married Suzette, my prowess with the ladies was rivaled only by my prowess with a pool cue."

Royce frowned. "You're not still hustling yokels for a few dollars are you?"

"It's in my blood."

"You can't be doing that shit, not now. We gotta keep a low profile here."

"Hey, I ain't no dummy. I know how to keep a low profile."

"You look like the love child of Kimbo Slice and Arnold Schwarzenegger. No way you can ever keep a low profile. You gotta cut that shit out. Now that Stone's in town, we might as well have big red targets painted on our backs. Take it easy, hear me?"

"Oh, man. I was just warming up these assholes down at this little dive. Getting ready to swoop in. Mothers wouldn't know what hit 'em. I'm in a couple hundred to 'em. You gotta let me get that back."

"Sorry, pal. Consider it the cost of bein' where you shouldn't have been in the first place." Royce stood and studied the table. Looking at the cards Bishop still held, he shook his head. "Kind of like this right here, better cut your losses and get out while you can."

Before going up to see China, Aiden let himself into the shed. The odor was worse than before. A new smell now mingled with the previous odors. So rancid it nearly dropped him to his knees.

When he moved closer, he knew why.

Layla's head lolled back, the old injury to her scalp joined by new ones. Fatal ones. She'd bashed her head against the wall behind the bench, over and over, until she'd died.

Damn. She really didn't want to give Royce up, or deal with the consequences of him thinking she had.

"Fuck me," Aiden whispered into the silent shed.

He'd have to figure out a way to get rid of the body. He wasn't concerned with doing it in a respectful manner. Someone sub-human such as Layla didn't deserve a proper burial. But letting her body be found would only lead to questions that could get China and the girl killed.

"Fuck me," he whispered again, backing out of the shed and locking the door.

He re-entered China's room the same way he had last night, via the balcony. Jimmying the lock with a credit card, he slid the glass door open.

He moved silently to the bed and watched her sleep, his body tightening with the urge to slip in beside her. His gaze traveled to the foot of the bed, and he grinned. Her feet poked out from beneath the blankets. Apparently, she still couldn't stand to have her feet covered. It could be twenty below in the room, and China's bare toes would be exposed to the chill.

He continued to allow himself the guilty pleasure of looking at her long enough that the blood in his veins heated, his heart aching with what-might-have-beens. Memories of how she'd betrayed him, left him without a backward glance cooled his lust.

He roughly shook her shoulder, clamping his other hand over her mouth. Her eyes flew open, first showing fear, then softening in a smile. His anger started to melt, and he felt himself weakening. He drew in a breath, steeling his resolve.

Releasing her, he stepped back from the bed, out of range of the scent of jasmine and citrus that was somehow hers alone.

She rose and climbed from the bed, rapidly blinking sleep from her eyes. The silky nightshirt clung to curves he ached to feel against him. "What's going on? Have you found out anything? Why didn't you contact me before now? Did Layla talk?"

He held up a hand to halt the flow of questions. "One at a time, lass. Give me a chance to breathe."

She fell silent, and Aiden told her everything that had transpired in the last twenty-four hours, ending with just a few moments ago when he found Layla. "Your prisoner was dead."

Her eyes grew wide. "Dead?" She shook her head. "I killed her?"

"She killed herself. It appears she smashed her head into the wall until it practically split open."

A visible shudder ran over her body. "Why would she do that?"

He lifted his hands and shrugged. "Maybe she didn't like her living quarters."

She brought a thumb to her mouth and chewed on the pad. "Dear God." Her voice was a choked whisper.

"You're bothered over the death of a demon who nearly slaughtered your child?"

"No. Of course not, I just can't imagine someone..." She shuddered again. Dropping her hand from her mouth, she looked up at him. "What do we do with her?"

"*We* do nothing. I'll take care of it."

"What can I do? I don't want to just wait around and feel useless."

"For now, taking care of your daughter and obeying the orders of these madmen is your job. I have a feeling they'll contact me soon. There's a point to this game, they want something from me. Until I know what it is, we just have to take it slowly. Unless..."

"Unless what?"

"I could just take you and the child—"

"Emma," she interrupted. "*Your* child."

He studied her, then said, "I could take the two of you and disappear. Take you somewhere safe and come back to deal with this on my own."

She was shaking her head before he'd finished the sentence. "No. That's not possible. Lucy and Spencer would still be in danger. Plus, they might find us anyway. And if we did get away, then what? Stay in hiding forever? What kind of life is that for Emma? And if we tried to just get Emma somewhere safe—" Her voice choked, and she sucked in a breath, waiting a moment before continuing, "—I've already tried that, with tragic results. We have to stay and see this through."

He narrowed his eyes, mulling over this new China. She wasn't as much of a coward as he'd once thought, but he didn't voice that discovery. He wouldn't show any signs of weakening toward her.

"You're right. As long as we appear to be cooperating, they won't harm you or the child. They'll want to keep you healthy to insure they get what they want. Whatever that might be."

"So, we wait and do nothing for now?"

"I suppose." He let his mouth curl into a contemptuous smile. "Besides, I still have to make certain for myself that you're not involved."

His words shafted through her heart, but she tried not to let their effect show in her expression. "You really think that? Think I might be involved?"

"Let's just say I've learned not to underestimate a woman's treachery."

"What do you think I have to gain?"

"Money. Revenge. I don't know."

"How would I have even hooked up with these guys?"

He shrugged. "Perhaps you cooked it up with Steve. He's supposedly the one who told you I'd died. Maybe the two of you are in on it together."

She threw her hands up in the air and let them drop. "Do you hear yourself? Steve was your best friend. He was destroyed when he thought you'd died. These assholes are terrorizing me, they've killed people. People I care about. How dare you!"

And still, as she hurled the words at him, as she stared into eyes that looked at her with hatred, she loved him.

She moved closer and lifted a hand to place it against his cheek. "Aiden, you're the only man I've ever loved, and God help me, in spite of your accusations, your hatred, I still love you. I would never be a part of something like this, and I think you know that."

His eyes held hers for several beats, then his hands rose to the buttons on her nightshirt. Her breath caught, and warmth spread through her blood. Her heart raced, her skin tingling in anticipation. Right or wrong, she'd been so long without his touch...

Slowly, he undid each button. Her gaze latched onto his dark eyes. She could scarcely draw air into her lungs, and her mouth went dry.

Cool air hit her skin where her nightshirt gaped open. She closed her eyes and swayed. His calloused hands skimmed roughly over her sides, her stomach. She blinked up at him in confusion.

His dark eyes glittered. In the silence of the room, his swallow was audible. "Checking for a wire," he said hoarsely.

Tears rose to her throat, and she tried to tamp down her disappointment. She lifted her chin, making sure the tears didn't fall. "Satisfied?" Her voice shook despite her efforts to control it.

His mouth quirked. "I wouldn't say *satisfied*, love. But, I think you're clean."

She stepped back and quickly buttoned her nightshirt. "So you believe I'm innocent? That I had nothing to do with what's going on?"

As she waited for his answer, she realized how much his response meant to her. Not only because she needed his help, but because she couldn't bear the thought of Aiden thinking the worst of her.

"I'll reserve judgment. For now, I'll give you the benefit of the doubt."

She frowned up at him. "Why do you want to think so little of me?"

"Want to?" He shook his head. "I never wanted to believe you were the kind of woman I know you to be. I learned the hard way. No, darlin', it's not that I want you to be deceitful, I just promised myself I'd never forget that you are."

She lifted a hand and wearily rubbed her forehead. "How many times do I have to tell you, I didn't mean to leave you. I thought you were dead."

"Yeah, but our love wasn't worth sticking around to find out if it were true or not. I wonder if you really bothered to *know* rather than just think. I thought we had something." He reached out and placed his forefinger between her breasts. This time, his touch was gentle, and it sent a warm quiver through her. "I thought you would have known, in here."

"Aiden, I—"

He brought up the same hand to silence her. "Enough. We have other things to discuss. Like what to do now. First, I'll have to get rid of the woman's body."

Thank God he would be handling that chore. "What next?"

"I'm not sure. I have a job waiting for me. I should just leave."

Her heart dropped to the pit of her stomach. "You would do that? Just...leave me and your daughter—"

"Stop saying she's my daughter," he growled. "None of this is any of my concern. I help you with the body, then I'm out of here."

She drew in a sharp breath. "You've really become a cold-hearted bastard."

"Seven years in hell will do that to a man." He winked. "Be glad I'm cleaning up your mess before I take off."

Chapter Twenty-Nine

The following evening after work, China hurried to Lucy's. Day care was closed, and Lucy had picked Emma up from school. She was anxious to see Emma. Lately, any time away from her made fear build until it nearly strangled her.

Lucy opened the door as China stepped onto the porch. "You look different, sweet pea." Lucy peered into her face. "Something new?"

She desperately wanted to tell Lucy about Aiden, but couldn't. For now, she had to keep his return secret. Besides, he would be gone soon. Might be gone already. The hope that had started to build was now crushed.

She smiled and gave a nonchalant shrug. "You always think you detect some kind of problem, some new emotion in me."

Lucy ran a hand over her wild red hair, setting her orchid hairband askew. "Yes, well. Your face is like an open book. Plus, you forget I've known you all your life."

"I didn't forget. And, you love me and want to protect me."

"With my life, sweetheart, with my life."

The words sent a pang into her chest. *Please don't let them be an omen...*

"Momma, Momma!"

Emma ran into the living room and launched into China's arms. China hugged her and kissed her cheek. "Hey, sweetheart. Have you been good for Aunt Lucy?"

"I'm always good for Aunt Lucy." She pushed her glasses up her nose. "I like Aunt Lucy's better than school."

China chuckled and touched her finger to the tip of Emma's nose. "I always did, too."

"Who's Gunnar?" Lucy asked.

Icy chills broke out on her neck and traveled down her spine. She forced her numb lips into a smile as she met Lucy's gaze. "What? Gunnar?"

Emma dropped her head and looked down at the floor. Oh God. What had she said about Gunnar?

Lucy nodded. "Yes, Emma said he was her new friend. That he stays at your house." She chuckled. "And that he's as big as a tree."

China gave a hollow laugh. "Oh, you know her imagination."

"Yes, but I've never known her to have imaginary friends. She talks about him as if he were real."

"Well." China took Emma's hand and headed to the door. "What fun would an imaginary friend be if they didn't seem real?"

Lucy frowned, but slowly nodded. "I suppose so."

At the door, Lucy said, "You remember this weekend, right? Emma's spending the night with me."

"I don't remember us talking about that."

"It's my birthday." Her lower lip trembled. "She spends the night with me every year on my birthday. Did you forget?"

A twinge of guilt shot through her. "Of course I didn't forget. I just have a lot on my mind."

"But she can come, can't she?"

How could she let Emma spend any more time alone with Lucy? She had already mentioned Gunnar once. With another opportunity, no telling what she might say.

Right now, she couldn't think of a legitimate excuse, so she nodded. "Yes, she can come. We'll talk more about it later."

China hugged Lucy goodbye, inhaling the sweet, comforting tropical-vanilla scent of orchids, then she and Emma headed to the car.

"Momma, are you mad at me for talking about Gunnar? I forgot to not talk about him."

"No, sweetie, I'm not mad. You didn't do it on purpose."

But, it certainly changed things. She would have to figure out a way to keep Emma home. Even her going to school was too dangerous. Royce would just have to understand. This whole thing had gone too far. Normal was no longer possible.

The body was heavy, slung over Aiden's shoulder like a bag of potatoes. Surprisingly, he felt sympathy—and even a little guilt— over disposing of Layla's body in such a callous manner. In spite of the kind of person she was, even she deserved a proper burial. She had family somewhere, someone surely loved her. When this was over, he would let the authorities know where her body was hidden. He might end up going to jail for it, but his conscience wouldn't rest if he didn't.

Moonlight trickled through the branches above his head as he tromped through the deep woods surrounding Draper Lake. He found a suitable spot and lowered her to the ground, then straightened. He rested his hands on his hips, drawing in air to ease his labored breathing. She didn't weigh much, but he'd traveled a good distance through the brush and over uneven ground, avoiding the path that wound through the woods.

He hurriedly dug a hole no more than three or four feet deep, optimistic that this would all be over before long, and she would only need a temporary resting place. The digging was easier than he'd expected. Recent rains had softened the ground and in no time, he was covering Layla's grave with the loose dirt. He trudged back to the rental car and tossed the shovel in the trunk, then headed out.

When he arrived back at the motel, he immediately took a long, hot shower. Just as he stepped out and grabbed a towel, his cell rang. The number was unfamiliar, but his gut told him he would soon learn what this big conspiracy was all about.

He answered, and the voice on the other line said, "Aiden, my brother. How goes it?"

He immediately recognized Royce Dolan.

"I've been better."

"Yes, but you've been worse, too, right? Seven years in a Tanier prison. Can't have been a fun time."

"You're a perceptive fellow. But I'm sure you didn't call to discuss my happiness or lack thereof."

"True. You just want to cut to the chase, huh? I guess you know who this is. I'm sure you've been to visit the lovely China."

"I know who you are, just not what you want. What you've got in mind."

"That, you'll learn soon."

Aiden rested the phone on his shoulder and wrapped the towel around his waist. "I'm waiting."

"Be at Eischen's Bar in an hour."

"Eischen's?"

"It's in Okarche. You know it? Oldest bar in Oklahoma. A historical site. I thought you might enjoy a little local flavor while we catch up. It's about forty-five miles from the city."

Forty-five miles. Royce wasn't leaving him much time to get there. Probably part of whatever kind of game he was playing. Showing who was in control. "It'll take me a while to get there."

"They close at ten, so we don't have much time. I'd suggest you leave now."

They ended the call, and Aiden dried off and pulled on jeans and a blue T-shirt. He didn't bother to wear a weapon. He likely wouldn't need it for this info gathering meeting. Besides, even if the bar allowed weapons, which was unlikely, Royce might pat him down. The trust factor would be nil if he showed up armed. They likely wouldn't trust him much anyway, but for now, he had to do all he could to show them he'd cooperate.

Wes had set him up with a tekky in town who'd provided a tiny wireless transmitter that fit in his ear so he could communicate details to Wes as he went along. That would have to be enough for now.

He arrived at Eischen's in just under an hour. The hardwood floors were worn, and the walls held vintage beer signs. In a room at the back stood a few pool tables. To the right were tables surrounded by metal chairs. Plastic upholstered booths lined one wall. The place was crowded for a Monday night. What would it be like on the weekend?

Royce and Bishop sat at a table. Royce stood and waved Aiden over like an old friend anxious for a reunion.

Aiden squeezed past the bodies waiting to be seated and headed to the table.

"Sit." Royce gestured to the chair across from him. "You remember Dan Bishop?"

"I do." Aiden slid into a chair.

Bishop inclined his head in a nod, and Aiden returned it.

Royce twisted around and draped an arm over the back of his chair. "I took the liberty of ordering chicken, okra, and Budweiser. They're world famous for their chicken. I haven't tried it, but since it's about the only thing on the menu, I figured I'd give it a shot. That okay with you?"

Aiden shrugged.

A thin, fifty-something waitress wearing tight jeans and a red blouse with the tail tied at the waist came over with three cans of Budweiser and sat them in the center of the table. "Chicken'll be out in a minute, boys."

Royce picked up a can and tipped it toward her. "Thank you, darlin'."

He was rewarded with a wide smile before she moved on to another table.

Aiden shot a look around the dining room. The other customers were so close he could reach out and touch them. He leaned slightly toward Royce. "You really think this is the best place to conduct private business?"

"I think it'll do just fine. The noise level will help drown out our conversation."

"Sides," Bishop cut in. "We had a taste for chicken. Folks around us are here for the same. Don't give a hoot what we're sayin'."

Aiden spread his hands out in front of him on the scarred table. "So, what's this all about? What do you want?"

"If you recall, we have a bit of unfinished business. A job about seven years ago where you never showed up at the rendezvous location to divvy up the payout."

Aiden snorted a laugh. "That's what this is all about? You think I ripped you off? I was in an explosion, ended up in the hospital. As soon as I came to, I went straight for the money. I was captured right after I collected. Arrested on some trumped up charge. The rebels took every bit of it."

Royce shrugged. "Maybe. Maybe not. We think you might have it hidden somewhere. We know you were thrown in prison, but we got a feeling you hid the money first. Now me and Bishop here, we're understanding fellas. We were willing to put it behind us. Then, I run into somebody who has it out for you. Hired us to get our own money back, how do you like that?" He chuckled. "Our boss expects a payout."

Aiden's gut roiled. These men were counting on money he didn't have, and China and her kid's lives were in danger if they didn't get it. He had maybe five mil Wes's accountant was holding, then if they'd give him time, he could do the job in Texas and get another mil. But the take from the job they'd done was fifteen. They wouldn't be satisfied with a third of that.

"What makes your boss think it'll do any good to use the woman and kid for leverage? Why would I care what happens to them?"

Royce grinned. "You're in love with the Beckett woman."

Stone's chest tightened. "That's a bunch of blarney."

He raised his brows and smirked. "Right. That's why you pined after her when you had to leave her behind to do the job in Tanier. Why you couldn't wait to get back to her sweet little body."

Anger simmered through Stone's veins. Royce was just trying to get a rise out of him. He had to keep his cool. "You've got it all wrong."

"Maybe. Boss man thinks you're enough of a sap you won't leave a woman and kid to fend for themselves, especially since the kid's yours."

Why did everyone keep saying that? Stone tried to keep his expression bland. "Kid ain't mine. You gents are barking up the wrong Irishman. I don't give two figs what happens to either of the females."

Royce threw his head back and laughed. "Come on, Aiden. Even if you aren't in love with her, and even if the kid's not yours, you are not the kind of man who could walk away and leave them to die. Especially over something you started."

Before he could respond, the waitress returned, her arms lined with food in paper containers. Efficiently, as if she'd done it thousands of times, she placed chicken, okra, bread, and a paper container of onions and pickles on the table, then laid a stack of wax paper squares down, which Aiden presumed were the plates.

"You boys ready for another beer?"

"You betcha. Thanks, sweetheart."

This time a blush accompanied the smile. "Be back in a jif. You holler if you need anything else."

After she disappeared, Royce and Bishop took turns picking out pieces of chicken and handfuls of okra, plopping them on the wax paper. Aiden's stomach growled. The chicken smelled and looked delicious.

He helped himself to a leg and a handful of okra. The food was better than it looked. Who would have thought an old bar in nowhere Oklahoma would have the best fried chicken and okra he'd ever tasted? But then, to be fair, he could count on one hand the number of times he'd had fried chicken and okra.

"Damn, that's good stuff," Bishop said, licking his fingers. "They weren't lyin."

Royce nodded, picking up his can of beer and draining it as the waitress brought them a second round. When she left, he said, "So, am I right? You won't leave China and Emma to die at our hands, now will you?"

Aiden pushed the chicken aside and picked up his beer, taking a long swallow from the can. They had him dead to rights. He wouldn't let a stranger die because of something he'd done. Despite China's betrayal, he damned sure couldn't let her and her kid come to harm on his account.

"You're right. So, what do we do? I won't have access to the funds for a few weeks, when my buddy's financial guy gets back in the country." He had to make them think he had the entire fifteen mil. At least until he could figure a way out of this.

"We'll wait. As you probably know, we've managed to acquire a bit of walking around money."

"The robberies. You must have gotten a pretty good take."

Royce took another swig of beer. "We did, but not fifteen mil. And we can't keep pulling jobs like that. Too visible."

"So, are you going to hold me prisoner until I can get my hands on the money?"

"Something like that. You'll be staying at the house with China and Emma."

Stay in the same house with China? And a kid everyone seemed determined to make out to be his? The Amityville horror house had more appeal.

"You really think it's necessary for me to stay with them?"

"You got a problem with it?"

"I'm not exactly fond of China Beckett. Don't care much for kids either."

"Maybe you're just saying that so we'll back off, so we won't believe she's good leverage in all this."

Aiden gave a humorless chuckle. "I don't want harm to come to anyone. I will do what I can to protect her, especially if it turns out she *is* the mother of my child. And, I don't want the child harmed. You have me where you want me."

Royce nodded. "Then that means you'll be a good boy and follow instructions. Check out of the motel and be at China's in the morning. When your guy gets back, Bishop here will escort you to Texas to collect, just to make sure you don't try anything funny."

"I thought you were threatening China and the kid so I didn't try anything funny."

Royce grinned. "Call this a little added precaution."

"If I show up with anyone, my guy will be ticked. He gets pretty antsy about people knowing his business."

"Oh, I have a feeling you'll figure out a way to overcome that little problem." He took a pull from the beer can and pointed it at Aiden. "After all, you know what will happen if you don't."

Aiden clenched his jaw. Wes wouldn't balk at his bringing someone, but he was hoping to get away on his own. Even with Emma's and China's lives on the line, he'd have a better shot at figuring out a way out of this if he were alone. Thing was, he didn't believe, even when he gave them the money, that they would let any of the three of them live.

So that meant he'd better figure out a way to outmaneuver them.

"How do I know you won't kill them—kill us all—once the job is done?"

Royce shrugged. "Call it honor among thieves. We have no reason to kill you once we have what we want. You won't go to the police. After all, you'd be charged right along with us. Besides, we'll be out of the country and it's not like we haven't skirted the law plenty of times."

Aiden smiled. "So, you're telling me you'll just let us all go when this is over? That, whoever is behind this doesn't particularly want me dead, he just wants the money?"

"That's what I'm telling you. Heck of a deal, am I right?" He clapped Aiden on the shoulder. "Just relax and enjoy the family time. In just over a week, it will all be done, and you can go your merry way. Or, if the domestic bug has bitten you, the three of you can settle down and live happily ever after."

Aiden grunted a laugh. There would be no happily ever after for him and China. When this ordeal was over—provided he lived through it—he would be out of here and this time, he would follow his instincts and *never* cross the Oklahoma border again.

He wiped his mouth and tossed the napkin on the table. "So, how does this work? I stay at the house, other people see me? I've come back from the dead, lots of questions, the kid talks. How you think you're going to manage all this?"

Royce frowned. "It is getting a little dicey with the kid. Hard to prevent a six-year-old from running off at the mouth. Her mother's done a good job so far of keeping her silent, but with a new addition to the household, someone she may or may not learn is her father, the kid's gonna spew at some point. Probably best to keep Emma and China sequestered until this is over."

"You don't think the school, China's job, her family, will wonder where they are? Will expect to see the kid?"

"The kid has asthma pretty bad from what we hear, she's nearly died from it a few times. We'll have China call in to school and her job. Say Emma's in a bad way, and they have to keep a close eye on her."

Aiden's blood heated at Royce's nonchalance about something so serious. He almost seemed pleased about a little girl's near death experiences. Aiden hadn't known about the girl's health problems. Must be rough for her and for China. Scary to think your child could literally stop breathing at any moment.

"That won't keep her family away. What about Steve? He seems to be sniffing around all the time." Aiden watched their expressions carefully. If Steve were involved, maybe their reactions would show.

Nothing. Not even a twitch.

Royce stood, and Bishop followed suit. "We'll leave that to you and China. If you can't manage it, we'll have to step in. If *we* keep them away, they'll be kept away permanently."

Chapter Thirty

Aiden gritted his teeth. Even with the severity of his current predicament, he couldn't get the thought out of his head that he'd be *living* in the house with China. How was he going to do it? When his fingertips still tingled from touching her, how was he going to spend so much time in close proximity with her and keep from doing it again?

He'd just have to. Somehow, someway. Giving in to his weakness when it came to China was far too dangerous to his peace of mind.

He pulled his bike into the small parking lot of Farrell's, the hole in the wall Wes had told him about. The seedy little bar was the kind Bishop frequented. If the big man was anything like he used to be, he wouldn't be able to stay away from the tables.

Stone wasn't sure what he hoped to learn, but he had time to kill before going to China's in the morning. Gathering intel was the only thing he could think to do. Maybe he could find out if Bishop had been here. If so, he'd likely be back. It was part of Bishop's hustle, picking out marks, losing a few bucks to them, then moving in for the kill once the stakes were high. If he could catch Bishop here one night, he could follow him to the hole the bastards were burrowing in.

He'd gotten back in touch with Wes, told him what was going down. Wes would do some extra digging on Bishop, since he'd be Stone's escort and therefore, the most likely way out of this mess.

He shut off his bike and pulled a skullcap over his head, to just above his eyes.

Pushing on the decrepit wooden door, he entered through a wall of cigarette smoke. Loud country music shook the small building. At the bar, he ordered a whiskey, then weaved over to a pool table where two men were in a game. One was middle-aged, a few inches taller than Stone with a beer belly. The other was shorter, in his early twenties, with spiked hair and a loose fitting leather vest.

Aiden purposely thickened his Irish accent and spoke too loudly. "Hey, gents, mind if I 'ave a go?"

The taller one frowned and took a cigar out of his mouth. The other laughed and pointed his pool cue at Aiden. "Hey, look, the leprechaun wants a *go*." He glanced around the bar to make sure he had an audience for his cleverness. "You got any money, *gent*?"

"Su—sure do." Aiden clumsily dug in his pocket and made a show of wincing, then gave a drunken smile and held up his bandaged hand. "These chums waylaid me good, but I still got a good 'and." He held up his other and withdrew a wad of bills from his pocket. "This e'nuf?"

The men looked at the money—five hundred in fifties and twenties—and exchanged a look. Stone could almost see dollar signs in their greedy eyes.

The older guy smirked. "Yeah, guess that'll be enough. Nice to meet you, pal. Name's T.J." He looked at his buddy. "Rack 'em, Neal."

An hour later, he'd lost two games and two hundred bucks. He'd been jabbering non-stop about nothing. Time to change the topic to *something*.

He missed a painfully easy shot and straightened, then swayed. "Sorry, lads. I'm usually better'n that." He grinned. "Guess I'm a wee bit buckled. " He staggered over and leaned against the wall. "By th' way. You gents know a big fella who hangs around 'ere? Woulda just recently started comin' 'round. Looks a bit like that Michael Duncan. The fella from Green Mile."

T.J. bent to shoot. "Sure. Dude by the name of Bishop. He a friend of yours?"

"Not 'especially. I hear he's a shark. Thought he could give me a pointer or two."

Neal shrugged. "He ain't bad."

Aiden took a swig of the whiskey. The rotgut almost made him gag, and he murmured a silent apology to good Irish whiskey. "How often does he come around?"

"Few times a week."

"Alone?"

"Yeah, why? You sweet on him?" He elbowed his buddy in the ribs, and they had a hearty laugh.

Stone stretched another drunken smile. "Jus' wonderin'." When the game ended, he scooped up the bills he hadn't lost to the buffoons and laid his cue on the table. "Iss been fun, gents. See ya' 'round."

"Ah, come on. You ain't leavin' yet? Don't you want to win your money back?"

Stone shook his head. "Don' think I stand a chance. Better hold on to the last few hundred I 'ave on me." He tipped a finger to his forehead and saluted them. "'Ave a g'night, boys."

He stumbled from the bar into the cool darkness, breathing in a lungful of the unpolluted air. The road was nearly deserted with only a few vehicles rumbling by.

He was almost to the corner when footsteps sounded behind him. *Predictable.*

A hand landed on his shoulder and whirled him around.

"You don't think you're getting out of here with the rest of your gold, do ya, leprechaun?" Neal chortled at his own joke, and T.J. grinned, then circled behind Aiden. "We tried to take it fair and square, but you didn't bite."

When T.J. was in place, Neal lifted a fist. Before he could swing, Aiden snatched his hand and bent it back at the wrist. The guy's eyes widened, and he went to his knees. T.J. lunged, and Aiden shot his leg out behind him, catching him square in the gut.

"What the hell?" T.J. dropped to the sidewalk, moaning and clutching his belly.

"Here's how it's gonna go down. You fellows do me a favor and let me know when Bishop shows up next, I won't break any bones."

Neal grunted, but didn't respond. Stone gripped his hand and bent it further back. He let out a yelp.

"Look," Neal gritted through clenched teeth. "Bishop's a lot scarier than you are, so we'll have to pass on your offer."

Aiden smiled. "Oh, so you thought it was a request?" He twisted Neal's arm until he squealed, then slammed his elbow into his face. Bones crunched, and Neal's hands flew to his nose.

"Arrgghhh, you broke my fuggin' nodes."

"*Only* your nose. You're welcome." He tucked a paper with his number written on it into T.J.'s pocket. "Are you going to let me know when Bishop shows up or do you want to find out how many other bones I can break?"

"Okay, okay," Neal panted. "We'll let you know. But how do you know we won't tell Bishop?"

"Because, in spite of your dumb lookin' mugs, I assume you have a little bit of sense. If Bishop even gets a hint that you were talkin' to someone about him, he'll be none too happy. And believe me, when he's unhappy, Bishop isn't near the sweetheart that I am."

Still clutching their injuries, they scowled up at him.

"You ain't drunk are you?" T.J. nodded at Stone's bandaged hand. "And you ain't hurt neither. You tricked us."

"That's right." Stone winked. "Never trust a leprechaun."

Chapter Thirty-One

China rubbed her temples with her fingertips, trying to ease the headache pounding there. Aiden staying here, in the house with her and Emma? This was just...too much. A week ago, she thought he was dead. Now...

Fortunately, Royce had instructed them to stay home until this was over. Like her, he was concerned about Emma saying something she shouldn't. China hadn't told him about Emma mentioning Gunnar to Lucy. She wasn't sure what the consequences would be.

She picked up her phone from the kitchen table and dialed the bank. Might as well get this over with. Her stomach knotted as she waited to be connected to Richard. She hated lying, and it seemed to be all she'd done lately. She'd become everything she despised. A liar and a killer—despite Aiden's reassurance that Layla had killed herself, China knew she was responsible.

Richard answered after a few rings. "China? What can I do for you?"

She drew in a deep breath. "I-I'm afraid I need to take some time off. At least a week. Maybe more. Emma is ill."

"Is she in the hospital?"

"No, I'm hoping that won't happen. She's just been suffering with her asthma lately, and it's getting worse by the day. The doctor wants me to keep her home for a while."

Richard was silent for several moments. Was he going to refuse her? If so, she'd have to take off anyway. Even if it meant losing her job. Finally, he said, "Of course. Take all the time you need."

She let out a relieved breath. "Thank you."

She called the school and told them the same story, and assured them she would provide a doctor's note. She wasn't sure how she'd come up with a note, but that was the least of her concerns at the moment.

The next call was one she dreaded the most—to Lucy.

When her aunt answered, China said, "I just wanted to let you know that you might not be seeing much of Emma and me for the next week or so. She's struggling with her asthma, and I've decided to keep her home from school."

"Oh my, poor little dear. Well, I'll come over and take care of her while you work."

"Thank you, but you don't need to do that. I'm staying home with her while she's ill."

"You are? Won't you get in trouble with the bank?"

China grimaced. At one time she'd have been worried about that. But that was before she really knew the meaning of trouble. "No, they understood."

"Well, since that nasty Sophie—God rest her soul—is no longer your boss, it's probably easier to get time off."

"Yeah, stroke of luck, right?" China couldn't keep the sarcasm from her voice.

"I didn't mean it that way, sweet pea. I hate to disrespect the dead, but she was an awful person."

"Yes, well, I just wanted to let you know about keeping Emma home. I'll call when she's better, and we'll come visit."

"This means she won't be coming to stay with me this weekend for my birthday." Disappointment filled her voice. "Doesn't she need to go to the hospital?"

"No, not yet. I'm just keeping an eye on her. We're letting her rest and not get excited and stay indoors to avoid pollen and all the other allergens in the air."

"I should come over and help you."

"No, that won't be necessary. She really just needs some quiet and rest."

"Yes, but I could be so much help to you. I'll just pack a few things and—"

"Lucy," China said sharply. "What don't you understand about her needing to rest? We'll be fine without you."

Lucy took in a swift, tearful breath. China had never spoken to her that way before, and it pained her to do so now, but hurting her feelings might be the only way to keep her away—to keep her alive.

"Well, if that's the way you feel." Her voice quavered with tears. "I won't bother you. Just let me know if you need anything."

China choked up too, but she kept her tone firm. "Thank you, Lucy. I will. Love you."

She hung up before her aunt could say more. Before she broke down and told her everything that was going on.

"That must have been difficult."

China turned to find Aiden standing behind her. She quickly wiped tears from her eyes. "Everything has been difficult lately."

Aiden had been in the house for twenty-four hours, and they'd barely spoken. It was odd, the four of them living together—she, Emma, Aiden, and Gunnar. They mostly co-existed. Aiden would watch Gunnar with a predatory look in his eyes, as if given the slightest provocation he'd pounce. Gunnar didn't seem intimidated—which made sense for a man his size. He returned Aiden's looks with equal intimidation, but neither man ever made a move on the other. After all, that wasn't part of the plan.

"Hopefully it will be over soon, and we can all get on with our lives."

China lifted her gaze to his. "Do you really believe that? That we'll make it out of this thing alive?"

Aiden shrugged. "I don't know, but I'm operating on that theory."

Emma swung the kitchen door open. "I'm hungry, Momma." She looked up at Aiden and waved her chubby hand. "Hi, Aiden. Want to have a snack with me?"

Aiden frowned down at her. "Not hungry, but thanks."

She frowned back. "Okay, want to read me a story at bedtime?"

China held her breath. Aiden was silent for a few moments, then shook his head. "I don't care much for children's books."

Emma climbed in her chair. "That's okay. You can read a grown up book, one you like. I just like to hear stories."

Aiden raised his gaze to China, as if pleading for rescue. She compressed her lips and said nothing.

"Sorry. No. Your mam can read you a story."

He left the kitchen, and Emma's puzzled gaze followed him. "What's a mam?"

"It's a word people in Ireland sometimes call their mothers."

She nodded slowly. "Is Aiden sick?"

"I don't think so, why?"

"His face always looks like his tummy hurts."

China laughed at her apt description. He didn't like being here, that much was clear. He barely spoke to her or to Emma. Maybe it was good that he didn't believe Emma belonged to him. She would hate for her child to know her father cared so little for her.

That night, after China and the kid were asleep, Aiden listened at his bedroom door for Gunnar to make his nightly rounds. Last night, the big Swede had patrolled the perimeter once an hour until finally going to bed at two a.m. and arising at four. Like Aiden, the man could get by on almost no sleep. Life in the military and prison would do that. He had no doubt Gunnar would perform the same routine tonight. He was an ex-soldier—

Aiden could spot them with his eyes closed—and would be a creature of habit. Strictly regimented.

Gunnar was using the guest room next to China's. Aiden had been given the room at the opposite end of the hall. Lucky for the mercs that China had a big enough home to accommodate their plan. Hell, the entire band of psychos could move in, and they'd never run into one another.

At exactly two, Gunnar's bedroom door opened and closed. Aiden hurried to his bed. He lay still as his door opened and Gunnar stepped inside, confirmed he was there, then left. Aiden resumed his vigil at the door, and fifteen minutes later, Gunnar returned to his room.

The jackass from the bar had called earlier and reluctantly revealed that Bishop was at Farrell's tonight. Stone let himself quietly out the back door and wheeled his cycle to the end of the road before starting it and heading to the dive. A peek through the grimy window confirmed the guy was correct. Bishop was there. The bar closed in half an hour, Bishop would leave before then. He wouldn't want to join the exodus of drunken patrons.

Sure enough, Bishop gathered his winnings from the man he'd been playing—a stocky, bearded guy whose expression said he'd like to whip Bishop's ass, but whatever common sense he possessed kept him from doing so.

Bishop walked to a dark-colored Lincoln Navigator and pulled out of the parking lot. Aiden followed at a safe distance through darkened streets. A light fog helped obscure his presence, but he had no trouble keeping Bishop in his sight. Half an hour later, the SUV turned onto a private drive.

Aiden waited five minutes, then cruised by and pulled off to the side of the road, parked his bike, and dismounted.

He had to hurry. His less than two hour window before Gunnar would rise was quickly dwindling. He sneaked through the bushes and trees. About ten yards from the road stood a sprawling ranch style home with a handful of vehicles parked around it, including a van and the Navigator. So this was HQ. Nothing much he could do right now, but at least he knew where to find them when the time came—when he had a plan in place.

Chapter Thirty-Two

China tossed the covers off and sat up on the side of the bed. Brushing tangled hair out of her face, she looked at the bedside clock. Four fifteen a.m. She was exhausted, but couldn't make herself rest. She'd dozed off and on, but hadn't been able to really sleep. Gunnar had just checked her room. The thought of him peeking in at her in the wee hours was unsettling. No point in lying back down. Trying to get back to sleep would be useless. Her nerves were taut, her mind whirling. Now that Aiden was here, she should feel safer, but she had an uneasy feeling that this thing wouldn't end well.

She stood and shrugged on her robe, then eased the door open. The hallway was dark, except for the meager glow of the nightlight in the outlet. Hoping not to run into Gunnar, she crept to Emma's room and pushed her door open.

Love swelled in her heart as she watched Emma's peaceful slumber. Although Emma didn't know exactly what was going on, she knew things were different in her world, yet she slept the sleep of the innocent. Would China be able to keep her innocent...safe? A shudder moved through her. She wasn't sure she could, but she would die trying.

As she headed back, she glanced down the hallway to Aiden's room. Without conscious thought, her feet took her that direction. She stopped outside his door and reached for the knob, but hesitated. She shouldn't wake him. He would not be pleased to see her. Besides, as much as she was happy he was alive, she was devastated that he despised her. The last thing she needed was more of his derision and insults.

She turned to leave, and the door opened. Her heart leapt to her throat when she looked back into Aiden's dark eyes. His hair was tousled, his jaw line shadowed with whiskers. He wore black pajama bottoms, but his chest was bare. Behind him, the room was bathed in darkness.

"China?" His voice was a low whisper. "What is it?"

Her face heated. "N-nothing. I was just checking on Emma and..."

His lips quirked, and the scar in his dark whiskers became more pronounced. "Emma's bedroom is that way." He jerked his head toward the end of the hall.

She twisted her hands together. "Yeah, uh..."

"Did you need something?"

She swallowed against a lump in her throat. *You, I need you, and I need all of this to just go away.*

"No, I was just restless. I couldn't sleep."

He was quiet for several seconds. She knew she should walk away, but her heart didn't want to.

Finally, he spoke. "Want to come in?" The invitation seemed to have been forced from him. "And talk?" he tacked on.

She gave a jerky nod. "Yes, sure."

He stepped back, and she passed through the door, brushing so close, she could feel the heat from his hard, half-naked body.

He pushed the door closed, and the sound made a quiver run through her stomach. Their aloneness closed in on her, and she swallowed loudly.

He crossed his arms and leaned against the door. Faint moonlight shone through the window, enough that she could see his lifted brow, his amused expression. "Was there something you wanted to say?"

She twisted her hands together and gave a jerky nod. "I just...wanted a chance to...explain."

"Explain what?"

"Why I left."

He remained silent.

"I—I thought you were dead." The pain of that time came rushing back, and a sob hiccupped in her chest.

The amused look never left his face. "Yes, you've said that. Perhaps you *did* think I was dead. But you didn't even wait until I was cold."

She sucked in a quick breath. The words hurt, but she couldn't deny them. "I was completely destroyed. I found out I was pregnant, and I didn't know what else to do."

His mouth twisted. "Of course you didn't."

"How...what was it like? Being in that awful place?" She couldn't believe, all these years, she thought he was dead, and he was suffering in prison. "If I'd known, I might have been able to do something, to help get you released."

His lips quirked. "Ah, no love. You had other things on your mind." He pushed off the door. "And, believe me, you don't really want to know what it was like." He walked toward her and stopped next to his bed. She noticed yet another scar in the hollow of his shoulder—a puckered, round white circle. A bullet hole? He followed her line of sight and chuckled. "As I said, you don't want to know. I suppose I owe you a thank you, though. Thoughts of you were all that got me through those first few years."

Hope bloomed inside her. He still cared about her, he must. "I'm glad you didn't forget about me."

He chuckled and shook his head. "Not much else to think about when you're locked in an eight by six hovel." He was silent for a few moments, then, his voice low, he said, "On the nights when cold rain poured into my cell through the bars in the window, I didn't mind, because it reminded me of you. Of how much you love the smell of rain." He shrugged. "I kept thinking I'd come home to you some day. That you'd be waiting for me. When I found out you hadn't waited, that you left while I was laying in the hospital, I learned how to hate you." His mouth twisted in a contemptuous smile. "Information somehow travels, even in the remotest of places. The guards delighted in sharing news of your happy nuptials. It was like being tortured all over again, only worse. At least when I was being tortured, I knew at some point that pain would end."

Heaviness weighted her heart, and tears flowed down her face. "Oh, Aiden."

He lifted a hand and flashed a smile that was more like a snarl. "No, save your sorrows, lass. I'm over it. One hundred percent. Once I stopped letting the emotion control me and I really thought about what you'd done, what you were, I learned to let go." He gave a sardonic, humorless laugh. "You were the first person—the only person—I ever loved. I gave you my trust. But I've learned my lesson about playing the fool. Never again."

She shook her head. "But, you don't understand. I never stopped thinking about you. Never stopped loving you." Knowing the pain she'd caused him, how they'd both suffered, cut into her like a knife. Her throat clogged until she was barely able to speak. "It was easy to marry Gary, because I didn't love him, didn't care. I was numb. I knew I needed to take care of the baby, and Gary did that. He was good to me, to Emma. Then when I realized what a mistake I made, I still tried, but he saw that I still—"

"Enough," he cut her off. "I don't want to hear your excuses. What's past is past. Right now, we need to focus on resolving this mess, so I can get out of your life, for good."

China held back any further pleas. This cold, bitter, hard stranger was not the man she fell in love with. Emma deserved to know her father, but only if he wanted to know her. And it was obvious Aiden didn't. She swallowed back tears and cleared her throat. "Yes, you're right. I won't mention it again. Once this is over, you'll leave, and we'll put all of this behind us."

"That's best for all of us. Now, if you'll excuse me..."

"Of course." She hurried to the door and let herself out. The realization that his love was truly dead finally sank in. That was okay, the pain in her heart would ease, eventually. She would have to grieve Aiden all over again, but she could deal with that. The only thing she couldn't deal with was losing Emma. No matter what it took, she had to make sure that didn't happen.

Emma chewed a mouthful of cereal and stared across the table at Aiden.

Without taking his eyes off her, Aiden said to China, "What does she want?"

China rolled her eyes. "She's a person. She understands English. She can even speak. Ask her."

He raised his brows at Emma. "So?"

"So what?"

"What do you want?"

She took another bite of cereal and chewed slowly. After she swallowed, she said, "Nothing. Just looking."

"Looking at what?"

"How'd you get that scar on your face?"

"Emma!" China said sharply. "We don't ask those kinds of questions."

"Why not?"

"Because it's rude, personal."

"Sorry." She went back to eating her cereal.

"I have a lot of scars. And each one tells a story." Aiden pushed the neck of his shirt aside and touched a scar on his shoulder. "This one I got when I was in prison. The guards were hurting a friend of mine. I tried to stop them, and they cut me with a big knife."

Sickness coiled in China's chest. No telling what kind of horrors he'd suffered. "Please. I don't think that's appropriate for a six-year-old."

"She asked."

"Yes, but that doesn't mean you have to—" The doorbell rang, and China's gaze flew to Aiden. "I'm not expecting anyone."

"I'll take Emma upstairs. Answer the door."

"I'm not finished with my cereal," Emma protested.

Aiden scowled. "Take it with you."

Emma slid from the chair and grabbed her bowl, following Aiden through the kitchen door and up the stairs.

China looked through the peephole. *Shit*. Steve. He'd called her a few times, and she'd made excuses about not seeing him, told him Emma was ill. He'd insisted on coming over, but she'd put him off. Or so she thought.

Taking a deep breath, she opened the door. "Steve? What are you doing here?"

"I wanted to check on Emma. Is she any better?"

She shook her head. "I'm afraid not."

"Should we take her to the hospital?"

She stood in the doorway, cracking it only enough to allow her to speak with him. "No, she's seen her doctor." She lied without flinching. "He just said for her to stay on the medication and remain inside."

He frowned. "Can I come in?"

"Well, I think it would be better if you didn't. Emma might be contagious."

He grunted. "Asthma isn't contagious."

"Right...but she's also got bronchitis." *Great*, might as well add pneumonia and consumption to her list of ailments.

He crossed his arms and narrowed his eyes. "China, are you upset with me?"

"No, no of course not."

"It's not like you to be so closed off."

He was Aiden's friend. She wanted nothing more than to tell him Aiden was alive. But there was no way she could risk it. Soon, maybe soon, she could tell him.

"I'm sorry, Steve. Things have been crazy lately. The robberies, Emma's illness. It's just a little overwhelming right now. I really need you to be a friend and just understand that I need time right now. I need to be left alone."

A shadow passed over his face. She'd hurt him. But not as badly as Royce and his men would hurt him if he didn't back off.

"Sure, okay. I'll leave you alone, for now. Just call me if you need me, okay?"

She nodded, and he leaned forward and placed a quick kiss on her cheek. "Take care, China."

She didn't let out her breath until he had climbed in his car and driven away.

Chapter Thirty-Three

Aiden frowned at the pages of the fairytale as he read aloud. He couldn't believe he'd let himself get roped into this. The kid had asked him the last few evenings to read her a story, and she'd finally worn him down. He'd made it clear, though. One story, and one story only. He'd elicited a promise that if he read her one, she'd never ask again. It would be worth it for her to leave him in peace his remaining time here.

He was at the part where the fairy godmother was using her magic to turn mice into footmen and a pumpkin into a carriage when he felt a light touch on his wrist.

"This is my favorite part," Emma said around a yawn.

He glanced up to find her small hand resting on his. His breath stalled, and a knot tightened in his gut. He moved his gaze to her face, and she squinted at him. "Is it a hard word? I can read a little if you need help."

He cleared his throat and shook his head. "No. not a hard word. I'm just..." He closed the book and stood. "I'm just tired of reading. Time to go to sleep."

A frown touched her mouth, and a dagger shot through his chest, but he steeled himself against the emotion. He still wasn't sure if she was his kid, but whether she was or whether she wasn't, he couldn't get attached.

"Will you tuck me in?"

He clenched his jaw. "I—"

"How are things going?"

He turned to find China standing in the doorway. An irrational flash of anger shot through him. "No, your mother will tuck you in."

He tossed the book on the chair he'd vacated and stalked past China out the door. Like a physical force, her anger and disappointment followed him all the way down the hall.

China rested her elbows on the table on either side of her coffee cup and rubbed her face. How could she be so tired, yet unable to sleep? Night after night, the same thing. Barely dozing, jumping every time she heard a noise. Tensing when Gunnar made his nightly checks. Last night, seeing the hurt in Emma's face after Aiden had been so abrupt had made it even more difficult to rest.

She took a drink of the strong, black brew. How could he be so cold to any child, let alone his own? No matter how much he despised China, Emma was just a little girl. None of this was her fault.

Her cell rang, and she picked it up to find Vanessa's number on the display. Hope lit in her heart. She missed her friend, badly.

When she answered, Vanessa said, "China, I—I just wanted to...talk to you. I hope it's okay I called."

China tried to keep the anxiousness from her voice. "Of course it is. What's up?"

"I'm calling to let you know, I've had time to think about it, and I shouldn't be angry with you. Miles chose to do what he did. I just wanted someone to blame."

Lightness lifted her spirits, and she squeezed her eyes shut briefly. "Oh, sweetie. I understand. And, I'm so very sorry. I loved him too."

A laugh that was part sob came over the line. "I know you did. I'm sorry I kept you away from his funeral. Is Emma okay? I heard you've taken some time off from the bank."

"She's having trouble with her asthma, but she'll be fine."

After a few seconds of silence, Vanessa said, "Miles refused to tell me what favor he was doing for you. But I have to know. Especially since it got him killed. You have to tell me."

China chewed on the pad of her thumb. How she would love to unburden herself to her best friend. But she couldn't. Not if she wanted her to live. "I can't. Hate me all you want, but I have a very good reason. I just...can't."

Vanessa let out a heavy sigh. "I can't hate you, China. I'm worried about you."

"Everything is fine, I promise."

"I hope so. I'd better get off here and get ready for work. You take care, and let's get together soon."

"Yes, soon. Love you."

China held the phone to her chest after they disconnected. She had her friend back. In spite of the crazy, awful circumstances she was in, there was a ray of hope.

The kitchen door opened, and she looked up to find Aiden entering. He wore sweat pants and a snug gray T-shirt. His dark hair was tousled, sexy. Just looking at him made her weak, but she resolved to hold onto the anger over the way he'd treated Emma.

"Mornin'."

She tightened her lips and didn't respond.

He grinned and ran a hand through his hair as he headed to the coffee pot. "Ah, I see you're miffed." He poured a cup and took a drink. "No matter. I'm not much for idle chatter anyway."

She was debating whether to let him have it, to tell him exactly why she was *miffed*, even though he didn't ask, when a sound in the living room caught her attention. Then, Lucy's voice carried to her. "China? Are you here?"

Fear iced her skin, and her gaze flew to Aiden's. All humor left his expression. "Who is that?"

"Aunt Lucy," she whispered. She jumped up and hurried into the living room.

Lucy must have used her key, because she was inside the house, looking around the room, hands on her hips.

"Aunt Lucy, what are you doing here?"

"I've come to check on you and Emma. Something's going on, and I want to know what it is."

China twisted her hands together and darted a glance out of the corner of her eye, making sure Gunnar wasn't coming downstairs. "Nothing's going on, other than Emma being ill. Please, you really should go."

Lucy narrowed her eyes. "See, that's not like you at all. Something *is* going on."

"Listen, I just need you to trust me. Please leave and don't ask questions."

"You think I'm just going to walk away when something's wrong with the two people I love most in the world? You always came to me with your problems. Why can't you share now? Is Emma okay?"

"She's fine."

"Then let me see her."

China took her arm and gently steered her toward the front door. "I can't right now. Just trust me, she's fine."

Lucy stopped and pulled from China's hold. Tears filled her eyes. "How can I trust you? You're like a stranger to me. This isn't right." She headed to the stairs. "Is Emma in bed? I'm going to see her, if it's the last thing I do."

And it just might be...

With a sigh of resignation, she followed Lucy up the stairs. She might as well let her see Emma, then she'd be satisfied she was fine, and maybe she'd leave.

Halfway up the stairs, Lucy stopped abruptly, letting out a small scream.

China looked up to find Gunnar standing on the landing.

"Who...who are you?" Lucy looked at China with raised brows. "Is he...are you and he..."

A sound behind her made China turn. Her heart dropped into her stomach when Aiden came into view.

"I heard a scream." He frowned. "Is everything okay?"

Lucy's eyes rounded. "Oh my God, Aiden? Is that you?" Lucy had met him once when she visited China and her parents in Liberia. So much for the hope she wouldn't recognize him. She said to China, "What on earth...? How can he...?" Her hands trembled as she twisted them together.

"I'm sorry, Lucy." Aiden halted at the bottom of the stairs. "It's a long story, but you really should listen to China."

"Please, Aunt Lucy. I'll explain all of this later. Just please go."

Gunnar spoke. "It is now too late. She cannot leave."

China gaped at him. "What? You can't mean to keep her here prisoner too?"

"I will phone Royce. We must find an alternate solution."

His meaning was clear. "Surely he wouldn't, you wouldn't..." Panic closed her throat. "Please, Gunnar. She won't say anything, I promise. Don't get Royce involved. Just let her go and pretend she never came here."

Lucy's eyes grew wide. "Who is Royce? What's going on here? Who is this man? How can Aiden be alive?"

China took her hands. "I will answer all your questions later, I promise. You won't say anything, right? For Emma's safety?" Her eyes implored her aunt to just go along.

Before Lucy had a chance to answer, Gunnar said, "I am afraid I cannot honor your request. Royce must know."

He took his cell from his pocket and dialed. China held her breath while he explained to Royce.

He listened, then said, "I do not wish to do so." He listened some more. "Yes, that is my preference." A few moments passed. "I am aware I do not make decisions."

China wrapped an arm around Lucy. Her aunt's frail body trembled.

Gunnar ended the call and nodded once. "She will remain here. But at least, for now, she will remain alive." He held out a hand. "I must take your cell phone. You are free to move around the house, but do not, under any circumstances, go outside."

"I—I don't have a cell phone. But I need to go to my house and get my things...my clothes."

"You will make do without them."

China put her arm around Lucy. "Come with me. I'll explain what's been happening before Emma wakes up."

In her bedroom, China told Lucy everything, from the day of the robbery to now.

Lucy shook her head. "I can't believe... And you've been dealing with this? My poor little baby, Emma." Tears coursed down her cheeks. "Surely there is a way out. The police can help. You can't mean to keep living like this, not knowing what will happen when it's over. If they'll let you live."

"We can't call the police. They have people all over town. I've tried everything. Trust me, I mean everything." She took a deep breath. "And people have died. It's only a few more days." She settled next to Lucy on the bed and took her hands. "You'll stay here until it's over. And everything will be fine."

Lucy wrapped her arms around her and squeezed. "I hope so. I love you, China doll."

A lump rose in her throat, and she returned the hug. "Love you too." She pulled away and wiped tears from Lucy's face with her thumb. "I'll see if Gunnar will let you stay in Emma's room."

"You have to have his permission for everything you do?"

"Yeah." China grimaced. "He's the one with the gun."

Chapter Thirty-Four

Emma was delighted to have Aunt Lucy stay with them. Especially since Gunnar allowed Lucy to stay in her room. To a six-year-old, it was nothing more than a fun sleepover. China envied her innocence. While she also loved that Lucy was with them, she couldn't help but feel they were sitting on a volcano that could erupt at any moment. She breathed a sigh of relief when the first twenty-four hours went smoothly, despite the tension in the house that everyone except Emma could feel.

Royce made his appearance the second evening into Lucy's stay. She and Emma were in the den watching television while China busied herself in the kitchen, cleaning up after dinner.

He waltzed in through the kitchen door, straight to the refrigerator, and retrieved a beer.

Flipping a kitchen chair around, he straddled it, draping his arms over the back. He took a long pull from the bottle, then tipped it toward China with a nod. "You're welcome."

She crossed her arms and leaned against the counter. "For?"

"For the choice I made in regards to your aunt. You're pleased, right?"

The other option sent a shiver of dread through her. "Of course I am." What else could she say? She poured a cup of coffee and looked him in the eye. "Are we really going to be allowed to live when this thing is over?"

"If everything goes according to plan." He took another pull from the bottle. "The boss just wants the money."

"I would say this is quite an elaborate way to go about getting it."

Royce shrugged. "There's a lot of money at stake. And he's not a man who does things in a small way."

"And I guess you're not going to tell me who's behind it?"

"You guessed correctly. Even the other team members don't know."

She took a drink from her cup. "So, if Aiden gets him the money, you all just disappear? You're not worried about us identifying you?"

"The police will never find us." He drained the bottle. "There is one thing I'd like to know, though."

She raised a brow. "What's that?"

He crooked a grin. "What did you do to Layla?"

Her legs turned to jello, and her breath stalled in her chest. "I—I don't know what you mean. Gunnar said Layla took off."

He tapped the beer bottle against the back of the chair. "At first, that's what I believed. Then I got to thinking about it. She is known for disappearing, but she was pretty gung ho about this job. I've contacted everyone who knows how to reach her, and she hasn't been seen." *Tap, tap, tap.* "Matter or fact, the last person who *did* see her, was you. What happened, you didn't like your new babysitter?"

She rose and went to the counter to refill her cup, avoiding his gaze. "I have no idea what happened to her."

"Right." He chuckled. "I'm just curious how you got the best of her. She's a bit of a bad ass. Maybe I haven't given you enough credit."

She turned back to face him. He grinned like they shared some fun secret. He knew. But he didn't seem angry.

"What are you going to do?" She regretted the question as soon as she asked. Did it sound like an admission?

He stood. "Nothing. Layla shouldn't have let you get the jump on her. I knew we'd lose a few in the operation." He chuckled again and shook his head. "I just had no idea one of them would be by your hand. I believe we underestimated you."

She bit her lip, not trusting herself to speak.

He stared at her for a few moments, then tossed his beer bottle into the trash can. "Now, let's go meet that aunt of yours."

"Is...is that really necessary?" Was this some trick, was he going to kill Lucy in front of her? Was he just pretending he was okay with what happened to Layla?

"Oh yes, quite necessary."

"Please don't hurt her." She tried to keep her voice strong, but the words trembled out of her.

He shrugged. "My original plan was for Gunnar to kill her, but he seldom asks for anything, so I allowed him this concession. You owe him a debt of gratitude."

Gratitude? She tightened her lips. If he hadn't called Royce in the first place, Lucy would be *truly* safe.

"I am grateful." She barely got the words out through gritted teeth. Thanking these bastards for anything wasn't easy.

She set her cup on the counter and led Royce to the family room. Emma was glued to the TV, watching *Frozen*.

Lucy was nowhere to be found.

"Emma? Where's Aunt Lucy?"

Emma glanced over her shoulder. "She had to go somewhere. She said she'd be right back."

"Go somewhere, like, upstairs?"

Emma shook her head and giggled. "She climbed out the window."

Terror clutched China's stomach. She shot a look at Royce. His mouth tightened, and he strode to the window and shoved it open.

"How long ago?" he bit out.

Emma frowned. "I don't know." She looked at the TV. "It was when the movie first started."

The movie was at the part where the ship was sinking during the storm. She'd been gone maybe ten or fifteen minutes. "Please," she whispered to Royce. "Don't hurt her."

His eyes were like chips of ice. "You'd better hope she hasn't gotten far." He worked his big frame through the window, and China rushed over and clutched the sill, looking over the back of the property, peering into the trees. Would Royce find her? Her shoulders caved. Of course he would. But what would he do? *Oh, God. Lucy, what have you done?*

"Momma?" China turned at Emma's voice. She was leaning with her elbows on the back of the sofa. Frowning, she pushed her glasses up her nose. "Is he mad at Aunt Lucy?"

"No, honey." Her legs trembled, and she held onto the back of the sofa for support. Touching Emma's cheek, she forced a smile. "Don't worry. Everything is fine. Just watch your show, and I'll go get you a snack, okay?"

"Okay." She nodded and turned around, dropping back onto her bottom.

China rushed out the door, nearly colliding with Aiden who stood in the hallway. He grabbed her arm. "What's wrong?"

She shook so hard, her teeth chattered. "It's Lucy, she..." Panic seized her chest. "She snuck out the window. Royce went after her."

He let out a heavy breath. "I'll go see if I can find them."

"Please don't let him hurt her."

He didn't speak, but his eyes told her the terrifying truth. Whatever was about to happen, he would be helpless to stop it.

With a gentle squeeze, he released her and headed out the back door off the hallway.

China went into the kitchen to get Emma's snack, but her mind raced with fear. Would Royce find Lucy before she told someone? And, if he did, what would he do to her?

She had to put her faith in Aiden. He would protect Lucy if he possibly could. She had to believe that he would. If not, she'd fall to pieces.

Chapter Thirty-Five

Twenty minutes later, China was sitting next to Emma on the sofa when Royce and Aiden returned. Lucy wasn't with them.

China looked from one man to the other. Aiden's dark eyes were shadowed with pain. Royce looked grim.

"You didn't find her?" The words echoed hollowly against the walls. The volume on the television became a distant blur, a faraway sound through a tunnel. Black dots edged her vision.

"I found her." Royce's voice was cold, flat.

Oh God... Despite all her efforts to keep Lucy safe, it was all for naught. Fear expanded in her chest. She rose unsteadily, terrified of Emma hearing what came next.

Arms wrapped her around her middle, she somehow made it out of the room before swaying. Aiden grabbed her, steadied her.

"Where is she?" She had to breathe. Oxygen would keep her from fainting. She drew in a breath that caught on a sob. "Where's Aunt Lucy?" Her gaze went from one to the other.

Aiden frowned. "I'm sorry, lass. I didn't get to them in time."

Royce's lips compressed. "I did what I had to do."

Her knees went weak, and she reached out a hand to steady herself against the wall, but it was too far away and she almost went to the floor. Aiden's hold tightened.

"No." Pain shafted through her chest. "No, no, no..." She gulped in a lungful of air. "Please, don't tell me, she's..."

"You knew the risks." Royce's smile was cold. "This little incident is on your head, not mine."

She tugged away from Aiden and, without conscious thought, drew her hand back and slapped Royce's face.

He jolted, then turned a look on her that stilled her heart. He stepped toward her, but Aiden moved between them. "You won't touch her." His voice was calm, deadly. "You've done enough."

Something in Aiden's tone or expression must have gotten through to him. He nodded jerkily, never taking his gaze from China. "That's one. The only one you get. Don't make that mistake again."

She glared at him, barely aware of Aiden's hand on her shoulder.

"I'll see to Emma," he said gently. "So she doesn't come out here and find you like this." Aiden skewered Royce with a look then headed down the hall and let himself into the family room.

"Come with me." Royce took China's upper arm and jerked her down the hallway and into the kitchen, releasing her with a shove.

She sank to a chair and dropped her face in her hands. Anguish ripped through her, opening a gaping chasm in her stomach. She sobbed, deep uncontrollable sobs that wracked her body. "She can't be dead." Tears poured down her cheeks, spilling through her fingers as she shook her head over and over. "Tell me my Aunt Lucy isn't dead."

"She did a very foolish thing. You should be glad I caught up to her before she told anyone."

"Glad?" She lifted her head and stared at him in disbelief, scrubbing violently at the tears on her cheeks. "Are you out of your mind?" Grief welled in her chest, cutting off her breath. "How could you? How could you just...oh my God. She's dead. Oh my God."

Gunnar came into the kitchen, his expression morose, but he didn't speak.

"You need to get ahold of yourself," Royce said calmly. "I'm going now. I'll have to take care of...the body."

"What? Take care of the body? No, no, she's going to have a proper burial. You aren't going to just dump her somewhere."

Royce chuckled. "It's sort of cute how you still think you have a say."

"You son of a bitch."

His mouth compressed. "You're pushing your limits, but I'll let that pass, since I know you're grieving." He turned to Gunnar. "Stay here and keep an eye on her." He moved to the door and looked at China over his shoulder. "Pull yourself together, China. We're in the home stretch now."

China did all she could to control her grief as she helped Emma bathe, then helped her dry off and dress in her pajamas. She went through the motions, like a robot, but her mind was screaming with disbelief, with pain. She tried to control her tears, but it was impossible. Her beloved Aunt Lucy, the woman who had practically raised her, was gone. Murdered. And she'd been helpless to stop it.

"Momma, what's wrong?" Emma's eyes were wide, frightened. How would China tell her that she'd never see Lucy again? She couldn't. Not now. Not until this was all over, and she could explain. Even then, how could she really explain? Senseless savagery had no explanation.

"I'm just not feeling well." China attempted a smile through her tears.

Emma put a hand on her cheek. "Is it your lady time?"

China laughed in spite of her paralyzing grief. "Where did you hear something like that?"

"From Brittany M's mom. She gets really 'motional when it's her lady time."

China hugged her to her chest, inhaling her sweet scent of shampoo and bubble bath. "Yes, that's it. It's my lady time." Her small, warm body felt comforting, her lifeline to sanity. No matter what else happened, she had to see that Emma was not harmed. Emma was her focus, her world. She'd seen what these bastards would do. She wouldn't let that happen to her baby.

Emma pulled free and looked up at her. "Aiden said Aunt Lucy went back home. I thought she was staying with us for some more days."

China swallowed a knot in her throat. "She was going to, sweetie, but she remembered some things she had to take care of at home."

"I liked having her here. Can she come stay with us again soon?"

China blinked, tried to force the words out, but nothing would come. She couldn't promise her daughter the impossible.

"Hey, there you two are."

China turned at Aiden's voice. He sounded...chipper. Something she hadn't heard from him since he'd returned from the dead. She knew it was forced for Emma's benefit, but it was still nice to hear. She could almost believe it was real.

"Hi, Aiden. I just had my bath."

"I know. You smell like tutti frutti."

Emma giggled.

"I was wondering if I could read your story to you tonight?"

Emma frowned. "But you don't like my stories."

"Ah, I didn't, but they've started to grow on me, lass."

"You talk funny."

Aiden scooped her up and tickled her. "Oh, I talk funny, do I? Just for that, you get the tickle monster."

She laughed and squirmed in his arms. "No, no, please."

Aiden looked down at China and winked. "I'll put her to bed."

Her heart swelled with gratitude. He knew what she needed right now. Some time to fall apart.

She rose to her feet and kissed Emma on the cheek. "'Night, sweetheart. I'll see you in the morning."

"'Night, Momma."

After Aiden carried Emma out of the room, China took a shower, letting the water wash her tears away.

She dried off and pulled on a robe, then dropped onto the bed. Moisture rose and spilled down her cheeks. How many tears could she possibly have left? Each time she thought the grief was ebbing, it would rise once more and threaten to choke her. She couldn't believe it. Couldn't believe Lucy was actually dead. Murdered. The nightmare kept getting worse. Only, it wasn't really a nightmare. With a nightmare, you eventually woke up.

The click of the door sounded. She turned to find Aiden entering her bedroom.

He moved to the bed, lowered to the mattress, and pulled her into his arms, against his hard, warm chest. He pressed her head to his shoulder and ran a hand gently up and down her back. "Go ahead and cry, lass. There's no one here but me. Cry until you can't cry anymore."

Something broke inside her. Even among all the horror, she was overwhelmed with a sense of safety, of security and relief. Her entire body relaxed, and she clung to him, and let herself cry.

Chapter Thirty-Six

Aiden hadn't been able to use his phone to call Wes since he'd been at the house, but with the transmitter, he'd managed to keep his buddy apprised of the updates and instruct him when a plan occurred to him. Although, so far, he was just winging it.

In two days, he would be leaving for Texas. How would he get them out of this mess, especially once Royce learned he didn't have the full fifteen mil? One way or another, this whole charade would be over. And not a moment too soon. Playing house with China and her daughter was starting to feel a little too comfortable. He was losing his edge.

He headed upstairs, wanting to take a long walk and purge some of the restless energy that plagued him. But he was as much a prisoner as he'd been in Tanier. The only differences were that this cell was larger, and this time, he wasn't alone.

He was passing Emma's open doorway when she called out, "Aiden, can you tuck me in?"

He gritted his teeth. What was up with the kid? She had no reason to like him, yet she somehow did. He considered walking on, but didn't. He'd tuck her in and be done with it.

He went into her room. "Did you already hear a story?"

She nodded. "Momma read me a story, and tucked me in, but I had to go to the bathroom, so I need tucked in again."

"You know, you're getting to be a big girl. You don't really have to be tucked in every night."

She pursed her lips. "I don't *have* to, but I like to. Would you hand me Red?"

"What's Red?"

"It's my bear. He's up there."

Aiden followed where she pointed and found a Teddy Bear in a Cincinnati Reds uniform. He walked over and picked it up. His hand stalled in midair. Around the bear's neck was a set of singed dog tags. *His* dog tags.

He picked up the toy and walked to the bed. "What are these?" He flipped the tags with his finger.

"They're doggie tags. They belong to my daddy, but Momma gave 'em to me."

A heavy boulder settled in his chest. "When did your momma give them to you?" Was this another of China's tricks? Trying to get to him through the kid?

Her face scrunched in thought. "Not this day...uh...it was..." Her face cleared, then she frowned. "It was about three bedtimes before Uncle Miles went away."

"Went away?"

She nodded. "To Heaven. Momma gave them to me after school on the first day after we had our weekend. Then, Uncle Miles took me on a trip, and the big man got me back from the trip, then Uncle Miles went to Heaven. I had the doggie tags for about three bedtimes before the trip."

A good week before China knew he was in town. Before she knew he was alive. She hadn't given them to Emma as a ploy to add credence to her story that Emma was his. She'd given him to Emma because she *was* his.

Emma took the bear and cuddled it to her. Her small, bare feet stuck out from beneath the covers. Just like China's always did.

Something loosened in his chest. Joy and disbelief and regret filled him all at once. He was a father. He and China had made this. Together. At the time, with love.

He swallowed back a lump in his throat and bent to place a gentle kiss on his daughter's forehead.

China had just stepped out of the shower and was slipping her gown over her head when her bedroom door opened. She whirled to find Aiden standing in her doorway. With a gasp, she yanked the gown down over her body.

His expression was stricken, as if his whole world had imploded.

"Aiden? What's wrong?"

He stood silently staring at her. Fear sped up her heartbeat. What could possibly be bad enough to affect him like that? "What's the matter? Please. Talk to me."

He pushed off the door and walked slowly toward her, shaking his head. "She's really mine."

She frowned. "Who? What are you talking about?"

"Emma. I'm her father." His voice was low, strained. "She's really mine."

Relief eased her tension. "Of course she is. I wouldn't lie about something like that." She wrapped her arms around her body. "What made you decide to believe me?"

"It doesn't matter. But I do."

She nodded. "Okay, then. I'm not sure how much it changes. I know you can't make yourself love her, but that's okay." Her breath caught on a sob, and she cursed herself for her weakness. "You keeping her at a distance helps me keep my distance from you."

He shook his head. "I never knew."

"I tried to tell you."

"I thought it was another of your lies. There have been so many."

She let out a laugh that was part cry. "No, you just choose to believe that. I never lied to you." She lifted a hand and rubbed her fingers along her forehead. "I'm sorry, Aiden, I don't know what else to say. I'm just too exhausted, too wound up and terrified to argue anymore. I didn't desert you, I thought you were dead, but there's nothing I can do to convince you. Nothing I can do to make you love me again."

He moved toward her, eating up the space between them in a few strides. He clamped his hands around her head and slid his fingers underneath her hair. "Oh, lass..." His dark eyes glittered like onyx. He shook his head and gave a little groan. He bent his head and his hot, firm mouth sliced over hers.

Her breath caught, and then she was kissing him back, pressing herself to him, not questioning why, just giving in to the moment, to the feel of Aiden's hard body against her. He dropped his hands from her head, slid them down her back, to her hips, pressing her to him.

Long dormant desire sprang to life. Her heart swelled with love. No one had ever—could ever make her feel the way Aiden did. His tongue tasted hers, devouring her, as if he couldn't get enough.

His hands stroked her through the gown, rubbing the silky material up and down, over her back, over the flesh of her bottom. A slow, hot ache started, deep in her belly.

She broke free long enough to whisper, "The lights."

His eyes were hooded, his breathing ragged. "No, love. I want to see you."

He tangled his hands in the folds of her gown and slid it slowly up her body, leaning slightly away and looking down, watching as more of her flesh was revealed. Her face burned, but she didn't stop him. Even if they only had tonight, and he went back to hating her tomorrow, this was Aiden, and she could refuse him nothing.

He pulled the gown over her head and dropped it to the floor. His rough fingers grazed the skin along her shoulders, down her arms, across her stomach.

He lifted his head and caught her eyes with his. "I've never seen anything so beautiful." His voice was husky, his Irish accent more pronounced.

She laughed self-consciously, then tried to swallow, her mouth suddenly going dry. "I've put on weight."

He crooked a grin. "I never did like skinny females. You're perfect."

She put a palm on his jaw and tiptoed, placing a kiss on his lips. Her hands found the edges of his T-shirt, and she tugged it up over his chest, then completely off. She traced each scar on his muscled chest with her fingertips. At least a few of them were a result of his saving her parents. Love for him rushed over her, so intense it nearly buckled her knees. This was Aiden, her Aiden. Tonight, she would give him all of herself.

He captured her hand in his and placed her fingers to his lips, kissing them one by one. His mouth moved back to hers, and he scooped her in his arms and carried her to the bed. He lowered her gently, then joined her, brushing a hand lightly over her hip. She reached for his belt buckle, and he groaned, helping her, shedding his pants, pulling her body over his. She kissed him, his rough stubble scraping deliciously along the skin of her chin, her cheeks.

Her head swam with euphoria. For now, she would shut out all the bad. Even with the horror, the grief, in this moment, all was right in the world. She was being loved by Aiden.

Chapter Thirty-Seven

Over the next few days, neither she nor Aiden mentioned their lovemaking, but things had shifted between them. Aiden seemed to have let go of the bitterness, the hatred. He hadn't said he loved her, and he hadn't touched her, hadn't kissed her since that night, but at least he'd stopped hating her. He was also treating Emma differently. He was more relaxed around her, although he still regarded her with a certain amount of reserve. Maybe he'd never love them like China wanted him to. Maybe it didn't matter. Maybe none of them would live long enough for that to happen.

They hadn't discussed when—or if—they'd tell Emma Aiden was her father. So much was going on, that it was difficult to make such a crucial decision with a clear head.

The night before he was to leave, he insisted on reading Emma her bedtime story. And this time, he got all the way to the end.

China watched them from Emma's door, and her heart squeezed. A tiny glimmer of hope that things would turn out okay sprang within her. Although she was destroyed over losing Lucy—a part of her knew she hadn't really grieved yet, that would come later, and it would be momentous—she was oddly content, even in the midst of this bizarre nightmare. Aiden was back, and he'd accepted Emma as his daughter. It wasn't everything, but it was a start.

She was stepping out of her bathroom after a shower, belting her robe, when the doorknob turned. Excitement jumped in her chest. *Aiden*. He was going away, and wanted to spend tonight with her. She smiled as she waited for the door to open.

Her smile faded, and fear shook her knees when she recognized Marcel, the perverted Frenchman.

She pulled her robe more tightly around her. "How did you get in the house? What do you want?"

His fleshly lips spread in a smile, and he clicked the door shut, turning the lock. Her heartbeat accelerated with fright. "I 'ave my ways, *cheri*. As to what I want." His eyes moved slowly over her body, then back up to her face. "I think you know what I want."

She shook her head. "You said you were waiting until this was over. Royce...he broke your hand after the last time. What do you think he'll do to you now?"

"He will not find out. No one is watching this time."

She made a break for the patio door, but he darted across the room and cut her off. Grabbing her arm, he twisted it painfully behind her back and clamped the hand with the cast over her mouth. She yanked her head away, trying to loosen his hold, and managed a muffled yell.

"If you scream, I will kill the child."

She fell silent. He would. She believed it like she'd never believed anything else in her life. Oh God, she was at his mercy. He was going to rape her...

He released her, then pulled a knife from a sheath at his waist and brandished it in front of her face.

"I cannot kill you, but I can kill the child. Do not be foolish."

She gasped out, "Gunnar and Aiden are in the house."

He smiled and nodded. "Yes, in their rooms, fast asleep. I checked. So, *ma cheri*, it is just the two of us."

Revulsion knotted her stomach. She could scream, she could fight him, but it was possible he would get to Emma before Aiden or Gunnar could stop him. A whimper left her throat. Was this really going to happen?

She clenched her jaw and gritted through her teeth, "Do what you will, but believe me, you will pay for this."

He laughed. "Oh, I think not. You will tell no one." He yanked the edges of her robe open, and she let out a yelp, then slapped her hand to her mouth. *Don't scream, don't scream. It will be over soon. Don't scream...*

He grabbed her breast and squeezed, then yanked her against him and smashed his mouth to hers. His breath smelled of garlic and bourbon. She gagged, closing her eyes, praying it would be over soon...

The door burst open and banged against the wall with a crack like a gunshot. Marcel released her and whirled. China jerked her gaze to the sound.

Gunnar came through the door, fists balled at his sides. His teeth drew back in a snarl, and with his scarred face, he was terrifying. He stalked toward Marcel.

Marcel lifted the knife. "Stay back, big man."

Gunnar growled like an animal and slapped the knife from his hand. He gripped Marcel by the throat and slammed him back against the wall. China scurried away, closing her robe.

Marcel frantically grabbed at Gunnar's hands. His voice strained, he gasped out, "Don't know why you got attached to these people, they're not long for this world."

"Shut up," Gunnar spat.

Marcel tried a laugh, but it came out as a squeak. "You think they are going to let them go? They will be killed."

Gunnar frowned and lowered Marcel to the ground, easing his hold. "I was assured the woman and child would be left alone once the job was over."

Marcel smirked. "You big dumb bastard. You surely did not believe this?" He looked at China. "Come on, Gunnar. Let me have some of that sweet stuff. I'm sure you've 'ad a taste yourself."

Gunnar's hand tightened again, then twisted. A sound like twigs snapping echoed in the room, and Marcel slumped to the floor.

China's hand flew to her mouth. "Oh my God. You killed him."

She wasn't sorry he was dead. She just couldn't believe she'd seen him die, just like that, in a matter of seconds. Life really was so fragile. So many people, dead, in such a short space of time.

Gunnar stood staring down at him for a few moments, then gave a curt nod. "It was necessary. He would never give up. He was like a rabid dog with a poisonous piece of meat. Even though he knew the meat would kill him, his need for it was so great, he could not resist." He withdrew his phone from his pocket.

"Wha—who are you calling?"

"Royce."

"No, please. You can't. He'll—"

"I am afraid I must." He turned his back to her and dialed. In a few seconds, he spoke into the phone, "Marcel is dead."

China's stomach clenched. He was telling Royce? Was he out of his mind? She waited, twisting her hands as Gunnar explained what happened.

He listened for a moment, then hung up the phone. "Royce has instructed me to get rid of the body."

"He wasn't angry?"

Gunnar shrugged. "He was displeased at losing one of the team, but understood."

"China? What the hell?"

She turned at Aiden's voice. He came into the room, looking at her, then to Marcel's body.

She lifted a hand wearily and rubbed her temples. When she described what happened, Aiden's jaw tightened. "Are you okay?"

"Yes, thanks to Gunnar."

Aiden gave Gunnar a quick nod. "I appreciate what you did. Thank you."

"I did not do it for you," Gunnar said. He looked at China. "I will take the body away. I will be back shortly."

"Where?" she asked. "How can you just...dispose of a body like that?"

"Royce has told me of a place nearby."

Probably the same place he'd taken Lucy. The strength drained from her legs, and she gripped the wall to keep from sliding to the floor.

Gunnar tossed the body over his shoulder and strode to the door.

God, she hoped Emma didn't wake up and see him carrying a dead guy...

Her entire body shook, quaking like she was having a seizure. She wrapped her arms around herself, but couldn't make it stop.

Aiden came to her and took her in his arms. "Shhh, lass, it's okay. Everything will be okay."

She nodded. Her teeth chattered so hard she could barely speak. "I-I tr-tried to fight him, bu-but he said he'd..." She sucked in a gulp of air. "He'd kill Emma." She pulled away from him, shaking her head from side to side. "I can't do this anymore. You were right. I'm weak. I'm falling apart and I—"

"No, you are not weak. I was wrong to say that. You're one of the most courageous people I've ever met, and I've fought in wars. You're raising a child on your own. You've suffered tragedies that would send many people over the edge." He stroked his fingers along her hairline and smiled into her eyes. "You are strong, lass. And I'm sorry I've been so cruel to you." His obsidian eyes glittered in the faint moonlight seeping through the windows.

She blinked up at him through a curtain of moisture. "You were hurt. I can't even imagine what you suffered. That was your pain talking. I know what kind of man you are, deep down. You were willing to risk yourself for me and Emma, even before you knew she was your daughter." She cupped his stubble-roughened cheek in her palm. "I forgive you."

He bent his head, and his lips found hers. His kiss was warm, gentle. She clung to his shoulders and returned the kiss. The trembling subsided. She felt safe, protected, confident that he was right, everything *would* be okay. But in reality, the danger was far from over.

She pulled away and squeezed her eyes shut, then looked up at him. "What happens now? Do you think we'll survive this?"

"I promise, I'll do everything in my power to protect you and Emma." He released her. "I'll be right back."

She resisted the urge to beg him to stay, to never leave her side again. When he was near, she could actually believe everything would be all right.

He returned in a few moments and extended a small flashlight toward her.

"What is this?"

"I should have given you something to protect yourself before now. This isn't much, but it's better than nothing. I can't give you a gun, because you wouldn't be able to hide it. This, you can keep in your pocket, and if they do find it, they won't notice it's anything except a flashlight unless they look closely."

She squinted at the flashlight. "I'm looking closely and still only see a flashlight."

He slipped a thin plastic ring off the beam end, exposing sharp, jagged edges. "It's also a weapon. The cover comes off easily. If you need to use it, don't hesitate. It likely won't kill anyone, but it will do enough damage that you should be able to get away."

She nodded and took the pen lite from his hand. "Thank you."

"I wish I could do more."

"I know you do."

Gently, he pressed his hand to her cheek. "Try to get some sleep." He released her and headed to the door.

"Aiden?"

He paused and turned back, eyebrows raised. "Yes?"

She might never see him again. He was leaving tomorrow, and who knew what would happen before this was all over. She'd lost him once, she could very well lose him again. Pride be damned, she had to know. "Do you...do you still love me?"

He hesitated a moment, then strode back to her, taking her shoulders and pulling her against him, his lips finding hers in a crushing kiss. After a few heart pounding seconds, he pulled away and growled, "Yes, I still love you. More than life itself. I tried to fool myself into thinking I didn't, but that's all it was. A foolish lie." He stroked a hand down her cheek. "I don't know what will happen, what tomorrow will bring, but we'll sort it all out later, okay?"

A spark of happiness lit in her heart. Maybe, just maybe there would actually be a 'later.' "Yes, later."

Chapter Thirty-Eight

Royce, Bishop, and a tall, bald man Aiden had never seen before arrived at the house late the following afternoon.

"Take Emma upstairs," Royce told China.

She shot a look at Aiden. He gave her a reassuring smile, and she smiled back, then took Emma's hand. "Come on, sweetie." Her voice trembled. Her face was pale, and bluish shadows showed beneath her cobalt eyes. This mess had taken a toll on her, but he'd been telling the truth when he said she was strong. Much stronger than he'd given her credit for. Still, he wanted to take her in his arms, assure her that everything would be okay, that he would get them out of this, alive. But he didn't. Not only because they had an audience, but also because he didn't want to lie to her.

He balled his hands into fists while China led his daughter up the stairs to the second floor. Would he ever see them again? All that mattered was that he protected them, saved their lives, even if he lost his own. Problem was, he couldn't guarantee sacrificing himself would save them.

"Sit down." Royce gestured to the kitchen table. "Take your shirt off."

Aiden grinned. "Sorry, ol' chap, you're not my type."

Royce chuckled. "Good to see you haven't lost your sense of humor. Now lose the shirt."

Aiden pulled his shirt over his head and dropped into a kitchen chair.

"Lean forward."

"What are you doing?"

"My friend here is inserting a tracker in your shoulder."

Aiden lifted his brows. "What? Don't trust me?"

Royce shrugged. "Not fully. We're sending Bishop with you, and we think you'll stay in line to keep your family safe, but we're adding a little insurance. A tracker on you and your bike, so even if Bishop loses sight of you, we'll know where you are."

Aiden rested his arms on the table, and the guy stepped behind him, utility knife in hand. A sharp pain made him flinch. He gritted his teeth as the tracker was imbedded beneath the skin next to his shoulder blade.

"All done." The newcomer spoke for the first time. He slapped a band-aid over the wound and stepped back.

Standing, Aiden shrugged into his T-shirt.

"Bishop will follow you," Royce said. "You make the least move out of line, and we kill them. Everything goes smoothly, you come back with the money, we go away."

Aiden didn't believe that, not for a minute. The plan he'd laid out through the transmitter to Wes would have to work. Even if Royce was telling the truth about letting them go—which he doubted—he didn't have the money they wanted. Once they learned that, Emma and China were dead anyway.

He followed the men outside and turned back to look at the house. A haze muted the afternoon sun, shadowing the trees that blanketed the house. Inside were his child and the woman he loved. Emotion clogged his chest. This had to work. Everything that ever mattered to him depended on it.

He straddled his bike and donned his helmet, then pulled out of the drive, Bishop behind him.

An hour later, Aiden put his signal on and took the Wynnewood exit.

In the rearview mirror, he saw Bishop do the same. He pulled to a stop at the back of a gas station.

Bishop jumped out of the Navigator and stormed toward him. "What the hell you doing?"

"Sorry, had to take a leak."

Hi big fists clenched and unclenched. "You stick to the plan, got it? You get out of line, and it all goes to crap. You know what that means for the woman and kid."

"Yeah, yeah. I'll be back. When you gotta go, you gotta go. No more unscheduled stops, okay?"

Scowl still in place, Bishop nodded. "I'll stand right outside the door. You have two minutes."

Aiden strolled to the men's room, searching in his peripheral for Wes. No sign of him. *Good.* Wes wouldn't be seen until he wanted to be.

He entered the restroom and let the door fall shut. Moments later, coming from outside, he heard a grunt and a strangled yell. He opened the door and found Bishop on the ground, eyes closed. Wes stood over him holding a leather sap. With Wes was a young guy with a lip piercing and shaggy hair.

Aiden clapped his friend on the back. "Good to see you, brother."

"Likewise," Wes said around a cigar hanging from his mouth. "Let's get this big lug out of the open."

Together, they dragged Bishop into the small bathroom and shut the door.

Aiden lifted his brows at the gent with Wes. "This is the genius?"

Wes grinned. "You really want to piss off a guy who's about to be digging around in you?"

"Guess not." Aiden grunted. "Come on, we don't have much time."

He lifted his shirt up around his neck and bent over the sink, his hands clamping on the porcelain. A sharp pain gouged his shoulder, much worse than when the device was inserted. He clenched his teeth and screwed his eyes shut. Blood trickled down his back. It seemed to take the kid an eternity, but finally, he whooped triumphantly. Aiden glanced back and saw him holding a tiny, bloody device.

"See, that wasn't so bad." Wes stuck a bandage on his bleeding shoulder, and Aiden pulled his shirt down.

Wes kicked Bishop's inert body a couple of times. "Wake up, sunshine."

Bishop groaned and opened his eyes. "What the...? What's going on?" He jerked to a sitting position, reaching to his side at the same time.

"You looking for this?" Wes held up a Beretta with a grin.

Bishop turned a scowl on Aiden. "You're signing a death warrant for the woman and the kid."

"Shut up." Aiden took a pair of handcuffs Wes offered and secured Bishop's hands behind him. Together, he and Wes managed to get him to his feet.

Aiden stepped out of the bathroom and scanned the parking lot. "All clear."

They shoved Bishop outside and into the passenger seat of the SUV.

Wes held up a phone in front of Bishop's face. "I have a little surprise for you. Check this out." He pressed numbers into his cell. In moments, the images of a woman and two children climbing from a car and heading into a grocery store came on the screen. "Look familiar?"

Bishop's face blanched. "I'll kill you."

Wes shook his head. "No, you got that wrong. You don't cooperate, and *we* kill *them*."

A bearded man's face came into the screen. "Hey there, Wes. Nice family you got me keeping an eye on. Woman's a real looker." He winked and lifted a gun. "Waiting on your signal."

Bishop roared and tried to come off the seat, but Aiden and Wes shoved him back down.

Aiden leaned toward him until their faces were only a few inches apart. "Now you know what it feels like for the lives of the people you love to be threatened. You help us, they live. You don't, they die."

Bishop's chest heaved rapidly up and down. "What do you want?"

"Tell us everything you know. What's the plan? Who's behind it?"

He didn't speak.

"One word," Wes said, "and your family dies, right now."

The big man looked from Wes to Aiden, then seemed to become smaller, to deflate in front of their eyes. "I don't know who's behind it. I swear. Royce wouldn't tell me. But, whoever it is wants Aiden dead and wants to take China and Emma out of the country."

Just as he suspected, they wouldn't be allowed to walk away. Who could it be? Steve? No, the guy might be a woman stealer, but he wasn't a killer. No matter, whoever it was, they were going down.

"Where is the exchange to take place?"

"I'm supposed to take you to China's with the money. Royce will kill you and take Emma and China to the boss."

Aiden grimaced. Royce would have to kill him to get to China and Emma. He just hoped that wouldn't be necessary. "First, we're going to the compound. I want to have a look around."

"You know about the compound? How?"

"I did a little recon. Followed you from Farrell's." Aiden grinned. "You should have known your billiard habit would get you into trouble."

Bishop scowled.

"We'll head to China's after. We don't have all the money, but you'll make them think we do and all is copasetic. One wrong move, your family will be blown to little pieces."

Bishop smirked. "You forget about the tracker, smart guy? You and your bike have to head to Texas."

"Got that covered." Aiden pointed to the guy Wes brought. "Genius here removed the tracking device. He will take it and my bike on to Texas."

Bishop blew out a breath and nodded.

Aiden shut him into the SUV and reluctantly handed his keys to the kid, then cringed when he climbed on the Harley.

Wes laughed and chugged him on the shoulder. "Chin up, dude. I'm sure Parker here will take good care of your bike."

With a smirk, the kid pulled on the helmet and revved the pedal, then squealed out of the parking lot. Aiden flinched. He'd probably never see the bike again in one piece.

He slid into the driver's seat of Bishop's SUV, Wes climbed into his Mustang, and they headed north toward Oklahoma City. He put the bike out of his mind. It was the least of his worries. If their plan didn't work...

No, he wouldn't even entertain the thought. China and his daughter had to survive. Anything else was unthinkable.

Chapter Thirty-Nine

"What's nine plus eight?" Emma frowned down at her paper.

China brought her attention back to the homework. Since Aiden left, she hadn't been able to focus on anything except the void his absence left and stark terror at how this would all play out. The flashlight he'd given her was nearby, in a kitchen drawer. She hadn't wanted to keep it on her in case they noticed and wondered why she carried a flashlight around. At least she could get to it quickly if the need arose, but the thought only brought a small measure of comfort. If the time came to use it, how successful would she be? She would have no problem plunging it into Royce or any of these other bastards. She just wasn't certain it would be enough. She prayed another solution arose, and she wouldn't have to find out.

She forced a smile. "That's what you're supposed to tell me."

"But I don't know, cause I ran out of fingers."

China laughed. "You shouldn't have to use your fingers. Just put nine in your head and count on eight times."

Emma tapped her pencil on the paper and propped her elbow on the table, leaning her chin in her hand. "Where's Aiden?"

China let out a sigh. She'd asked three times since lunch. "I told you, he had some business to take care of. Now, come on, we have to do your lessons. You're missing more than a week of school, and you don't want to be behind." She hoped that was all she'd miss. That next week, their lives would be back to normal.

Right. With Lucy gone, Aiden back, and all the horror they'd experienced these past few weeks, life would never be normal again. She pushed thoughts of Lucy from her mind and swallowed back tears. "Now, try again."

The doorbell rang, and her shoulders tensed. She was tempted to ignore it. Whoever was on the other side would be in danger. They would also put her and Emma in danger. Maybe it was Detective Boyle? He hadn't been around in a while. His lack of attention made her almost as nervous as his hounding her had.

She rose and went to the door. Looking through the peephole, she gritted her teeth. *Steve*. Would he never listen? She'd told him to stay away.

Releasing a sigh, she opened the door.

Early evening sun glinted in his red-brown hair, and a bright smile lit his face. He held a bouquet of carnations and a pizza box. "Hey, hope you don't mind. I missed you guys, thought we could share a pizza like old times."

"Steve, I'm sorry, I told you, Emma's ill, and I don't think—"

"Steve!" Emma's voice sang out from behind her, and China cringed. *Damn*, she was hoping to send him on his way before Emma found out he was here. "I missed you!"

Steve smiled down at her. "I've missed you too. You seem to be feeling better." He cast a suspicious glance at China then looked back at Emma. "Want some pizza?"

"Yes!"

Reluctantly, China opened the door and allowed Steve to enter. She took the flowers and went into the kitchen to get drinks while Steve and Emma settled in the living room.

She had to admit, it was nice to have Steve around. Unlike Aiden, he didn't stir desire, but he also didn't stir unease. He was comfortable, a rock. Exactly what she needed.

They finished the pizza, and Steve stood, picking up the box. "I'll take this to the kitchen. You guys want anything?"

China shook her head. She'd barely been able to choke down a few bites of pizza. "No, thank you, I'm good." *Or will be when you leave...*

"Can I have a cookie?" Emma asked.

Steve grinned. "One cookie, coming right up." He disappeared through the kitchen door.

"I like Steve better'n Aiden," Emma said. "Aiden's grumpy, but Steve never is."

"Yes, well..." What could she say? It wasn't as if they were trying to decide between the two men. She wasn't sure what would happen with Aiden, but she could never be with Steve.

A shout came from the kitchen. Steve's voice. Then, a loud crash.

China's heartbeat stalled, and she jumped to her feet. "You stay here," she told Emma.

She rushed into the kitchen. Steve lay on the ground, and Royce stood over him, holding a gun. A large man she'd never seen before was with him.

Steve's startled gaze went to her. "Stay back, I'll handle this." He glared up at Royce. "What are you doing here, Dolan? What do you want? If it's money, please, just take it and go. Don't hurt her."

Royce slowly shook his head. "You got it all wrong." He smiled at China. "Looks like lover boy is the last victim in this little scenario."

Her knees trembled, and chills washed over her skin. Who else would be caught up in this madness before it was over? "No! I'll do whatever you ask." She looked into Steve's bewildered face and sniffed back tears. "Please, please, don't kill him."

"I don't understand." Steve shook his head. "China? What's going on?"

The kitchen door swung open, and Gunnar appeared. He saw Steve and grimaced. "I apologize. I should not have allowed him in."

"It's okay," Royce said. "I wanted you to stay out of sight. This is on China."

Her shoulders sagged. He was right.

"Who's this?" Steve's voice quivered. "What the hell is happening?"

"I'll explain later. Please, just do what he says." She looked at Royce, her chest knotting with fear. "You don't have to kill him. There's been enough killing. It's almost over."

Royce seemed to consider for a moment, then gave a brief nod. Without looking at his companion, he ordered, "Secure him, Joseph."

The man took handcuffs off his belt and snapped them on Steve's wrist.

"Where's Emma?" Royce said to China. "I don't want the two of you out of my sight until this is over."

"Please, let me take Emma to my sister's. She doesn't need to be a part of this."

"A part of what?" Steve scowled and shook his head. "What's going on?"

"Shut up." Royce whacked the butt of the gun into his chin. Steve's head jerked back, and he grunted in pain.

China gasped, her hand flying to her mouth. "Stop! You don't have to hurt him."

"Get him up," Royce said to the bald guy. He lifted the gun toward China. "Take me to Emma, now."

On trembling legs, she left the kitchen, the men following behind. Emma lifted her head, and her gaze moved around the group until it landed on Steve. "Steve? You're bleeding!" Tears brimmed in her eyes. "What's the matter with Steve?"

China's heart splintered at the look on her child's face. As much as she wanted to, she could no longer protect her from the cold hard reality of the horror that had taken over their world.

Aiden slowed the car, pulled into the ranch house drive, and stopped at the gate. Bishop touched a button on the control panel of the Lincoln, and the gates slid open.

Aiden peered through the windows, scanning the grounds. The evening had grown dark early, and black clouds hung low in the sky. He didn't see a soul around. Bishop had told the truth so far. Good thing. No way in hell would they kill his family, but as long as the big man thought they would, he would be cooperative.

During the trip up, Aiden removed the handcuffs, and Bishop had made a few calls to Royce with updates, making him think all was going according to plan. He seemed convinced he had to help them for the safety of his family. Time would tell just how convinced.

Aiden climbed from the car and glanced around. His plan had to be in place before Royce expected to hear back from Bishop. He'd learned from Bishop that there were four men left on the team, including him. With Marcel and Layla's departures, Royce brought in the big bald guy, Joseph. Aiden didn't know him, didn't have time to check him out. But, having an idea of what he was facing was helpful.

Aiden intended to convince Royce—torture him if need be—to tell him who was behind the scheme. If that didn't work, he'd take Royce out, then do his best to protect Emma and China. If necessary, he'd force them to go away with him until he could smoke out the leader.

Bishop exited the SUV and slammed the door, crossing his massive arms over his chest. "You'll get us both killed."

Aiden shrugged. "What can I say? I'm a risk taker." He gestured to the house. "Let's go."

Bishop led him into a large living room with sparse furniture and no decorations. A big screen TV dominated one wall. The only other furniture was a sofa, two recliners, and a couple of tables.

The house was all one level, but spread out. Aiden walked through, searching for any clue as to who else might be involved.

Bishop trailed behind him as if concerned he'd rob the place. "I don't know what you expect to find."

Aiden shrugged. "Maybe nothing."

He rifled through dresser drawers, kitchen drawers, every potential hiding place. Nothing set off his warning meter.

"I guess that's it then. Let's go."

They stepped outside, and Aiden glanced around the big, wraparound porch. A small table sat between a couple of chairs. On the table lay a tobacco pouch.

"You smoke?" he asked Bishop.

"No way, nasty habit."

"Royce?"

Bishop shook his head. "Why?"

Aiden shrugged. "Just asking." He picked up the pouch and stared at the monogram. He kept his expression impassive, but rage pounded through his blood as the answer clicked into place.

"I don't know what you expected to find. This is my place, and I can tell you, whoever is behind it hasn't been here."

Aiden held up the tobacco pouch. "I believe your pal, Royce, has been entertaining while you were away."

Bishop frowned. "I don't know who that belongs to."

Aiden ground his teeth together. "I do." Satisfied he'd learned all he could, he shoved the pouch in his pocket and headed for the Navigator. "Let's go find Royce."

"Won't do you any good. Unlike me, Royce has no Achilles heel and no amount of torture can get him to talk."

He was right, but he had no idea how determined Aiden was. "Then I'll kill him."

Bishop's shoulders drooped, and he nodded. "I'm all in. I'll do whatever I have to in order to save my family."

Aiden knew exactly how he felt.

Chapter Forty

China sat on the sofa next to Emma and put her arms around her. "I'm sorry, sweetie. But it will be okay. Steve's fine."

"Yes, I'm fine, Emma. These men just need to keep an eye on us for a little while. Just be a good girl and do everything they say, and it will be okay." He smiled, but it ended in a wince. The busted chin had to hurt. "Can you do that, can you be a big girl for me?"

Emma wiped her eyes and slowly nodded.

China's heart filled with warmth for him.

"Sit," Royce commanded.

Steve plopped down on the sofa next to China.

"Is anyone going to tell me what's going on?" He shook his head. "Does this have something to do with me? Why would you come after China and Emma?"

"Nothing to do with you, you just got caught in the crossfire. This is about Stone."

Steve frowned. "Aiden? What about him? He's dead."

Emma's head shot up. "Aiden died?" Her lip trembled. "How did he die? Did he go to Heaven like Uncle Miles?"

China tightened her arm around her. "No, sweetie. He didn't die. He's fine."

Steve's frown deepened. "How does she know—"

"Aiden didn't die in Tanier," China said softly. "He's alive. He's been here the past week."

"What?" Steve's eyes rounded, and he shook his head. "That's impossible. The doctor...his dog tags..." He shook his head again. "Why would they lie about it?"

"I don't know. I wondered that myself."

Royce grunted a laugh. "He's alive all right. Son of a bitch ripped us off on the last job. We intend to get the money back."

"That's what this is all about?" Steve snorted disbelievingly. "Money Aiden stole? Why put China and Emma through all this?"

Royce shrugged. "We knew the only way to get to him is through them." He settled in the easy chair. "No need to concern yourself with it. You do what you're told, and you'll get out of this alive. All we want is the money."

China prayed that was true. "You mean to tell me you just walk out, and no one else dies?"

"All of that depends on your boyfriend. He screws up, all bets are off."

She didn't trust that Royce was telling the truth, but had to hope that, somehow, Aiden would find a way out of this with no one else dying.

Royce looked at his phone. "They're here."

"Who?" Steve asked.

"Aiden and Bishop. With the money." He grinned. "See. It's almost over."

The front door opened, and Aiden and Bishop came in, Aiden carrying a leather messenger bag over his shoulder.

China sprang from the sofa and rushed over to him, throwing her arms around his neck. "I was so worried about you," she whispered.

He pressed his lips to her temple. "Everything will be okay, love."

She pulled back. "They have Steve."

Aiden's gaze went to the sofa. "I see they do."

Steve smiled. "You're alive, buddy. I can't believe it. Best news I've heard in years."

Aiden nodded. "Yeah, I'm alive."

"I'd shake your hand, but..." He twisted to show his cuffed hands.

Aiden gave another nod, then slid the bag off his shoulder and extended it to Royce. "The money."

Royce stood and took the bag. Opening the flap, he thumbed through the contents. "This isn't nearly all of it."

"No, it's not. I have some hidden. Once you let Emma and China...and Steve go, I'll take you to it."

Royce shook his head. "No deal." He looked at Bishop. "You been with him the whole time?"

"Most of it."

"*Most* of it? I told you not to let him out of your sight. Were you with him when he hid the money?"

Bishop sighed. "No."

"Why the hell not?"

"He got himself in a little pickle," Aiden said. "I kind of forced his hand, and he had to go along with me."

Royce's eyes narrowed. "What do you mean, forced his hand?"

"He got Suzette and the girls." Bishop's voice was dead, defeated. "Some dude is watching them. Said they'd kill them if I didn't follow orders." He slid a gaze to Aiden. "And you know they would have."

Royce pursed his lips and slowly nodded. "Yes, I know they would have." He slung the bag over his shoulder. "And *you* know there's no room for traitors in this operation." His hand went to the gun in his holster.

Bishop's eyes widened, and he licked his lips. "But, they were going to kill my family. I had no choice."

Royce drew the gun and pointed it at him. "Sorry, old friend, neither do I." A small explosion went off, and Bishop dropped to the floor. Blood oozed from his chest.

China screamed, and Emma cried out. China rushed over to her and picked her up, burying Emma's face in her shoulder. "Don't look, baby. Just hold onto Momma. Don't look." Emma's small body trembled, her shoulders shaking with sobs.

Dear God, if he would shoot a friend down in cold blood, what would he do to them?

Royce stared at Bishop for a moment, then wiped his sleeve across his eyes and turned from the sight of his dead friend.

Aiden clenched his jaw. "Let China and Emma stay inside. I'll take you to the money."

Royce's gaze narrowed, and he seemed to consider for a moment, then he shook his head. "We all go."

Aiden heaved out a breath. *Showtime.* Wes was in place, so with a little skill and a lot of luck, they might just survive.

"The trees aren't good for Emma's asthma, plus it can be dark in there," China said. "Let me grab her inhaler and a flashlight."

Aiden inwardly smiled. *Good girl.*

Royce jerked a nod. "Fine, make it quick."

She disappeared into the hallway and returned in moments.

Aiden led the group out of the house, cursing himself for not figuring out a way to keep China and Emma away from this. His daughter had seen a man die. What kind of damage would that do to a six-year-old child? He couldn't worry about that now. He had to keep her alive. At the moment, long-term trauma was the least of his worries.

They headed across the back yard and into the trees surrounding the property. He and Steve were up front, China and Emma behind them, with Royce and the big man bringing up the rear. Aiden had to plan very carefully, make sure he got everyone where they needed to be so that when Wes did his part, Emma and China weren't caught in the crossfire.

The temperature had dropped as evening approached, and a cool breeze blew. Fog hovered over the ground, making the trees look as though they rested in a blanket of cotton. The dim visibility would hamper Wes's line of sight. He'd have to tread cautiously.

Thirty feet into the woods, Aiden stopped where he'd left the shovel. The rest of the money—less than what was in the bag—wasn't actually in this spot. But for now, he had to make Royce believe it was.

"It's here," he said.

Royce moved next to China and Emma. "Dig it up." He inclined his head toward Steve. "Your buddy will help."

Aiden picked up the shovel. "There's only one shovel."

"Then I guess it's all you, but make it quick. I'm losing patience."

Aiden chuckled. "Funny you should say that. So am I." He whipped the shovel around Steve's neck and yanked him against his chest. Steve gagged and struggled, but Aiden tightened his hold.

"What the hell?" Royce raised the Ruger.

"Drop it, or I kill him." Aiden's muscles strained from holding the handle against Steve's neck with only enough pressure to keep him immobile and not kill him. He wanted to decapitate the son of a bitch.

Royce laughed. "You're threating to kill one of my hostages? Go ahead."

Aiden shook his head. "He's not a hostage, he's behind it."

China gasped. "What? No, it can't be."

"Yes, I'm afraid so. It all makes sense. He's the one who told you I was dead. He's the one who wants me out of the picture."

"The—the doctor said you died." Steve gasped. "I swear."

"Shut up!" Aiden took one hand off the shovel long enough to pat Steve's pockets. Pulling out a .38, he released Steve, but trained the gun on him and said to Royce, "Now, drop it and let China and Emma go. We'll settle this between the three of us, as we should have all along."

"No!" China's face was streaked with tears. "Steve, tell him it's not true. Tell him he's mistaken."

"I-I don't know what he's talking about." Steve forced just the right amount of bewildered panic in his tone. "Please, buddy. You got it all wrong."

"Yeah? Then why the gun? Why didn't you pull it earlier?"

"I was just waiting for the opportunity. China, you have to believe me."

China turned her stricken gaze to Aiden. "Aiden...you're mistaken. Steve wouldn't do that. He just wouldn't."

Aiden reached into his pocket and pulled out the tobacco pouch, holding the side with Steve's initials up for China's inspection. "Recognize this?" She nodded. "I found it at the house these assholes have been using for headquarters." He pointed the .38 at Steve's head. "Explain that, you son of a bitch."

Steve's eyes widened. "I don't, I just—"

Aiden shoved the barrel against his head. "Tell her the truth!"

Steve cut his gaze to Royce, then back to China. A few moments ticked by. Finally, his shoulders lifted and dropped. "Sorry, China. This wasn't how I meant it to go down. He's right. I planned the whole thing."

"You...you what?"

"I knew he was alive. I was well away from the house and barely got a scrape in the explosion. But Aiden was injured, near death. I took his dog tags off him, came to see you in Abidjan, and told you he'd died. My plan was to go back to the hospital, be there when he woke and wait until he had the money from the job he'd done with Royce and Bishop, then kill him. But when I got to the hospital, he was gone. The next thing I heard, he was in prison."

She shook her head. Her expression was ravaged with pain. It killed Aiden's soul to see her suffer. "But why? You were his friend."

"We were once friends, but I grew to hate him. He always had everything I wanted. Success, friends, then you. I fell in love with you the moment we met, but before I could make my move, Aiden had you."

"You sorry bastard." Aiden strengthened his grip on the gun, resisting the urge to pull the trigger. "You did this out of jealousy?"

"I wanted China. I wanted the money. With you out of the picture, I could have both. I came to the states and found China, but she'd married that asshole. After he left, I thought we had a chance." He looked reproachfully at China. "But you didn't want me like that. You only wanted a friend. I bided my time, waiting for Aiden's release."

"And cooked up this elaborate scheme?" China shook her head. "I don't get it."

"It was perfect, actually. Royce and Bishop wanted the money Aiden stole from them. I wanted you, and a few million for us to start over somewhere. I figured I could make you love me once we got away, once you saw how I saved you and Emma. Even though Aiden had to die in the process." He swung his gaze to Royce. "I was none too pleased to find out Royce had Aiden stay at the house, but once it was done, I decided to let it slide."

"Yeah, my bad. Sorry about that." Royce grinned like he wasn't all that sorry. "What now? Kill the child? My man, Joseph here isn't squeamish about that kind of thing."

Steve nodded. "I'm sorry, China. But I have no choice."

"No!" China shoved Emma behind her body. "You'll have to kill me first."

Joseph pulled a Beretta from a shoulder holster. "Want me to kill them both?"

"Not the woman," Steve said.

Aiden grabbed Steve by the hair and jerked him down to his knees, then pressed the barrel tight against his skull. "I'll blow a hole through him if you harm one hair on that child's head."

Royce swung his aim toward China. "Drop the gun right now, or she's dead."

Aiden's insides vibrated with the urge to drive a bullet into Steve's brain. Wes had a weapon trained on them at this very moment, but he couldn't take the shot yet. No matter which ones Wes took out first, the others could kill China and Emma before he could get to them. And the fog hadn't lifted. He wasn't sure how clear a view Wes would have.

Hesitating only a brief second, he released Steve and stepped back.

"Drop the gun, Stone," Royce demanded. "Nice and easy."

Aiden let the .38 fall to the ground.

Steve straightened away from him and snatched the gun. "This could have all been so simple. I was going to be the hero, Aiden would, unfortunately, be killed in the process. I would take China and Emma out of the country, in order to keep them safe. Now, Aiden screwed all that up." He narrowed his eyes. "As punishment, I think maybe your daughter should die in front of you." He nodded to the bald guy. "Do it."

Aiden lunged forward. A shot rang out. Fire burned in his shoulder, and he stumbled to the ground. Blackness crowded his vision, but he shook his head vigorously to clear it. He could not pass out, not now, not when they needed him...

China screamed, shielding Emma with her body. "Aiden!"

"I just winged him," Royce said. "Can't kill him til we find the rest of the money. Emma, however, is another story. Move. Now, China."

Emma's sobs shattered Aiden's soul. He was almost grateful for the burning pain in his shoulder. It was nirvana compared to the searing agony in his heart.

"You can't possibly think I'll love you after this," China sobbed.

Steve laughed. "Like you could have ever loved me. This way, you see the product of your incessant love for this asshole die in front of your eyes."

Aiden struggled to his feet and staggered toward the bald guy. Something hard landed on the back of his head, and he went down.

Chapter Forty-One

Emma cried out as Aiden fell. China's breath panted in and out so hard, she thought she'd pass out. This couldn't be happening. Oh my God. Her baby...

Steve barked out, "Move out of the way, China. You can't protect her."

Her stomach heaved with terror. "You...you can't. I will die before I'll let you hurt her."

Joseph grabbed her by the hair and nearly pulled her off her feet. He slung her to the ground, where she landed with a grunt. Her spine felt like it had caved in. The impact knocked the air from her lungs, but she was back on her feet in seconds.

Aiden rose as well. But it was too late. The bald guy lifted the gun, pointed it at her child... Terror clutched her insides. From the corner of her eye, she saw movement. A body hurled across her vision. A blast went off, and China's heart ripped in two. *Gunnar.*

Gunnar landed with a thud in front of Emma.

Emma screamed out, "Gunnar!"

Blood soaked the front of his shirt, but he rose and sprang toward Joseph, his face a mask of rage. Joseph raised the weapon again, but Gunnar had him in his grasp. He twisted the gun around. Another boom went off. Joseph toppled to the ground, a hole pumping blood from his neck.

Gunnar crashed to the dirt next to him.

Emma dropped to her knees beside Gunnar and threw her body across his, sobbing like her heart would break. Tears welled in China's throat. She knelt beside Emma and felt Gunnar's neck. He was gone. She sniffed back tears. The man had been a criminal, but he'd given his life to protect her daughter.

She pulled Emma into her arms and stroked her hair. "It's okay, sweetie. It's okay." She glared up at Steve. "Don't you dare touch my child. You should know, if you hurt Emma, I would kill you or myself, I wouldn't live one day without her."

Steve sighed. "Fine, enough of this. Just do what I say, and no one else gets hurt." He pointed his gun at Aiden. "Where. The. Fuck. Is. The. Money."

"Let them go, and I'll take you to it."

Steve laughed. "You have absolutely no leverage here, got it? Tell me now, or I start shooting off little pieces of your body, or maybe of theirs, until you talk."

Steve stalked over to China and grabbed her arm. Jerking her to her feet, he pulled her against him. "Come on, sweetheart, tell him. Tell the greedy asshole to cough up the money or I start shooting."

China's gaze slid to Royce. He held a gun on Aiden. Emma was a few feet away, still crouched over Gunnar's body. She met Aiden's eyes. He looked down toward her pocket and gave an almost imperceptible nod. Now was the time. She hated to leave Aiden, but they wouldn't kill him until they knew where the money was. Besides, her number one priority was Emma. Always and forever.

She eased her hand down to her pocket and slipped the flashlight out. With her thumb, she flicked the plastic ring off.

Drawing air into her lungs, she brought her hand back over her shoulder and jammed the jagged edges into Steve's cheek, just below his eye. He released her with an agonized cry and clutched his face.

Aiden dove for Royce and knocked the gun from his hand. The two men struggled. China grabbed Emma up into her arms and took off toward the trees. Her shoulders tensed with expectation. Could she make it into hiding before Steve recovered and shot her dead?

She crashed into the trees without looking behind her. Emma clung to her. And China ran, ran as fast as possible. Branches whipped against her, but she shielded Emma from them the best she could. She panted with exertion. She wasn't in the best physical condition. Never had been a fast runner. Carrying Emma slowed her progress even more. Steve would catch up to them. Royce too, if Aiden couldn't subdue him. Or...maybe they'd already killed Aiden? Maybe it was just her and Emma?

No, they would want him to lead them to the money. They would keep him alive. She had to believe that.

For now, she had to find a hiding place before they caught up to her.

She spotted a grouping of three trees with shrubbery growing up between them. She didn't know what kind of creatures might dwell in the space behind them, but they would be better than the creatures pursuing them.

She ducked behind the trees, crouching with Emma in her arms. She was no longer crying, but she was coughing while struggling to take in air. Oh God, an asthma attack.

"Shhh, sweetie. It's okay. I have your inhaler." She barely whispered the words, listening for cracking branches and footfalls as she dug the inhaler from her pocket.

So far, nothing.

Emma tilted her head back, and China placed the opening of the device into her mouth. She pressed the pump, and Emma breathed in. China took the inhaler from her mouth, watching for signs that it had helped. Emma sucked in a gasp and coughed again.

Come on, baby, hang in there, breathe...

She was so intent on Emma's condition, she didn't hear anyone approach, but Steve's voice boomed out, "China? Come on, I know you're close. Might as well come out now."

She held her breath, hoping he wouldn't hear. But Emma's wheeze was loud enough to attract attention.

"This is the end of the line. Aiden almost had Royce, but his bad shoulder and the blow he'd taken to his head must have zapped his strength. Not quite the warrior he was when we worked together before. Between Royce and me, your lover didn't fare too well."

Oh God, they hadn't... Aiden couldn't be dead. They wouldn't kill him, not without the money. Would they?

"China... I'm losing patience. Show yourself now, and I might not hurt Emma. You know I'm fond of her, but you're starting to piss me off."

Fond of her? He almost murdered her moments ago.

Emma took another pull from the inhaler, wheezing at the same time. China tensed. Had that been loud enough to carry to Steve?

"Ah, I hear her." He chuckled. "Huh, asthma *is* deadly isn't it?'

Footsteps drew near, and China squeezed her eyes tightly closed.

Please, please, don't find us, please...

The shrubs in front of them parted, and Steve stepped loomed in the gap between the trees. He smiled down at them. Blood had smeared down his face from the wounds she'd inflicted. They were deep. Likely painful. A glimmer of satisfaction took hold inside her.

"Good try, but not quite good enough." His expression darkened, and an evil light came into his hazel eyes. "Get up and come with me. I've had enough of the bullshit." He grabbed her arm and jerked her to her feet.

Emma slid from her lap, and China gripped her hand. "Is Aiden okay?"

Steve's lips twisted. "Figures you'd be concerned about that son of a bitch. I can see you and I are going to have a rocky relationship. But, I've decided to let Emma live to keep you in line." His gaze dropped to Emma, then back to China. "However, I'm going to have to teach both of you a little lesson when this is all over with. You need to understand you can't defy me."

Rage heated her blood. She gritted her teeth and captured Steve's gaze. Softly, she said, "I don't know when. I don't know how. But one of these days, I will kill you. That's a promise."

Steve let out a belly laugh. "I can see there won't be a dull moment with you around." He tugged her out of her hiding place. "Now, come on. Let's get this thing done."

Moments later, they emerged from the trees into the back of the property where Royce waited, with a very much alive Aiden, thank God. Aiden's shoulder dripped blood, as did his face.

His dark eyes found hers, and he winced. "I'm sorry, love. I wanted to save you."

She nodded. "It's okay. We'll be okay."

"Enough screwing around." Steve shoved China aside and put the gun to Aiden's temple. "Tell us where the money is right now, or you die. Then, Emma dies. And I'll make China my sex slave until I tire of her worn out, whore of a body and then, she dies too. So, what's it going to be, tough guy?"

China's body sagged with defeat. She held onto Emma's small hand. Her breathing had stabilized, thank God.

This was it. The end of the line. No choice now, except to give in to their demands. But, she would do all she could to make sure Emma was safe. "Wait. Please. We can work this out. There's been enough death. This just needs to be over." A sob caught in her throat. She swallowed it back and made her voice as strong as she could. "Let Emma go with Aiden. Right now. Let's end this. I will come with you, no arguing. Aiden will tell you where the money is. You and Royce can split it, and this will all be over."

Steve was silent for a few moments, then he nodded. "Fine, fine. Let's just do this."

Aiden's pain-filled eyes met hers. "I can't let you go."

"We have to think about Emma. As long as she's okay, I'll survive."

A suspicious sheen of moisture hovered in his eyes. His voice was hoarse when he spoke. "I'll find you."

She couldn't muster a smile, though his promise filled her heart. "Just take care of our daughter."

Emma's tear-streaked face lifted. "Is Aiden going to be my new daddy?"

China squatted and pulled her small body into a hug. Maybe for the last time. Through the knot of pain in her throat, she whispered, "Aiden is your only daddy, sweetheart. I didn't want to tell you like this, but he's your real daddy."

Emma pulled back and looked into her face. "My dog tag daddy?"

China laughed in spite of the crushing weight on her heart. "Yes, your dog tag daddy. I want you to go with him. Be a good girl and never forget how much Mommy loves you."

Emma lifted her hand and pressed it to China's cheek. Tears swam in her eyes. She wiped at them behind her glasses. "I want you to come with us."

"I'll come back as soon as I can, I promise." She rose to her feet and looked at Aiden. "Tell them where the money is. Please."

Chapter Forty-Two

Aiden's chest nearly exploded with a mixture of rage and grief. He couldn't lose China. The bastards. What would they do when they learned the money wasn't all there?

He had to hope Wes had repositioned himself. Had to hope for a miracle. At least the odds were better now, with only Royce and Steve left. But, he'd been of little effect against Royce earlier. His injured shoulder made his right side almost useless, and once Steve had joined the fray, he was helpless as a newborn lamb.

"This way." He led them across the large yard, toward the spot next to the shed where he'd buried the money. The bag he'd given Royce held five million. All that remained was a million. When he dug it up, they would see. And probably kill him. But maybe Wes could take them out before they hurt China and Emma.

He stopped when they arrived at the shed. The money wasn't buried all that deeply. He could dig it out with his hands. He knelt next to the disturbed dirt and slowly scraped through it.

"Get the hell out of the way," Steve barked impatiently. "Royce, get the money."

Aiden backed away, and Royce squatted next to the hiding place. Aiden slid a look to where Steve stood a few feet from China, who held tightly onto Emma. Steve stood closer to Aiden than he did to China and Emma. Perfect.

He looked out toward the trees and cocked his head toward Royce, giving Wes the signal.

Royce pulled a money pack out of the ground and held it out, scowling. "This can't be ten mil. Where the hell is the rest of it?"

A loud pop sounded, and a hole appeared in the center of Royce's forehead. His eyes widened, then he toppled forward into the pile of dirt, the money trapped beneath his body.

Steve whirled toward the trees where the shot came from, his wild gaze searching, then back to face Aiden.

Aiden launched into him and drove him to the ground. The .38 skittered from Steve's hand. Aiden pounded the fist of his good arm into Steve's face. Flesh met flesh, his knuckles splitting Steve's lip and the skin on his cheekbone. Steve bellowed out an agonized scream. All the rage that had been building inside Aiden burst forth, gathered in his muscles and detonated into a flurry of punches to Steve's face, his throat, his chest...

Steve bucked and tried to knock him off, but Aiden planted himself over his body. He slammed his elbow into Steve's jaw. Steve grunted and punched Aiden's injured shoulder, dislodging him. Pain sparked a path from his shoulder into his chest, followed by a burning so intense, dizziness rose and swam in his vision.

Steve staggered to his feet and snaked his arms around Aiden, driving him into the ground. Over Steve's shoulder, China held the gun with both hands, pointing it at them.

"Shoot," Aiden gasped out.

China shook her head. "I might hit you." Tears streamed down her face, and she brushed at her cheek with her shoulder.

"Doesn't matter," Aiden grunted. "As long as you hit him. Fire and keep firing."

Steve's fist slammed into Aiden's jaw, jerking his head to the side. "You sorry mother fucker. Die already!"

Blood trickled down to Aiden's ear, and fierce pounding exploded behind his eyes. With his good arm, he plowed upward, driving his fist into the area just below Steve's chin. An agonized grunt left Steve's throat, and he fell backward. Aiden came to his feet and weaved toward him. His strength was waning. He'd lost a lot of blood. If China didn't shoot soon, Steve would get the best of him. Wes wouldn't want to take the shot with Aiden so near.

"Shoot, dammit," he growled.

Steve pushed to his feet and started toward Aiden. Aiden kicked out, catching him in the sternum. Steve stumbled back, but came at him again.

From his peripheral, Aiden saw the .38 shaking in China's grip. Emma clung to her leg.

"Take him out, Wes," Aiden shouted.

Wes emerged from the trees and pointed his gun at Steve.

Steve whirled back toward China. "Don't let him kill me. You know I would never really hurt you or Emma. Please, we have a history. Don't let him kill me."

China sniffed back tears. Her gut told her to tell the man to pull the trigger. Her heart told her she couldn't let her child see someone else die. Especially someone she once loved.

China shook her head, staring at the man before her, his face looking like ground hamburger, and tried to reconcile him with the kind, caring person she'd known all these years. The man who'd brought pizza and flowers and cared for her and Emma like family.

But it had all been a lie. A sadistic ploy. He'd not only threatened their lives, he'd betrayed her trust, her daughter's trust. People she loved had died because of him. Aunt Lucy...

She ground her teeth together. "If it weren't for Emma, I'd let him shoot you down like the dog you are. But she's seen enough death. I'll let the authorities handle you." She squatted and lowered the gun to the ground, then picked up Emma and held her to her breast. Relief made her legs go weak. It was over. It was finally over...

Aiden swayed on his feet, and fear gripped her. He didn't look good at all. She rushed over and put her free arm around him. "Don't worry. I'll call an ambulance." She'd have to go inside. The bastards had taken her cell.

"I'll be okay, love." His eyes blinked shut, then back open. "Meet my buddy from Texas, Wesley Faulkner."

Wesley gave a quick nod, then strode over to Steve and jammed the pistol into his side. "I'd like nothin' better than to blow a hole through you, but if the lady says I can't, I guess I can't." He lowered his voice. "But just flinch, mother fucker. Just blink your eyes, and swear to Christ, I'll do it."

Steve's mouth compressed, and his eyes shot hatred as he looked at each of them in turn. "I'll make you pay. Somehow, someday. All of you. I'll make you pay." He laughed, the sound evil and chilling. "You have no proof I'm guilty. None at all. Cops already suspect China. So you'll have hell proving she and her ghost of a lover aren't the ones behind all of this."

Anger heated China's blood. He was right. The sorry, malicious bastard who had terrorized her and her child might walk away scot-free. And she and Emma would never, ever be safe.

She looked at Aiden, then at Wesley. "I'm going into the house to call an ambulance." She paused. "And I'm taking Emma inside with me." Her gaze locked onto Steve. "Did you hear that? Emma, who I didn't want to witness your death will be inside the house. With me." She smiled.

Steve's eyes widened, and his gaze darted from Aiden to Wesley. "No, you can't. Please. You can't leave me with them."

She turned her back on him and headed to the house. Each step seemed to take an eternity. No room for second thoughts or regrets. Her mind and heart had been through so much these past few weeks, and with Steve's threat ringing in her hears, she couldn't think about it in any other way than the only way.

Shortly after the door closed behind her, she heard the unmistakable pop of a gunshot.

China sat with Emma asleep in her lap in the hospital waiting room. Against Aiden's vehement protests, she'd insisted he be seen by a doctor. An ambulance had come, along with a couple of squad cars. Wes had disappeared before they arrived. Apparently, the man liked to keep a low profile.

She was exhausted, physically and emotionally drained. Part of her couldn't believe it was really over. That they were finally safe. Could finally take their lives back. She'd deal with Lucy's funeral, whether or not they recovered her body. Grief clutched her heart. Her sweet, loving aunt. Gone.

She placed a gentle kiss on Emma's forehead. At least she was safe. Traumatized, most likely, although she seemed to be coping fairly well. Now, to figure out how to get on with their lives. Would Aiden want to be a part of that? He'd said he loved her, but he'd also made it clear he never wanted to be a father. Maybe too much had happened for them to be able to have a life together. Maybe Aiden wouldn't even want to try.

If not, she would accept that. She had her child—alive, safe, and warm in her arms. Anything else, she could handle.

Aiden came into the waiting room, and China stood, adjusting Emma on her shoulder. She raised her head and blinked sleepily.

Aiden's shoulder was bandaged. The blood had been cleaned from his face, but the bumps and bruises remained.

He peered at her from across the room. His gaze went to Emma, then back to her, his expression inscrutable.

"Miss Beckett?"

China nearly groaned when she recognized Detective Boyle's voice. She'd been so focused on Aiden, she hadn't seen him come in.

He stalked past Aiden and over to her. Aiden followed.

The detective lifted his brows. "So, this is the long lost ghost, huh? I've heard sketches of what went down from the first responders who came on the scene, but there's a lot of dead bodies." His narrowed his gaze on Aiden. "And some not dead that used to be. I need you all to come down to the station with me and answer some questions."

Aiden stood next to China. "You'll find answers at a ranch house out at the end of Prosper road."

Boyle nodded. "I still need to question the two of you." His mouth tightened. "Extensively."

"Later." Aiden took Emma from China with his uninjured arm and slid his other hand around China's. "Right now, I'm taking my family home."

Epilogue

One week later...

The sky was a hazy gray due to the rain clouds hiding the sun. China clutched Aiden's hand, grateful for his quiet strength on the saddest day of her life.

Pastor Timothy ended his graveside prayer, giving China a sad, sympathetic smile.

She stood, holding a bouquet of orchids, and stepped up to the casket where her dear Aunt Lucy rested. Her body had been found, and they were able to lay her to rest.

China held the lovely pink and purple flowers to her nose, inhaling the delicate scent that would forever remind her of Lucy. She gently laid the flowers atop the gold and white casket.

"Goodbye, Aunt Lucy," she whispered, the words catching on a sob. She squeezed her eyes shut against the tears cascading down her face. Her lungs ached with grief so strong, she didn't know how she would contain it. Her heart seemed about to burst with the weight. She could almost hear Aunt Lucy saying, *"You'll be fine, China doll. You're stronger than you know..."*

The past month had made her realize she *was* strong, but losing Lucy had left her soul with a permanent void, and her heart would never stop hurting for the woman who had been more of a mother to her than her own mother.

When Emma's small hand slipped into hers, she bent to place a kiss on her cheek. Emma would miss Lucy, too. But at least she had her daddy now.

China worried about how the trauma from all the violence she'd witnessed might affect her. So far she seemed okay, although perhaps slightly more subdued than normal. They were going to see a counselor next week—one who specialized in working with children. Hopefully, she would emerge from all of this emotionally unscathed.

Aiden stood behind Emma, looking handsome in his black suit with a haircut and clean shave, his dark eyes shining with loving concern. He'd been her rock during the planning of Lucy's funeral. And, he doted on Emma. The harsh lines in his face seem to have melted away, and he and his daughter were forming a bond.

She and Aiden hadn't spoken of marriage. He hadn't said what he intended for the future. Would he, now that Lucy's funeral was over? He was a nomad, maybe settling down wasn't in his plans. Although she secretly hoped he'd stick around, maybe even want to marry her, she wouldn't push. If he didn't want to be a part of their lives, she wouldn't beg.

They had all been through a great deal. With or without Aiden in her life, China would slowly heal, as would Emma. Thank God they'd survived, physically, even though the mental toll was yet to be determined.

"Miss Beckett, I'm sorry for your loss."

China looked behind her to find Detective Boyle standing under the canopy. "Thank you."

She still wasn't sure if any charges would be filed against her or Aiden. Wes had slipped away, and the authorities didn't know about his part in it. But, for the past month, she'd more or less aided and abetted criminals. Aiden had committed his share of crimes as well.

Boyle frowned and cleared his throat. He wore a clean suit, his tie free of stains, but somehow still appeared rumpled. "Also wanted to tell you, we almost have the investigation wrapped up. Evidence suggests you were being held hostage, forced and threatened to go along with what these criminals wanted." He looked down at Emma and smiled, then lowered his voice as he raised his gaze back to China. "Your daughter's life was at stake. We're recommending the DA not pursue any charges."

Thank God. Although she wouldn't have done anything differently—she'd rot in prison the rest of her life to protect Emma—she was exceedingly glad she wouldn't have to.

Aiden stuck out his hand. "Thank you, Detective. We'll do all we can to assist you in finalizing the investigation."

"Appreciate it." The detective settled a worn fedora on his head and took off for his car.

China accepted the well wishes of countless friends and family, hugging Spencer and Destiny more tightly than the others. She needed to work on cultivating a closer relationship with her sister. Family was important.

When everyone cleared out, China, Aiden, and Emma slowly walked to China's Camry.

Before getting inside, Aiden took her hand, then Emma's. "I have something to ask you two."

"Yes, Daddy?" Emma's inquisitive face turned up to him, and China absent-mindedly pushed her glasses up her nose.

"I was wondering if..." He let out a sigh. "I know it's not the time or the place, but I can't wait any longer to know."

"Know what?" China held her breath. What was coming? Was he leaving? Staying?

He knelt on the dirty ground, the knees of his new suit resting on gravel. His mouth quirked in a grin. "To know if you will marry me."

Before China could speak, Emma cried, "Oh yes, Daddy." She threw her arms around his neck, nearly toppling him over. "We will marry you!"

Aiden laughed and rose to his feet. "Well, that's one down." He looked at China, his expression hopeful and vulnerable. "How about your mother?"

Love swelled until she thought her heart would burst. They'd come a long way, had been through a lifetime of pain in a short time. They'd weathered the worst, she hoped. Now was their time to grab for happiness—the three of them.

She stepped forward and placed a kiss on his warm, firm lips. "Her mother would be ecstatic to marry you."

Also by Alicia Dean

Without Mercy

Watch for more at www.AliciaDean.com.

About the Author

Alicia Dean lives in Edmond, Oklahoma and is the mother of three grown children. Alicia loves creating spine-chilling stories that keep readers on the edge of their seats. She's a huge Elvis Presley fan, and loves MLB and the NFL. If you look closely, you'll see a reference to one or all three in pretty much everything she writes. If she could, she would divide all her time between writing, watching her favorite television shows-such as Dexter (Before it ended, boo hoo), Vampire Diaries, Justified, and True Blood-and reading her favorite authors...Stephen King, Dennis Lehane, Michael Connelly, Lee Child, and Lisa Gardner to name a few.

Please follow Alicia on Twitter: @Alicia_Dean_ and visit her website: AliciaDean.com, or feel free to drop her a line at: AliciaMDean@aol.com.

Read more at www.AliciaDean.com.